Origin time: March 11, 2011, 2:46 p.m.

Great East Japan Earthquake

Personal Account of Mayors from Disaster-Struck Municipalities

Tachiya Hidekiyo, Mayor, Soma City

KINDAISHOBO

Introduction

On the chance that a large tsunami would come, I mede orders from the Disaster Management Headquarters that we had set up immediately after the earthquake to fire brigades in coastal areas to direct people to evacuate toward high ground. I will never forget as long as I live the sense of panic I felt when those worries became a reality beyond anything I had imagined.

Even today, I still have flashbacks as I remember finally managing to get myself back on an even keel in the face of the damage situation as I pictured it in my head and the dreadfulness of the actual reports that had us constantly redrawing the measures being devised in response. I struggled with a bottomless well of anxiety over how many people the disaster had turned into victims, while at the same time admonishing myself not to panic.

At that moment, it seemed to me that the first response an ordinary man like myself could take in a role as head of a disaster response headquarters was to not show any signs of the panic that I was in fact feeling.

Listening to one damage report after another the evening of the earthquake, I explicitly laid out a concrete course of action on what needed to be done immediately and what would have to be dealt with in time to come in order to rebuild the community. My objective was to see Headquarters staff come together as a team working with the conviction that their purpose was to protect the disaster's victims and Soma City. I believed that everyone there would firmly held on to those objectives for their actions. We waited to gather information because we probably would have been overwhelmed by the enormity of the damage.

We laid out our course of action on a single sheet in the middle of the night. The things that needed to be done immediately were grouped into categories with the responsibility for each of these items divided up among the staff. Everyone shared their objectives and information. On those occasions when new information came up, I consolidated the thinking of everyone on the Headquarters team as a means of revising our course of action.

I believe that we were able to unite at the time based on the fundamental strategy of moving ahead together on disaster response and recovery as a wheel-and-spoke-type organization with Headquarters' chief at the center. Everyone sharing the same sense of purpose, and no one flinching from the enormity of damage. That approach to the battle that began that evening continues unchanged to the present.

June 2011. Visualizing what conditions will look like after recovery, I drew up a plan unique to Soma City.

With the idea that recovery means rebuilding the lives of disaster victims back to that stage in life that they had been at prior forming its basic policy, the initial recovery program put together a plan of operation covering tangible and intangible aspects in a way that could anticipate the wishes of the community and security in people's lives.

Naturally, as the Disaster Management Headquarters, we also had to run through the PDCA cycle to improve our efforts to respond to the various issues and changing conditions that emerged as we pursued recovery such as new measures for dealing with collateral damage like measures to cope with unattended deaths and changes in the government's response to radioactive accidents. Furthermore, we got expanded assistance from the Reconstruction Agency and other government ministries and agencies, powerful support from friendship municipalities and support groups, and above all the power of a populace trying to band together in response to the crisis. With each such development we created a new and improved version of the recovery program.

We also received tremendous support from elsewhere around the country and the world, along with a variety of forward-looking suggestions about recovery.

However, for Soma City it was the ideas promulgated through the early 19th century Hotoku movement led by agrarian reformer Sontoku Ninomiya—who had been asked for lessons on how to recover from the great famines of that era when warrior rule was coming to an end—that would serve as the spiritual pillar for its government and people. Accordingly, we made it our basic policy to work steadily at maintaining the bonds among people so as to forestall the emergence of collateral victims of the disaster such as people committing suicide or dying alone, and to band together as we steadily pushed recovery forward one step at a time. I've been believing that assessments of whether we are going slowly or quickly aren't really an issue. The very fact that we were steadily pushing ahead on a recovery program that was just right based on actual conditions in Soma City was the important thing.

More than six years have passed since that time.

That day is still feels like it was just yesterday, and also seems like a memory from the distant past.
I believe that many of the misfortunes we experienced were unrivaled in the history of disasters however far we go back.
In addition to the damage caused by the earthquake and tsunami, there was also the nuclear accident that followed. That was a grueling situation that itself should be termed a major, multiple disaster not only due to its tremendous scale but also because it wove together in a complicated fashion many difficulties. It was the largest predicament that Soma City had ever faced since its founding.
With multiple countermeasures called for to deal with the respective issues, we have had six years of the Soma City team puzzling the problems out to the utmost and going through repeat cycles of trial and error as it puts its heart and soul into maintaining and managing residents' health and rebuilding their ways of life.

Today, we see that for the most part on work preparing the major tangible components such as equipment and facilities has been completed. In particular, disaster recovery public housing was finished off on higher ground so that victims could have a place to rebuild their lives; the City Hall buildings have been reopened after renovations undertaken in light of the fact that they were at risk of collapse in the next major earthquake; and the fishermen's guild freight handling building that had taken a direct hit from the tsunami and was destroyed has been rebuilt, along with the cluster of facilities adjacent to it. All these developments and others signify that Soma City has now created itself anew.
However, when it comes to the intangible factors, there are a number of ongoing issues that require our constant attention. Primary industries face the problem of how to recover the value of their commodities due to the reputational damage caused by the nuclear accident. While no problems have

been seen to date when it comes to exposure doses, the safety of children needs to be verified on an ongoing basis through internal and external examinations. Measures need to be taken to cope with post-trauma stress disorder (PTSD) in view of the fact that the possibility of problems at the nuclear plants flaring up once again cannot be excluded. Elderly disaster victims now living on their own need to support to maintain their health and also to forestall the prospect of anyone dying alone. Facilities need to be developed to secure a nonresident population in place of the tourism resources lost in the tsunami, and they need to be put to use or with private cooperation operated effectively.

There is also one more important job that must be taken care of as we go about recovery.
That is our obligation as the Soma City—which survives today having confronted this tremendous earthquake and disaster—to pass on to the future generations of Soma residents how we as a local government reacted to this historic crisis that faced our birthplace and how we handled it.

Starting six months after the quake and continuing every year since, Soma municipal employees have participated in the creation of an Interim Report that is sent to every household in the city and to the organization and volunteers who have given us their support. As the city's government, we plan to continue this practice for as long as the recovery and renewal period lasts.

Meanwhile, at each juncture along the way I have been issuing the "Soma City Mayor's e-mail newsletter 'Mayor's Essays'" as way of both sharing my basic thoughts and impressions with our residents and the people who work for the city, as well as making entreaties and reports to our supporters from outside the city. Now, these essays have been pulled together and combined with documentary photographs into this personal account you hold in your hands.
Based on records of the instructions I gave as Disaster Management Headquarters chief and photographs. I have also written in my own words a description of how events were unfolded and an explanation of what happened both during what should be termed the period of hyperacute crisis of the first 24 hours after the disaster as well as during the two following

weeks when the disaster entered its acute phase.

I believe that with the tremendous assistance received from experts we also came up with every measure imaginable for dealing with the various radiation-related problem arising due to the nuclear accident. At the end of this account, I have included a record of the developments in this area and explanations for them based on a log of Soma City's actions and the data collected.

Our disaster response proceeded with many varied issues woven together in complicated ways. Accordingly, there unavoidably are overlaps and duplications in the account presented here. Likewise, the essays from my e-mail magazine had places where I was forced to overwrite passages with new facts and revised ways of thinking due to changes in conditions as we went along. The descriptions in these places get a little irritatingly repetitive, but I used the e-mail magazine as a means for delivering information and so it stands as is as a record of the time. Accordingly, it might make for difficult reading, but I ask for your forbearance.

The positions that I describe people as having in the text are the ones they had at the time. By all rights, I should annotate their current position, and for this, too, I ask you to make allowances.

In preparing this book for publication, I'm ashamed to note oversights made due to my being an amateur such as clumsy pieces of writing, rambling constructions that run on, and duplications in content. However, I wanted to leave behind a record of this disaster as much as possible in the voice of someone who was on the scene before my memories fade, so I and my local friends and associates compiled these materials as is.

As the record of one local government leader rocked by an enormous and unprecedented disaster, I hope it will be of some use both for future residents of Soma and also for efforts at disaster response and crisis management in the future including the Nankai Trough Earthquake that is predicted for Japan's future.

Midsummer 2017

contents

■**Introduction**

■**Chapter 1　Hyperacute Period**
24 Hours After Earthquake ················15

(1) Immediately after the earthquake / 16
(2) Initial systematic action guidelines / 24
(3) The reality I observed / 28
(4) Emergency medical care systems / 32
(5) Aid from friendly municipalities / 34

■**Chapter 2　Acute Period:**
The First Two Weeks After Earthquake ···············37

(1) News report about the nuclear accident / 38
(2) Soma City official records from March 12th to March 14th
　　(original text reproduced as written) / 41
(3) A Frightening experience / 46
(4) Soma City official records from March 15th to March 19th
　　(original text reproduced as written) / 46
(5) Reasoning with residents and insufficiencies in foodstuffs and
　　goods / 54
(6) Soma City official records from March 21th to March 25th
　　(original text reproduced as written) /　58
(7) Medical care / 63
(8) Volunteer activities / 66
(9) Encouragement from Taro Aso and Junko Mihara / 67
(10) **Castle under siege** (First email magazine after the disaster
　　issued on March 24th) / 68

March 11, 2011　　I. 24 Hours After Earthquake　　March 12, 2011

II. Acute Period: The First Two Weeks After Earthquake　　March 26, 2011

■Chapter 3　Evacuation Shelters
(A record from March 26 to June 27, 2011) ·······75

(1) Opening of psychiatric outpatient facilities (March 29) / 76

(2) The "Saigai FM" station starts (March 30) / 77

(3) Starting construction of temporary housing (March 26) / 78

(4) Restarting schools and dividing partitions / 78

(5) Free legal consultations (April 11 onwards) / 80

(6) **If not for the power plant** / 82

(7) The nutrition control menu at evacuation shelters (After implementation of the meal service - April 18 onwards) / 84

(8) Restarting the schools (April 18) and measures to counter PTSD (Post Traumatic Stress Disorder) / 85

(9) **The Earthquake Disaster Orphan Scholarship Fund ordinance** / 88

(10) The first induction into the temporary housing (April 30) and crisis headquarters support / 91

(11) **The feelings of the Emperor and Empress** / 93

(12) **A new village** / 95

(13) Radioactivity countermeasures and briefings (from May 22 onwards) / 98

(14) Measures against sludge and dust (effects on worker health and residents' lives due to dust scattering) / 99

(15) **For the futures of the children affected by the disaster** / 100

(16) Completion of temporary housing (1,000 units for Soma city) and closure of evacuation shelters / 103

(17) Hiroaki Omoto / 104

■Chapter 4　Temporary Housing
(June 18, 2011 to March 26, 2015) ·································· 105

(1) Temporary housing basic operating policy / 106
(2) Distribution of dinner dishes to all households (from June 18, 2011) / 108
(3) City of Soma Reconstruction Meeting and expert Reconstruction Advisory Board Meeting (from June 3, 2011) / 109
(4) **City of Soma Reconstruction Plan** / 111
(5) Haragama Morning Market Club / 116
(6) **Carts** / 117
(7) 2011 Soma Nomaoi (wild horse chase) / 121
(8) **Ayane's determination** / 122
(9) **Soma Idobata Nagaya** / 125
(10) Beginning operation at the disaster waste intermediate processing facility (from October 28, 2011) / 132
(11) **Portraits of families standing together** / 134
(12) **His majesty, the king of Bhutan** / 138
(13) Poll on disaster prevention group transfer and conference with disaster-stricken residents (Thorough discussion covering 79 sessions) / 143
(14) Speech at the United Nations (UN performance of HIKOBAE stage play) (March 12, 2012) / 145
(15) **Emergency supplies storehouse** / 147

(16) **Soma Terakoya School** / 151

(17) **Your future is bright!** / 156

(18) **Fishery warehouse** / 159

(19) Completion of the new community center (October 7, 2013) / 163

(20) **Soma City Folklore Museum** / 165

(21) **Duty and sentiment (Friendship with supporting local governments)** / 169

(22) Operation of the temporary incinerator for disposing of disaster waste materials (February 20, 2013) / 174

(23) **Support from the Tokyo University of Agriculture** / 176

(24) **"Wada Strawberry Farm" agricultural corporation** / 182

(25) **FIFA Football Center preparation** / 185

(26) **PTSD countermeasures and Louis Vuitton** / 192

(27) **Soma Tourism Reconstruction Information Center and Thousands of Visitor Hall** / 198

(28) **Strong Bones Park** / 203

(29) **2014 Manifesto Awards Grand Prize** (November 14, 2014) / 208

(30) The "Soma Kids Dome" bringing smiles to the faces of kids through the power of sports (December 18, 2014) / 212

(31) **Eastern Rebuilding Association (all units of public disaster housing complete)** / 213

(June 18, 2011 to March 31, 2015)

■Chapter 5　Rebuilding Period
(Starting March 27, 2015) ································· 219

(1) Completion of public disaster housing (March 26, 2015 - All 410 units in 9 areas completed) / 220

(2) **Reconstruction and regional revitalization** / 221

(3) Residential complex meeting place - Completed in 5 areas / 225

(4) Tobu Children's Community Center (Opened on October 31, 2015) / 226

(5) Coastal rain drainage measures / 227

(6) Haragama Joint Distribution Center (Completed December 17, 2015) / 228

(7) **Neighborhood watch** / 229

(8) Isobe Seafood Processing Facilities (Completed February 18, 2016) / 232

(9) **Bringing the best wishes of the people in the food truck** / 233

(10) **News from a far-off town** / 237

(11) **Five years of life at Idobata Nagaya and strong-willed young doctors** / 241

(12) Haragama goods handling facility / seawater purification facility (Completed September 18, 2016) / 244

(13) New main building at Soma City Hall (Completed October 5, 2016) / 245

(14) Tohoku-Chuo Expressway - Abukuma Higashi Road open for traffic (March 26, 2017) / 247

(15) **My grandfather and a bicycle laden with vegetables** / 248

(16) **The Flowers Bloom (City Hall community gallery)** / 253

(17) New community pool (Completed March 22, 2017) / 257

(18) Seibu Children's Community Center (Completed April 5, 2017) / 258

Chapter 6　**Fighting Radiation** ·································· 259

(1) Preparing for worsening conditions at the nuclear power plant / 260

(2) Tap water countermeasures / 261

(3) Radiation dosage measurement and information disclosure / 262

(4) Vagueness of the Japanese government's expressions and their effects / 264

(5) Limits of city handling / 265

(6) Meeting professor Masahiro Kami / 265

(7) Information sessions in local areas on radiation and its health effects (from May 15, 2011) / 266

(8) Tamano Elementary and Junior High School schoolyard top-soil replacement (May 24 to 27, 2011) / 268

(9) Tamano area residents' health examinations (May 28 and 29, 2011) / 269

(10) Start of detailed investigation at all city schools and top soil replacement (from June 16, 2011) / 270

(11) Distributing high-pressure washers and decontamination information session in the Tamano area (August 10, 2011) / 271

(12) Food contamination testing / 272

(13) Radioiodine countermeasures / 273

(14) Systematic survey of radiation in all areas of the city and later progress (Starting June 18, 2011) / 275

(15) Start of education on radiation at schools (Beginning May 2011) / 278

(16) External exposure survey and countermeasures for all schoolchildren in the city / 279

(17) Whole-body counter / 285

(18) The necessity of radiation education / 287

(19) International symposium (May 7 and 8, 2016) / 289

■**Afterword** / 293

■**List of Reference Works** / 295

Index / 297

Chapter 1
Hyperacute Period
24 Hours After Earthquake

(1) Immediately after the earthquake

At 2:46 p.m. on March 11, 2011, returning to the City Hall after a meeting on land improvement districts, I pressed the elevator button to go up to the mayor's office on the third floor and was immediately assaulted by a powerful wave of shaking.

It was an abrupt jolt, that occurred without any time to feel any initial tremors. The lamp indicating the floor of the elevator that should have come down blinked out suddenly. It took only seconds for the power to cut out after the shaking began, I noticed immediately that it must have been a quite big earthquake.

The earthquake tremors gradually grew stronger, and looking around the interior of the first floor of the government office showed objects strewn everywhere across desks, which seemed as if they might come flying this way at any time. I remember turning to the staff and members of the public who were in uproar on the first floor, and yelling at them to stay calm and hunker down.

However, I also found too hard to keep standing.

Unlike a normal earthquake, this one was characterized by the strong tremors that continued for a long time. According to records later, the shaking continued for approximately four minutes, but I felt it was like thirty minutes or an hour.

I wondered "if this government building is going to be OK? But we can do nothing - this is our life. What I can do is only waiting to stop.. I hope it's soon."

The shaking continued so long until subsiding. When it was over, I felt relieved to survive. I rushed to the office of the manager of general affairs on the third floor.

"This is an emergency situation. We have to have a crisis response meeting right away."

Even before they heard my order, the people responsible for disaster response were hurrying towards me.

"Where is the head of the committee?"

"We can't get through to his cellphone."

"Is he OK?"

"If he is, I'm sure he will be here as soon

Hyperacute period

Chapter 1

as he can."

Shortly after, fire chief Tadao Ara with his sunburned face came towards me in his fireman's garb. Nine minutes after the shaking had stopped, I noted the visages of deputy chiefs Isamu Kanno and Yukio Yamada, who came in a little late.

Everyone moved from the general affairs section to the government office meeting room.

"We are now going to establish a Disaster Management Headquarters. I would like everyone to follow the disaster response manual and begin their assigned tasks. However, I have a special request for the fire brigade. Some buildings may have collapsed, so I would like brigade members in each area to check all of the buildings in their respective districts. There is currently a tsunami warning in effect. We are told that there may be a tsunami as high as three meters. Those brigades in inland areas should check collapsed buildings and rescue any injured people, third, seventh, and ninth brigades should evacuate citizens to high ground. The evacuation sites in the disaster manual are fine. In any case, however, tell people to head for places in elevated areas."

In response to my words the fire chief, deputy chiefs, and other city staff began contacting the ten brigades.

Before long, reports on the damage caused by the earthquake began to stream in, and it was apparent that there were almost no houses without any damages from the disaster.

Reports arrived of fallen utility poles blocking the streets, and of collapsed walls in various locations around the city obstructing vehicle traffic. "If ambulances can't get through, then the only thing we can do is have fire brigades and rescue teams carry the injured on stretchers. How far will that get us? If a fire breaks out with the roads in this state we don't stand a chance!" Such were the thoughts that preyed on me.

Thirty minutes later, some information arrived that left us horror-struck. A woman had been struck on the head by a collapsing wall in a supermarket and left unconscious and seriously injured. We checked ambulance access and the availability of a hospital to

take her in and I thought "The only thing we can do now is pray, and hope that no one else has been hurt."

People in coastal areas were already being instructed to evacuate to high ground. Fire brigade members and the head of the administrative district were going to the various communities in the area to tell people to evacuate.

We were asking everyone in areas closed to the sea to evacuate to high ground, so in addition to the Isobe elementary and junior high schools in Isobe district that were sit-

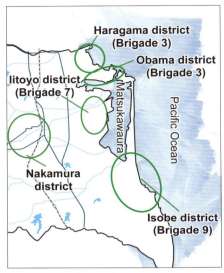

Soma city coast

uated in higher areas. The gym at Nakamura Daini Elementary and Junior High School and the Tobu Community Center, which are closed to Haragama and Matsukawa districts. The gyms and multipurpose facilities in inland areas of the Nakamura district were also used as evacuation areas.

There were no records of anyone dying in a tsunami in Soma City since the city began keeping records in the Meiji Era (which began in 1868), which is the reason that no one living near the coast, including myself, had any great fear of tsunamis. However, this was a big earthquake, and we were left fraught with the knowledge that it went beyond the levels depicted on the hazard maps, praying that people would flee to high ground.

The City Hall was luckily enough not to suffer from a power outage, so everything played out on the television screen, which announced the imminent arrival of a tsunami in the Sanriku area.

When we asked people in Soma to move to elevated areas as quickly as possible due to the likelihood of a tsunami hitting the region, a report burst in stating that a tsunami had penetrated four kilometers inland and was about to overflow onto the National Route 6 bypass. I found this difficult to believe, but the next report was from the head of the third brigade, saying that the Haragama district had been obliterated, and that a tsunami of unimaginable size had come.

Hyperacute period

When I raised my voice to ask him if the members of the third sub-brigade were safe, he reported that most of the group had escaped to an elevated area nearby, but that they were unable to confirm that everyone was okay.

Hurriedly, I contacted the ninth brigade from the Isobe district, but neither the brigade chief nor his deputy responded.

We were able to contact the seventh brigade, who told us that citizens of the area had fled to higher regions and were safe. "The tsunami has swallowed the houses next to Matsukawaura, but all of the brigade members are also all right."

There were elevated areas adjacent to the Iwanoko and Kashiwazaki districts for which the seventh brigade was responsible, and thus residents did not need to travel far to find shelter. Although flat and full of paddy fields, the Niida region lies far from the coast, and thus there were few reports of buildings being damaged by the tsunami.

However, the Osu and Seriyachi areas of Isobe were far from areas with high ground. I was filled with foreboding, but there was absolutely nothing I could do, and of course there was no response to our calls to cellphones or landlines. I requested calls to be made to those residents of the Isobe district living in elevated areas, but we were unable to obtain any information over the phone.

Amidst the building frustration, a stream of detailed reports of the damage was arriving at my feet. This was information from citizens who had somehow managed to get through to us, and via the fire brigade radio from the third sub-brigade who had managed to escape to higher elevations.

"A woman has been swept offshore."

"I saw a van from the Council of Social Welfare floating away."

There was more than one tsunami. I thought that after the drawback of the first tsunami, the second tsunami was incredibly powerful. Many of the people who fell victim to this wave were swallowed by it after returning to their homes to retrieve their valuables after the first wave.

Among the information we received were strained

19

requests for help. "I'm cut off. I escaped to high ground okay, but I'm hurt, and I need help quickly." At the time the technology to dispatch a drone immediately like we can nowadays didn't exist, and it was very difficult for us to gain an understanding of the disaster in its entirety.

The time was a bit after 4 pm. In another hour sunset would be on us, and we had to gather as much information as we could. We continued with preparations to work with the Self-Defense Forces, who we had already contacted, to rescue people who had been cut off. At the same time, we faced the pressing issue of providing warmth and water to victims of the disaster who were gathered in the evacuation sites.

We had made a request directly to the Self-Defense Forces immediately after the tsunami for taking action, and had informed the prefecture of this. Although we were supposed to route requests for cooperation through the prefecture, we were in a race against time, and didn't have the leeway to work with the prefecture acting as an intermediary. When the head of the general affairs department placed a call directly to the Camp Fukushima of the Ground Self-Defense Forces, he was told that they would firstly send an advance team on motorcycles, and then move in with mobility vehicles.

The help of the Self-Defense Forces was essential if we were to rescue those people who had been cut off. We had received information that there were many survivors who had been stranded in two- and three-story buildings that had not been swept away in the tsunami seawater, but we were waiting on tenterhooks for the arrival of the Self-Defense Force mobility vehicles that would help to get through the rubble and seawater to perform rescue operations. Until then we had to gather data on how many people were cut off and where they were, and gain as much information on the state of the rubble and the areas of flooding as we could before sunset.

The evacuation sites that opened when the tsunami warning was issued and the evacuation directive went out toward community centers in high areas, some elementary and high schools, the Arena sports facility, and the "Hamanasu-kan" welfare facility. Thinking that residents would have to help each other at the evacuation sites, we directed entire communities to

20

Hyperacute period   Chapter 1

evacuate to a single location.

One hour after the tsunami, the evacuation sites were already full, and the reserves of food, water, and blankets (700) stocked by Soma City were completely insufficient. We handled the difficulties with food by securing all of the products at supermarkets in the city with which disaster cooperation arrangements had been made, but still there was nowhere near enough.

Several hours after the tsunami, the situation at the evacuation sites was extremely fluid, and it was almost impossible to grasp how many people were there. However we were already anticipating that we would have to operate the evacuation sites for a considerable length of time. Thus we needed to have an idea, even if approximate, of how many people they housed. Additionally, information from evacuees who had been rescued from areas close to the tsunami was invaluable.

In order that the Self-Defense Forces be able to start rescue work as soon as they arrived, we had to record and collate a great deal of information that the City Hall was receiving from residents, and at first we struggled in chaos.

So we decided to write things one after another on a single whiteboard as time passed, even if it had to be done in a random manner. This single whiteboard was entirely covered in an instant, so we arranged for the next whiteboard and unified information gathering in a chronological manner. Furthermore, I instructed to take pictures of the whiteboard as time passed.

The capacity of designated evacuation sites was, at base, the number of people that the community centers and school gymnasiums were able to hold, but as we gained an understanding of the situation we faced, it became clear that based on normal assumptions these facilities would be nowhere near adequate.

Moreover, we felt that school education would be impossible for quite long time, and accordingly we opened all of the classrooms of the Nakamura Daiichi Elementary School, a school with wooden buildings that had only just been completed. I directed that the Hamanasu-kan wel-

21

fare facility also be opened in its entirety as an evacuation site.

As the emergency headquarters, we tried to estimate the scale of the disaster based on the number of disaster victims gathering, but because the numbers were increasing moment by moment, we faced enormous difficulties in providing water and blankets, and preparing food.

However, those residents in areas that had only been damaged by the earthquake and had not been affected the tsunami were extremely cooperative with regard to the city's disaster response measures.

Since it was on March, still cold days, blankets were blankets were particularly important. Night had already fallen, but we sought the cooperation of the city's public relations vehicles and large quantities of blankets were delivered to the City Hall. The blankets were provided to victims at evacuation sited randomly, therefore there are no accurate records of the relevant quantities remaining unfortunately. I saw the blankets streaming in and felt the latent power of the community in Soma though.

I visited the evacuation sites to see how things were going, but conversely was met by encouraging cries of, "Mayor! It's times for you to do your best and hold everything together!" from the victims. I returned to emergency headquarters, wondering to myself if there wasn't anything we could do to turn this situation around. How could I put myself into the fight?

At emergency headquarters, Takashi Watanabe, the section chief in charge of planning policy was working away diligently in his seat. Although we had received information that his father, the head of administration for the Isobe district, had been taken by the tsunami while

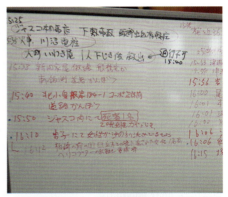

Goods collected First floor lobby

Hyperacute period — Chapter 1

Blankets and bedding collected from city residents

giving evacuation instructions, Watanabe was struggling resolutely to deal with this awful fact.

I was also not in a situation which I could ask someone about the welfare of my younger brother, who lived in Haragama district and whose whereabouts were unknown. Watanabe was conveying to me wordlessly that I, as mayor, should lead the struggle before worrying about my family.

(2) Initial systematic action guidelines

With everyone at city hall bewildered by the earthquake information that was gradually coming to light, I felt that I should encourage myself by giving my goals to achieve, and find the will to do my job. The only way to prevent myself, and the emergency headquarters along with me, from being overwhelmed by the crisis, was to give our goals and objectives regarding the fears and anxiety preying on us, and to fight to achieve them.

After 24 hours we began formulating action goals and putting all of our affairs in order. The television showed footage of the disaster that had struck along the entire pacific coast of eastern Japan, plunging hundreds of thousands of people into crisis.

How far would the support from the government and the Self-Defense Forces stretch in the face of so many victims? We needed temporary housing, but how much was there to be found across the country? If we hesitated now, would there be any left for us?

We couldn't afford to lose if competition to build temporary housing emerged. That was what turned me around. We couldn't afford to lose the competition, and we couldn't allow ourselves to give in to the disaster.

However, before I looked to the future, my immediate concerns where the people cut off and waiting for rescue, and the more than 4,000 people at evacuation sites who had been displaced from their homes. The most important thing was to safeguard the lives and health of these people. Things like the construction of temporary housing would come after that, but I had to be very aware of them as objectives.

That was when I decided to establish countermeasure goals to protect the citizens and the victims of the disaster, splitting them into those for immediate action and those aimed at rebuilding the region and disaster-struck areas.

My first objectives, as our immediate response, were
1) Rescue of people who were cut off.
2) Gathering of information on the disaster, and confirmation of survivors.
3) Supply of water, food, warmth, medical care and governance to evacuation sites to insure that no deaths occurred among those who had managed to escape from the disaster with their lives.
4) Acquisition of water trucks to supply water to areas outside those struck by the tsunami.

Hyperacute period

5) Losing out to other disaster-afflicted areas in acquiring necessities would mark my failure as a leader.

My second objectives, for medium-term response, were

1) Ensuring the availability of apartments and unused residences for disaster victims, and creation of a database of those affected by the disaster and confirmation of their contact details to facilitate this.

Obtaining the cooperation of all real estate agents in the city area to hold all open apartments, and beginning negotiations to use company dormitories and employment promotion accommodation that was relatively unused due to its worn state.

2) Quickly request cooperation from friendship cities with which we had concluded disaster prevention agreements since there were insufficient city hall staff and city businesses to reopen roads that had been affected by the disaster, and rapidly begin to remove as much rubble as possible to establish routes for traffic.

3) Since there would probably be a struggle to obtain building materials for temporary housing, apply to the prefecture that day.

This application would be predicated on obtaining land to build on, and thus we needed to begin drawing up plans using idle city land. If we were able to borrow idle land from businesses, we should begin negotiations right away. Businesses holding land within the cities were probably mostly companies.

4) Since most evacuees came to the evacuation sites with nothing but the clothes on their backs, they probably wouldn't even have enough money to buy a tooth brush, so they should be given 3,000 yen each.

However, when doing so we should check their identification and ask for their contact details, and compare these with the basic resident register so that we had materials to create a database.

5) Apart from the problems of tsunami damage, make plans to get water and sewerage services, electricity, and gas restored, to restore lifelines, and re-look at all of these in the entirety while doing so.

It was at 1 a.m. by the time I wrote all of these ideas down in itemized form and gave them to deputy mayor Norio Sato.

Once they received my instructions, the paperwork done by Sato, the deputy mayor, and Kenichi Koyama, the chief of the construction department who was also present due to his secondment from the Ministry of Land, Infrastructure, Transport and Tourism, was something to behold.

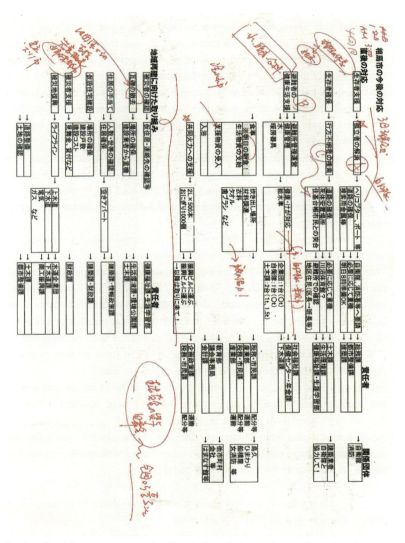

The fourth crisis response meeting/Excel sheet listing action goals and assignments

Hyperacute period — Chapter 1

They transformed my directives into items on a vertically formatted Excel sheet, with specific action items spreading across the sheet horizontally, assigned responsibilities to departments, and brought it to me.

This format communicated the instructions of the general manager and made the roles and responsibilities of everyone at emergency headquarters clear, all on a single sheet. They also finished a strategy and plan document defining our action goals. This provided the emergency headquarters, which had heretofore been reeling under the scale of the disaster, with a clear strategy that allowed us to fight back. With this in mind, I convened the fourth crisis response meeting.

At this meeting, which started at 2:45 a.m., we decided on short-term response policies for lifesaving and maintaining the health of city residents, and settled on policies for the long-term rebuilding of the region as action goals. These were shared with everyone at emergency headquarters. With affected personnel and staff at City Hall sharing the same sense of purpose, a team was formed at Soma. We received information and concrete recommendations from headquarters staff during discussions in meetings, and I also made my own additions, stating, "There is going to be competition for coffins as well, so for now, please order 500 tomorrow."

I myself felt that this was a contest, and a fight to rebuild. My feelings that we must not lose in the struggle with other regions changed to a determination that we absolutely must not give in to the crisis.

Disaster response headquarters meeting
(March 12, 2011, 2:45 a.m.)
(Author's photograph)

(3) The reality I observed

Night passed without me being able to get even a moment's sleep. In morning we had meeting to check action plans for each department. After the meeting, fire chief Tadao Ara, deputy chiefs Isamu Kanno and Yukio Yamada, and myself headed to the Haragama district, which had been hit by the tsunami.

We thought that we had gained a general grasp of the state of the damage from the reports received from Koichi Tachiya, chief of third brigade, but nothing brought the truth about the difference between the images in our heads and reality home as strongly as that moment.

Three bodies had already been placed in the Haragama fire station where we stopped the car. A single glance revealed that they were elderly women, but their faces were distorted and had turned an earthen color. Almost all of the older women in the Haragama district were patients at my clinic, so I should have remembered their faces, but in death these three looked completely different and I was unable to recognize them.

For now, I brought my hands together to pray for them, all the while repeating, "I'm sorry, I'm sorry" in my head. When we moved into the back yard of Yukio Tachiya, a former member of the city council whose home was on high ground, the scene of the tsunami devastation hit me full force.

For as far as the eye could see, not a single house stood standing in the areas of Haragama and Otsu, which had been engulfed by the tsunami, and there were heaps of rubble strewn everywhere. Below us and to our right

Hyperacute period — Chapter 1

The sign from the Tachiya Miso and Soy Sauce
store that was swept away

should have been the miso and soy sauce store where I was born and raised, but I was unable to discern where my home had been.

I was barely able to see the signboard of the miso and soy sauce store where it had been carried in front of the reinforced concrete offices of the fishermen's union. It flashed into my mind whether my younger brother and his wife, who had taken over the family business, had escaped or not, but I was unable to voice my thoughts.

The Tachiya household had lived on this land for generations, and Haragama was where I grew up. I was shocked at the change, and my mind was blank.

Six and a half hours ago, I had been formulating strategies at the crisis response meeting to deal with the emergency, and the determination to win this battle had been such an inspiration to me.

Could I really hope to rebuild the lives of the people who had suffered such a terrible loss?

How on earth can we to deal with all this rubble?

I was shocked with immobility.

The next thing I knew is that was clutching at my back and sobbing. It was Yukio, the eldest of my relatives.

"Haragama is gone. The soy sauce store is gone."

I came to my senses immediately.

"It's okay. I'll take care of it. Don't cry."

29

Next, we set out for the Matsukawa district. Rubble was scattered around Matsukawaura, and there were houses that had been swept away by the tsunami rising up out of the water.

Vehicle passage through the area near the entrance to the Matsukawa district was impossible, and although we tried to clear the rubble away with our hands and feet to get through, the fishing boats that the waves had carried up onto the surface of the road blocked our path.

As we threaded our way carefully over the detritus, all the while being careful of nails and fragments, we encountered a fisherman with an octopus dangling from his hand. "I couldn't dock in the port, so I looked for a sand bar and jumped into the sea. There's not a trace left of my home, so I have to go to the evacuation sites to search for my family." He said no more after that.

We bade him farewell and tried to proceed, but the rubble thwarted us and we were unable to make any progress. I had to see how other areas were doing, and we were about to turn back, but deputy chief Yamada tried to go forward on his own, saying, "My daughter married and went to live in Matsukawa. I don't know where she is. I have to check on her house."

Although this was the first I had noticed it, the deputy chief had been holding back his concern for his daughter since the previous evening, trapped in emergency headquarters.

Prompted by the expression on his face, all four of us attempted to press on, but eventually Yamada declared, "Mayor, we can't just search for my daughter. Let's go to Iwanoko and Isobe." The other three of us signaled assent with our eyes, and set out for the roads of Wada district, which were on high ground and led to Iwanoko.

Because the Iwanoko district had a community at the base of a reef

Hyperacute period — Chapter 1

continuing down from a higher area, evacuation from the tsunami had been comparatively smooth, and thus we understood from reports on the day that no deaths had occurred.

However, the reclaimed land in Iwanoko that had been a prominent grain producing area was now covered in huge accumulations of pine trees and sludge that precluded any vehicle traffic, so

Iwanoko area

we were unable to make any progress. The masses of pine trees that we saw had been turned into driftwood were enveloped in mud, scattered across the paddy fields in a terrible spectacle, making the revival of any agriculture seem like a hopeless dream.

We abandoned our attempt to travel to Isobe from Iwanoko and tried to approach from the Nittaki area. Even the area, which was relatively far inland, had been inundated with rubble pushed in from Isobe, most likely, with even the paths between the paddy fields filled with detritus.

A fireman noticed me, saying, "Mayor, there are bodies in here. We contacted the police and they told us not to touch them and to wait until the police arrived."

When I looked, I could see bodies submerged in the seawater under the rubble. I was tempted to say, "That's outrageous, I'll do it myself!" but at the same time my heart was pained by the notion that this was someone from Isobe, and dread at the thought of what might have happened to the area.

There were large quantities of rubble and driftwood in the Isobe area, and on that attempt we were unable to reach our destination.

We thought it best that the bodies be placed temporarily in a gymnasium borrowed from the old Soma Girls' High School, which had been closed down. Therefore, I made a request to the prefecture and received approval.

Although the members of the police and

31

Self-Defense Forces were extremely caring and diligent in the search for bodies, I requested to the fire chief, head bowed, that local fire brigade members taking part in wearing their happi coat uniforms in a manner visible to the local citizens. I believed that this was an issue of pride for the people of Soma. With every family affected by the tsunami and earthquake, the members of the fire brigade continued to show themselves in this guise to the citizens of Soma.

(4) Emergency medical care systems

When I returned from observing the state of the afflicted regions, there was some information waiting that gave me great courage.

Since gathering survivors in evacuation sites and securing food, water, and warmth took precedence over everything else on the night of the 11th, I had that thought that anything but dealing with emergency cases of sick people was a job for the second day. However, almost all of the doctors belonging to the Soma medical association had assembled of their own accord at the evacuation sites set up by Soma at the Hamanasu-kan and Sports Arena Soma facilities.

Normally I got on well with them, but I had never felt them to be such a source of strength until that moment.

Shortly thereafter Yoshito Sengoku, formerly Chief Cabinet Secretary with the Democratic Party administration of the day, called my cellphone, saying "Mr. Tachiya, I'm glad you're okay. How is the damage to Soma? Do you need us to arrange for a DMAT?" (Disaster Medical Assistance Team) Beginning with that phone call, I stayed in touch with Sengoku and his confidant Ryu Matsumoto, who was to be the first Minister for Reconstruction; we contacted each other every night.

There are two hospitals in Soma city. Public Soma General Hospital, of which I am the director, and the privately running Soma Central Hospital. Both hospitals were in a flurry trying to deal with issues such as low water pressure and damage to equipment caused by the earthquake, spending a sleepless night treating people who had been injured in the earthquake, or

Hyperacute period

Chapter 1

emergency patients who had fallen ill. Taking into account measures to counter secondary health hazards to the victims of the disaster, I felt they faced a grave shortage of medical personnel. I requested the immediate dispatch of a DMAT. I think that Sengoku's overwhelming kindness and assessment of the situation surpassed everyone else in the government of the day. Matsumoto, to whom the task of assisting with the dispatch of the DMAT fell, turned out to be an extremely nice person. We were the same age, and I think that we will remain friends for the rest of our lives.

Although the primary task of the DMAT would be to provide health care for emergency cases and disaster victims, doctors cannot provide effective care without a venue, and so we settled on Soma Central Hospital to act as their base of operations, including accommodation, and I instructed them to use the medical equipment, supplies, and other items as they saw fit. The DMAT remained there for around a week, and proved extremely capable at working in the battlefield-like medical conditions present in the acute phase of the crisis.

24 hours after the event, we had a rough idea of the scale of the emergency and the state of the victims. Working reports from each fire brigade and map data possessed by city hall, we conjecture that there were around 5,000 victims, with the Isobe district, which had lost the Osu, Seriyachi, and Ohama communities in their entirety, having been hit particularly hard. Communities that had lost half or more of their households were Kitaharagama, Obama, Minamiharagama, Iwanoko, and Koisobe.

Approximately 4,500 people were gathered at the evacuation sites. The death toll was estimated to be between 500 and 600 people. While some people had evacuated to stay with friends and relatives, some residents in areas outside those that had been hit by the tsunami were seeking help from evacuation sites due to the power outages and water shutoffs caused by the earthquake. Therefore it was impossible to know exactly how many there were. Thereafter, we made changes in step with checking disaster victim certificates and the basic resident register, but this early on we would institute actions based on our initial estimates.

33

(5) Aid from friendly municipalities

As early as the morning of March 12, supplies of blankets, rice, and emergency food such as "alpha mai" (instant rice that can be eaten immediately after water is added), water, and hard biscuits were arrived from our sister city of Nagareyama in Chiba prefecture, and Tokyo's Adachi ward, with whom we had concluded a disaster prevention agreement.

Since this was before the Self-Defense Forces started emergency rice distribution, we were extremely grateful for the alpha mai and water. Aid materials from Yonezawa city in the Tohoku region's Yamagata prefecture arrived the following day. Since the earthquake crisis affected all of Tohoku, I pictured the face of the mayor of Yonezawa as I thought about how difficult it must have been for Yonezawa city, which was also dealing with water shutoffs and damaged homes. Nagano prefecture's Komoro city, which was battling a truncated election vote count period was also quick to send goods. The gratitude I felt when we received aid supplies from friendly

municipalities in the difficult times immediately after the earthquake remains with me to this day. This led to the overall policy of Soma city that, "The quicker the better when sending aid goods."

We printed the names of the municipalities who had provided us with aid on sheets of A4-size paper, and posted them on the wall at city hall.

Thereafter, aid from friendly municipalities continued to arrive. When unloading it, we had to keep accurate records of what materials had arrived and from where. City employees who had acquired ISO9001 certification were already accustomed to keeping records, and I think they did a great job in the midst of such chaos.

I asked them to create a database of the aid we received using Excel sheets. Creating a database gave us a good understanding of what goods we were short of, and what was consumed rapidly. Next, we waited for the Internet to be connected, and listed the goods we needed on the city website.

Additionally, I set a written request for aid to the chairman of the city mayors' association of which I was a member, asking for aid. Although the circumstances were such that we didn't know when the letters would be delivered or if the logistical systems would serve to get the supplies to us, I was happy that there was someone I could ask.

I was keenly aware of how much one needs friends.

物資残数（各方面からの支援物資状況含む）

食料品関係

品　名	単位	アルプス	女子高	低温倉庫	市民会館	川俣体育館	計
サバイバルフーズ	箱			338		665	1,003
アルファ米	食			450			450
お米	kg			131,103		59	131,162
パックごはん	食				482		482
塩	kg					12	12
レトルト丼	箱			1			1
レトルト食品	食				8,766	186	8,952
レトルトカレー	ケース				2		2
カップメン	個				1,587	25,682	27,269
カロリーメイト	箱				4,128	2,380	6,508
缶詰	缶				2,205	71,740	73,945
お菓子類	袋				4,253	9,293	13,546
チョコレート	箱				8	300	308
せんべい	袋				852		852
かんぱん	食			47	640		687
クッキー	食(箱)			20	414		434
粉ミルク	缶				59	1,240	1,299
さとう	kg				10	24	34
パン	食			80			80
スープ	食				9,086		9,086
みそ	箱				33	100	133
味噌汁	食			27	21	6,800	6,848
水	ℓ			128,226		1,220	129,446
牛乳	本				684		684

Compilation of a database of relief supplies

Chapter 2
Acute Period: The First Two Weeks After Earthquake

(1) News report about the nuclear accident

Starting March 12, Kenichi Koyama, the chief of the construction department, began using a computer to take notes on my statements made at the crisis response meeting and the details of our discussions. They comprise a precious resource, serving as a record of the period of acute crisis for the disaster. I wrote the content of this chapter based on those records (the original versions).

News organization began reporting over and over starting around 20 hours after the earthquake occurred that Fukushima Daiichi Nuclear Power Station (hereafter Fukushima Daiichi) had been hit by the tsunami.

With Soma City separated from the station by about 45 kilometers, initially we thought that the nuclear disaster in Futaba district would be a problem for some other place. At a moment when we were doing our utmost to provide food, medical care, and a place to stay for more than 4,000 evacuees and protect their lives and their health, we thought it would just be a nuisance with the nuclear station being in Futaba so far away. We were too busy worrying about Soma.

But then we heard reports first that the nuclear source material could no longer be kept cool owing to a fault in the electrical power systems at Fukushima Daiichi and then a hydrogen explosion had occurred. In response, starting the evening of March 12th, people from Minamisoma City's Odaka Ward began surging into Soma City's evacuation sites. This forced us to take the nuclear accident into account in the courses of action we pursued.

At first, I thought that the nuclear accident should be a problem for the national and prefectural governments to deal with. However, following on reports about the risk of radiation spreading the situation became one that even Soma City 45 kilometers away would have to confront in earnest.

More than 20 years before when I was in my first year as a member of prefectural assembly, there had been a great debate about whether Fukushima Prefecture should accept a plutonium-for-thermal-use project. What I learned at the time was that content percentage of the

Kenichi Koyama, the chief of the construction department

Acute Period

Chapter 2

uranium 235 that would become nuclear fuel within natural uranium is less than 0.7 percent. When it concentrate to a level of 3% to 5%, it undergoes fission if unattended. The heat generated under such conditions is turned into energy. This is how nuclear power is generated. Coolant water is used to control the nuclear reaction. A nuclear power station constitutes a system for controlling and converting energy. On the other hand, making a nuclear bomb that will explode in an instant requires condensing uranium 235 to a level of 90%. This nuclear-enrichment technology is something that nuclear weapon states were the first to come to grips with. These required levels are the reason why a nuclear explosion cannot occur at a nuclear power station.

That is the basic knowledge I learned about nuclear power stations. The plutonium-thermal project had the objective of glass-hardening fission product from uranium 235 and burying it 500 meters underground. However, it easy to imagine that the fission products contained in the nuclear source material would scatter into the outside air should the fuel rods melt. I knew from my profession that the human body would receive a dosage as a result, the effects of which were expressed in millisieverts. We physicians work within an acceptable range of up to 50 millisieverts annually.

When the nuclear accident was first reported, we didn't think we would have to go so far as to consider the effects of fission product being scattered in the air. However, the situation changed completely with the hydrogen explosion at the reactor building.

At that point when we were thinking that the radiation leaking from the nuclear station would not reach Soma 45 kilometers away and there was no expectation of the nuclear source material exploding, we were confronted with the reality that radioactive materials lofted by the wind into the air would be pouring down.

Since Soma General Hospital had radiation counters in case of any exposure in the hospital itself, on March 13th, Director Yoshinobu Kuma hurried to us with the data collected. The data showed that the level of exposure on March 13th stood at 3.25 microsieverts per hour, and on the following day at 1.25 microsieverts per hour. If conditions arose such that these figures rose continuously, we would be forced to consider evacuating the entire city including the patients in the hospital. Director Kuma and I decided that a rise in the range of 20 to 40 microsieverts per hour would indicate that we should temporarily evacuate while keeping an eye out on what the national government was doing and the prefecture directed. Still, as a rule we also agreed that even if the figures were lower than that we would have to go along with whatever the national government directed.

However, the government drew a concentric circle around the plant and used that to set its standard for evacuation. It issued no clear comments about doses. The only thing it said was that "at this stage they are not at a level that will immediately be harmful to health."

This way of putting things left Soma residents and many Japanese ill at ease.

As a matter of fact, massive numbers of people from Minamisoma City have descended upon Soma. Having residents of Minamisoma mixed in with Soma residents at Soma evacuation sites would create confusion when it came to management of disaster victims. I asked the prefectural government for permission to designate the classrooms in the buildings of the defunct Soma Girls' High School a new evacuation site, with the thought that we would have no choice but to supply food and other supplies to them just like we do to Soma City residents.

After 24 hours had passed, it fell as though everyone at emergency headquarters had steadied their nerves to look to the road ahead. We had discussed the problems and issues as topics of concern for everyone, all of the HQ staff were aware of what was going on in each section, and methods had been settled upon for sharing response measures.

When there were differences of opinion or a lack of information made decision-making difficult, the HQ chief would settle the issue and make a decision. Given that disaster response requires coming to a conclusion in order to move ahead, I had the repeated experience of taking responsibility as HQ chief and being decisive when the team could not make a decision.

Acute Period Chapter 2

(2) Soma City Official Records from March 12th to March 14th (original Japanese text reproduced as written)

●March 12th, 2011 (Saturday), 9:00 a.m. 5th Disaster response headquarters meeting (HQ chief's instructions and discussion)

▷Substantial amount of human remains. Next issue is the search for missing persons and the collection of human remains.
There are corpses floating in the ocean. Situation is we can get boats to pick them up, but they can't reach shore.

▷At present we have 150 coffins, which will not be enough so we need to get more made quickly.
Contact undertakers in the Nakadori area and secure dry ice.

▷Survey of evacuation site needs currently underway. We are collecting towels, toothbrushes, snowsuits, etc. from local residents.
Water is being distributed from the civic center.

▷Schools will have to be closed for a while.

▷Prepare and utilize the employee housing facilities for people to live in them from next week.

▷Consolatory payments of 30,000 yen per person. Must be disbursed as quickly as possible.

Scene at the city hall with disbursal of city-provided assistance grants (30,000 yen per person)

●**March 12th, 2011 (Saturday), 3:30 p.m. 6th Disaster response headquarters meeting (HQ chief's instructions and discussion)**
▷Fuel will run out in three days. Won't be able to come from Sendai Harbor, so we must also think about not being able to obtain fuel.
▷Should lease private apartments quickly. Also hurry up with getting employee housing facilities prepared.

● **March 13th, 2011 (Sunday), 8:30 a.m. 7th Disaster response headquarters meeting (HQ chief's instructions and discussion)**
▷Search for missing persons at the same time as clearing rubble. Create evacuation routes while clearing rubble. Have police check when human remains turn up.
Be deferential in transport of human remains, in principle done by using three police station wagons. No choice but to settle on the method of viewing at the mortuary itself to confirm the identity of the corpse.
▷Need to match the deceased whose identities have been confirmed with resident registries. The same goes for survivors.
People left over in the middle (do not correspond to either group) are missing persons.
The administrative work won't move forward if the sorting into these three groups is not finished.
▷Establish the zones swallowed up by the tsunami. How many people lived in there?
In Haragama, Kitaharagama, Matsukawa, Obama, Isobe, Iwanoko, Niida, and Kashiwazaki.
Need to hurry with task of matching residential maps with resident registries. Make lists of zones and names of people to be searched and match with list of evacuees.
Have accurate list of evacuees drawn up and manage carefully.
▷Build 1,000 units of temporary housing as quickly as possible.

Tsunami damage in the Obama district (taken March 13, 2011)

Acute Period   Chapter 2

● **March 13th, 2011 (Sunday), 3:30 p.m. 8th Disaster response headquarters meeting (HQ chief's instructions and discussion)**

▷ Provide 29,000 yen subsidies toward leasing private apartments.

▷ Nuclear refugees are coming to Soma City. Particularly from Odaka Ward. Several dozen came last night, and more are coming today.
House them in the defunct Soma Girl's High School.
There are toilets there, and can already accept 150 people.
Get everyone other than Soma City residents stay at the Girl's High School.
Marumori Town says they can take in 500 people.

Clearing roads

▷ Items to ask for when other municipalities provide assistance include emergency rations, canned goods that serve as side dishes, blankets, bath towels, futons, rice, powdered milk, diapers (both children and adult), toilet paper, etc.
Request assistance from Mayors' Conference on Medical Issues, Mayors' Association to Consider Social Capital Improvements, and the participating municipalities of the Hotoku Summit.

▷ Put up notice at entrance to the city hall about municipalities from whom aid has been received. "Thank you, XXX Town, for YYY (rice, etc.)" sort of note.

43

● **March 14th, 2011 (Monday), 8:00 a.m. 9th and at 6:00 p.m. 10th Disaster response headquarters meeting (HQ chief's instructions and discussion)**
▷ Sort out short-term, mid-term, and long-term responses for separate consideration.
▷ Currently, there are approximately 4,000 people at evacuation sites. The density of people at sites is high. We must think about problems related to mental health, privacy, and food, clothing, and housing.
 On housing, we will prepare as quickly as possible temporary housing and apartments.
▷ Coffins. City has 100, police have 50. Asked prefectural government for the remainder. For the moment, expect that the city will be able to secure 550.
▷ The Water Supply Authority should think about how to go about water distribution.
▷ To help evacuees with daily life, push forward on relocating them to employee housing facilities and Alps Electric's dormitory for single employees.
▷ As to formulating an ordinance on living support grants, propose to the Assembly 30,000 yen per person assistance grants and 100,000 yen in condolence money.
▷ To get information to residents, publish and distribute a Notification Edition (Extra) twice weekly.

Koho Soma Extra Edition

Acute Period   Chapter 2

The nuclear accident forced people from one after another neighboring municipality to flee. Starting on the 13th, the large number of evacuees coming from Minamisoma City for the time being were housed in the defunct Soma Girl's High School. The mayor of Minamisoma City asked us to look after people from that city's Odaka Ward, who had been ordered to evacuate, along with people from other city neighborhoods who made the independent decision to seek refuge. "Municipal employees are also evacuating and we can't maintain control," the mayor said. "I'm sorry, but we need Soma's municipal workers cope with the situation."

Having to operate evacuation sites for the people from Minamisoma put sizable burdens on the stamina of our municipal workers besides working day and night. Minamisoma, however, had taken the initiative in calling on its residents to seek refuge. Therefore we had no choice to look after these evacuees.

In response to my request for assistance with manpower, All-Japan Prefectural and Municipal Workers Union (JICHIRO) Secretary Yasushi Konno put in efforts that resulted in the dispatch of administrative staff including public health workers. Furthermore, through JICHIRO and thanks to a request for assistance made to the prefectural headquarters of the Japanese Trade Union Confederation (known as "Rengo"), workers from around the country gathered together as volunteers. Thanks to their assistance, Soma municipal employees were able to get back to their original task of responding to the disaster. This truly helped us. Later, on the occasion that I made a report in an address delivered at JICHIRO's headquarters in the prefecture, I bowed deeply to them in appreciation.

45

(3) A Frightening experience

The evening of March 14th, I experienced the greatest crisis of my life.

I would stoically listen to the news of the hydrogen explosion at Fukushima Daiichi's number 3 reactor. That's because based on what I knew a nuclear explosion like that of an atomic bomb could not occur with uranium 235 in the concentrations found in nuclear source material.

However, at 9:00 that evening 100-plus Self-Defense Forces members imposingly outfitted with protective cloaks worn over their camouflage uniforms and carrying gas masks began rolling in the city hall.

The municipal conference room at the City Hall was already being used as liaison center for the Self-Defense Forces, so there were usually five or six soldiers on standby anyway. The newcomers' arrival at first wasn't that surprising. On the other hand, their numbers even had me mystified, so I went to the office of the director of the general affairs section and gave instructions to find out what this detachment had been sent here to do and make arrangements. That's when it happened. The unit's leader walked briskly alongside me and said, "You need to direct all Soma City residents to evacuate. We will be their escort."

Looking around, I saw the eyes of every worker on the third floor of the city hall were gazing at me intently.

"What happened? On what grounds are you telling me to do this? I haven't heard anything about this from either the national or prefectural governments."

"They are orders from higher ups."

It occurred to me that I hadn't seen that many reporters around during the day, nor had there been any of the liaisons from the Ministry of Land, Infrastructure, Transport, and Tourism, or any of the other support staff dispatched by the national government. The Ministry's Construction Department Chief Koyama Kenichi in town on temporary assignment was the only one there.

We quickly confirmed that dosage levels in Soma had not abruptly risen, and so far we could tell from the news on the television. It did not seem like some sudden development had occurred at Fukushima Daiichi other than the hydrogen explosion at the Number 3 reactor building. I directed the head of the general affairs department to contact the prefectural government right away and check whether or not a state of emergency was in effect.

Acute Period Chapter 2

I left the general affairs section and from the mayor's office placed a call to the cell phone of Yoshito Sengoku, a leading figure in the ruling Democratic Party. I thought I would be able to confirm what the government's thinking was. Mr. Sengoku told me that no one around him had issued such directions, but he could not get his hands on information coming from other places.

The head of the general affairs department reported that the prefecture had not ascertained any particular changes in the situation.

The prefecture's opinion regarding the Self-Defense Forces instruction to get people to evacuate was to leave it up to me as mayor to make my own determination.

I could not get a clear answer from either the national or prefectural governments. The one worrisome thing was that the support workers the national government had dispatched had all disappeared. However, I had to give an answer to the Self-Defense Forces unit in front of me.

If I issued an evacuation order to people at 9:00 p.m., we could expect a situation of relative chaos and accidents.

I knew in my head that an evacuation calls for planned behavior, and you cannot order one without also deciding what your destination is. All things considered, this was not a matter of airborne radiation rising. The hydrogen explosion at Fukushima Daiichi was not something to lose our presence of mind over. Though it might be the Self-Defense Forces, it would not do to just follow their instructions. I was the mayor, and the chief of the emergency headquarters. The answer to give, I thought, was, "No."

This what my intellect told me. However, the alarming appearance of these 100-plus soldiers and the resolute tone of voice had enough power to make me wonder if by chance some relatively terrible thing was going on. In my head, I weighted at 60% my thinking that I would say "no" on the grounds that it would be a real mess if I followed the their instructions, versus 40% for the thought that perhaps some serious situation that I could not conceive is occurring and we should follow their instructions.

My feelings fluctuated wildly between these two alternatives. I had never thought such excruciating thoughts in my life before.

However, while this experience was one had I never thought, when I gave word to that 60-40 thinking, it came out 100-0.

Tachiya "If I give the order to evacuate now, it will cause a lot of chaos. For that reason, I will not order people to evacuate. Please, leave the city hall immediately."

Self-Defense Forces "We have our instructions from our superiors."

Tachiya "Only the Government of Japan can give me orders. I as the mayor make decisions for Soma."

Self-Defense Forces "If we are to withdraw, where would like us to go?"

Tachiya "I'd like your assistance if we learn that some new situation has developed. For the moment, please be on standby at the Civic Center across from the city hall. Only, please gather all your troops into the municipal conference room first and line-up before withdrawing. General affairs Director, please take the lead and guide them to the civic center."

As we watched, they marched out in double file and headed in neat order to the civic center. I don't think I will ever forget the sight as long as I live.

The third floor workers had watched the whole thing from beginning to end without taking their eyes off of me, but once the Self-Defense Forces unit had left they calmly went back to work as though nothing had happened.

It brought home to me the fact that they rely entirely on the mayor's decision, and I also, should have faith to come to a decision. This is something our workers taught me without saying a thing.

The next day, we received a report from the Self-Defense Forces that order to evacuate immediately was an erroneous report. But I already knew from my exchange of messages afterward with Sengoku that this was not the government's policy, and that criticizing the Self-Defense Forces who are working together with us on disaster response would lead to nothing. Therefore, I just let it go in one ear and out the other.

We talked about evacuation chaos in our conference the following morning (March 15th), and in the end we reaffirmed our policy on evacuation would be to follow the national government's instructions.

Acute Period Chapter 2

(4) Soma City official records from March 15th to March 19th (original text reproduced as written)

●March 15th, 2011, 8:00 a.m. 11th and 6:00 p.m. 12th Disaster response headquarters meeting (HQ chief's instructions and discussion)

▷How do we handle the nuclear accident? Last night, there was talk from the Self-Defense Forces that we should evacuate, but it was refused on the grounds that the city follows the national government's orders. Minamisoma City and Iwaki City are of the same view.

If we should evacuate, we will get support from the national government for the plans to do so. The prefecture is avoiding a definite decision.

If there are no evacuation instructions, we will follow the plans we've had until now without a word.

▷Thinking of radiation, wear raincoats, masks, work gloves, etc.
Use disposable raincoats. Have people wash faces.

▷With respect to restoration of essential utilities, show electricity and telephones on a map display and post evacuation sites.

▷We had a request from the mayor of Minamisoma City to take in 500 and agreed to it.
I asked Marumori Town to also take in people.

▷If we create a place to take in volunteers, physicians and nurses will come.

▷As to how to make the most of the volunteers, also have them assist at evacuation sites.

Volunteers hurrying in from around and outside the prefecture

● **March 16th, 2011 (Wednesday), 8:00 a.m. 13th and 6:00 p.m. 14th Disaster response headquarters meeting (HQ chief's instructions and discussion)**

▷There will be no nuclear explosion at the nuclear power station. For that reason, radioactivity levels are not going to suddenly, explosively rise.

Drivers are saying they don't want to come to Soso Bureau (Soma and Futaba). Arrange for drivers and go get them.

▷Fire brigades as well as the squad leaders and vice-leaders. Give them directions.

Need to get acquainted with the area.

▷We need to think not only of Soma but also Minamisoma and the broader Soma region. Artificial dialysis situation is critical.

Minamisoma could not hold on.

Seriously injured also will soon be at extremes. Biggest reason is because medicines are not being brought to Minamisoma.

Trucks gone out to collect relief supplies

Acute Period — Chapter 2

●**March 17th, 2011 (Thursday), 8:00 a.m. 15th and 6:00 p.m. 16th Disaster response headquarters meeting (HQ chief's instructions and discussion)**

▷Distribute gasoline for worker use at Morinomiyako, Veterans' Circle, and Fukinoto-en (senior care facilities), as well as medical personnel and caregivers.

Caregivers are unable to make home nursing visits.

▷Regarding health management for disaster victims, psychological care is going to become quite problematic.

▷Be open about radioactivity concentrations.

▷Today, I held a mayors' meeting with the mayors of Shinchi Town and Iitate Village. Said we would solemnly act in accordance with the national government's decisions regarding the nuclear station.

In that event, we said we would get support from the national government and act.

▷If Soma collapses, then Sendai will collapse. Tokyo will collapse. Japan will collapse. We have to hold out.

▷2,000 meals worth of "alpha rice" were given to Shinchi Town.

40,000 liters of water were given to Iitate Village.

▷In the event that the Uda River system becomes the only source of drinking water, work out which zones are affected and amounts of water needed.

There will be no nuclear explosion at the nuclear power station.

For that reason, radioactivity levels are not going to suddenly, explosively rise. Drivers are saying they don't want to come to Soso Bureau (Soma and Futaba).

Arrange for drivers and go get them.

Bottles of water stored at the civic center

51

●**March 18th, 2011 (Friday), 8:00 a.m. 18th and 6:00 p.m. 19th Disaster response headquarters meeting (HQ chief's instructions and discussion)**
▷Supply of water is increasing, but with earthquakes every day the leaks are growing and the supply doesn't move forward.
▷5,000 coffins have arrived from the Ministry of Economy, Trade, and Industry, among others. Includes share for Minamisoma.
▷Materials for general public are lacking. Rice (people out in the town), canned goods, kerosene, gas, etc.
Request canned goods and rice to prefecture.
▷Need to think systematically about pulling out of evacuation sites and lives ahead while keeping a close watch on the nuclear station.
▷Difficult to hold opening ceremonies on April 6, but must think about narrowing down evacuation sites to start school somewhere.
Must think simultaneously about plan for closing evacuation sites and plan for reopening schools.
▷Quite a few relief supplies have been accumulated, but storage locations are becoming a problem.

Line of people waiting to get gasoline

●**March 19th, 2011 (Sunday), 8:00 a.m. 20th and 6:00 p.m. 21st Disaster response headquarters meeting (HQ chief's instructions and discussion)**
▷Evacuation of the patients in Minamisoma City largely settled. Soma will be the front line. We will protect this zone.

Acute Period

▷ Distribution of goods for the most part is functioning. Based on circumstances at the nuclear power station, we will hole up like in a castle under siege. Prepare emergency stores.

▷ If advice to evacuate comes, that will be the time to prepare for the worst. I don't think it will happen. The possibility of Soma City being instructed to evacuate seems low.

Until then, calmly and coolly go about dealing with the disaster.

▷ Don't worry about the outlays for cremations. Also ask Yonezawa City for help.

▷ Talk came up at the physicians' conference about whether they must go as far as Minamisoma.

I asked them to please lend a hand since they're having problems there, too, and got the attendees' assent.

▷ Kerosene will be on sale to the general public starting tomorrow. Time not set, location to be the parking lot at Niraku.

Prioritize areas with hospitals and people vulnerable to disaster.

▷ Must think about support for people vulnerable to disaster. Includes nursing homes, Fukinoto-en, hospitals, etc.

Think about it as administrative units. What do we do about the bedridden in the area?

Make a list of these people and deliver foodstuffs.

Perhaps can get help from fire brigades. What do we do about people who require looking after?

▷ If morale at the city hall drops, we could not do anything. It seems that Iitate Village has also started to evacuate.

Chain of command and employee morale are important.

March 18th, Obama district

March 18th, Haragama district

(5) Reasoning with residents and insufficiencies in foodstuffs and goods

I had already decided that our basic response to the nuclear accident was to follow the government's decisions and instructions, but preparations needed to be made in the event of an actual evacuation. The first groups of people we had to take into consideration above all else were the seriously ill at hospitals. The seniors at care level 4 and 5 in the care facilities, and the bedridden throughout the area. There were 46 bedridden seniors in the city. We prepared an equivalent number of stretchers to prepare for their evacuation and placed them at their bedsides or deployed them to fire stations, and assigned the firefighters who would be charged with carrying them.

We needed to prepare for a worst-case scenario by starting discussions with the facilities and the local fire brigades while also working up explanations for Soma resident, who were growing uneasy. In particular, those disaster victims who had barely escaped the disaster by fleeing with only the clothes on their backs were extremely worried.

On March 19th, accompanied by the chair of the City Assembly and the chief of the fire brigade I went around to three evacuation sites to explain the city's policy. I told people the present situation was not such that we had to escape but if radiation levels rose and evacuation became necessary I would lead everyone to a safe place. In going around, I saw that people at the evacuation sites were serious and concerned about what was coming. I was the one giving the explanation, but I was frantic, too. There are photos of these events that I think captured all of this clearly.

With the distribution of goods having stopped with the news reports about the nuclear accident, we now had to struggle with the inconveniences of

Acute Period

nothing coming in.

It felt as though I spoke every evening by cell phone to Lawson' President Takeshi Niinami to prod him to get goods in and reopen their shops, but they needed another week before they could do so.

There was an episode involving President Niinami that occurred on March 26 when he came to Soma to coincide with the reopening of the Lawsons' Awazu outlet.

Niinami "Mayor Tachiya, I'm sorry for the problems we created for you. I've come to take the lead in getting this shop reopened. I know it won't wipe away the problems that we've created by taking so long, but please accept as partial compensation 'makunouchi' box lunches from Lawsons for the 4,500 people at the evacuation sites."

Tachiya "I'm grateful, but I would like to decline the offer. With people having to put up with trials daily, what would be better than a one-time thing is for Lawsons to stock those box lunches at the store on an ongoing basis. I would be grateful for that." I make these kinds of requests when I am truly distressed, so I'd like you to withdraw the offer."

Niinami "Mayor, I understand what you are saying. Please tell me whenever you need to."

Three weeks later. The schools reopened on Monday, April 18th. The first two days of school were to be morning-only half-days, but starting from April 20th the schools had to start their lunch service.

However, school superintendent Norio Ara came to me to say that the work to resume lunch service had not gone well and they would not be able to provide meals until the following week. "Can we get 'makunouchi' box lunches for the three days this week?" he asked. I agreed that we had no choice, but then I suddenly remembered the promise with President Niinami. I called him with Ara right there in front of me. "Oh, sure, that's fine," he said. It's for the kids, right? Three days' worth? Leave it to me. I'll see to it that we deliver three days' worth of box lunches for 3,500 kids."

The box lunches that came were very carefully made. There were three different combinations of items for lower-year elementary school students, the upper-year students, and for junior high students, and each of the lunches even came with desserts. Most of all I was delighted at the friendship he had expressed toward Soma.

It was around this time that the amount of information gathered in Soma

Response instructions spreadsheet from 10 days after the disaster

crisis response meeting Excel spreadsheet that the disaster response headquarters meeting had been using since late the night of the disaster had really increased and the data was becoming detailed. The Disaster Response Headquarters had segment the entries into even greater detail; did its best to consolidate objectives, methodologies, and results onto a single A3 page; and then distributed it to all parties involved. Soma City had acquired ISO9001 certification two years before the disaster, and municipal workers made their way through the PDCA cycle at daily meetings in the morning and again in the evening.

The measures for dealing with the issues raised at the evening meeting were pulled together and organized overnight, and those results were then presented to everyone at the following morning's meeting. The results of having operated for a day based on those guidelines were then reported at the evening meeting. In this way, we went through the PDCA cycle every day.

The size of the text on those single A3 sheets used as meeting handouts gradually shrank and the amount of information contained rose, but we have continued to use this approach for going on six years at this writing.

The lack of goods reached its peak around March 20th, the tenth day of the disaster. Rice and other foodstuffs went out of circulation, and it became necessary to distribute the rice and water received as relief supplies to the populace. Additionally, if the nuclear accident worsened further and this

Acute Period

led to the tap water becoming contaminated (there were fears of this possibility since the source of the water was in Iitate Village), we would have to immediately distribute bottles of drinking water to all households. I asked friendship municipalities and mayors with whom I was friends to send us water.

On the other hand, I was worried about whether or not we would be able to smoothly distribute it to all city residents since we had no experience with rationing out foodstuffs and the like. Accordingly, I decided that we would try to distribute water and rice to all households also for training.

Distribution of Rice
(March 24th, 2011)

(6) Soma City official records from March 21th to March 25th (original text reproduced as written)

●**March 21st, 2011 (Monday), 8:00 a.m. 24th and 6:00 p.m. 25th Disaster response headquarters meeting (HQ chief's instructions and discussion)**

▷Be thinking that we are creating the systems for a castle under siege. We're setting up a distribution system. We have been overoptimistic about managing goods. If we do things properly, there are a lot of things like rice on hand. Rice is lacking from people's lives. I want to try to get supplies like water out, with a focus mainly on foodstuffs like rice.

▷Figures for radioactivity in Iitate Village have risen. There seem to be people in Soma also who are resistant to drinking tap water. We may need to distribute bottled water.

However, we can't distribute it if we don't have a distribution system. The system will continue from now on. I asked the vice-minister of Ministry of Agriculture, Forestry and Fisheries.

Inventory control needs to be handled properly.

▷Have the Assembly of Ward Mayors meet quickly to get a distribution system set up.

▷I had a phone call from a responsible party at Lawsons Tohoku. The Soma Awazu outlet will be opening.

▷Besieged castle system = distribution system. How do we divide up 500 bags of rice?

▷One 2-liter bottle of water per household, and several 500-ml bottles. Starting tomorrow, distribute as quickly as possible. Tomorrow I will hear what the ward mayors' views are.

May not be able to do things well, but what's important is doing something. We will clearly convey our policies to the populace.

▷Clothing should also be distributed. Also towels, shampoo, soap, toothbrushes, etc.

▷Get people living in apartment quickly. Putting that into effect is important.

▷No water is getting to Minamisoma. Repair workers are not coming, either. People vulnerable to disaster remain. We will lend Soma's water supply vehicles to Minamisoma.

Acute Period — Chapter 2

● **March 22nd, 2011 (Tuesday), 8:00 a.m. 26th and 6:00 p.m. 27th Disaster response headquarters meeting (HQ chief's instructions and discussion)**

▷ With respect to the distribution of goods in Soma City limits, how do we go about distributing what we've collected? We need to reconstruct the administrative name register. Generally, a government starts trying to distribute items once they confirm there are no problems, but we will distribute in order to find problems.

If there is chaos, say the mayor's fault

Please do what we can do now.

▷ Organize stock. Iwaki City also seems to be running out of goods. The prefecture seems to have quite a lot. How do we distribute these to the populace?

▷ Artificial dialysis is becoming a problem. Can we procure medicinal solution? Ask help to Minamisoma City, and set up a system that can procure it.

People from Minamisoma who are on dialysis are scattered around town.

A nationwide call has gone out for physicians experienced with artificial dialysis, they will come starting the 28th.

▷ Hand out moving kits to people who are moving to apartments, etc.

Create moving kits that include toweling blankets, futons, etc. and pass them out.

Tell the new tenants that the city has prepared futons.

▷ We have to think of ourselves as a castle under siege and come up with distribution systems. I went to look at the storehouses. We need to quickly hand out powdered milk and other items.

▷ I want communications with residents to go through the Assembly of Ward Mayors.

▷ Put the content of the disaster prevention emails sent to cell phones up on the website, too.

Relief supplies and other items sent from around the country

● **March 23rd, 2011 (Wednesday), 8:00 a.m. 28th and 6:00 p.m. 29th Disaster response headquarters meeting (HQ chief's instructions and discussion)**

▷ We estimated that living assistance grants would go to approximately 5,000 people. They've gone to 2,683 people so far.

Subtracting the approximately 200 people who have died and approximately 500 people missing leaves around 1,700 people who might not know they could get the money, but maybe they have evacuated to places farther away.

▷ From today, we begin distributing rice and moving people into private apartments.

▷ The question of when schools will be able to get the new school year underway is connected to how quickly people can move from evacuation sites into temporary housing.

▷ We have no choice but to store relief supplies in warehouses. Continue working to pass them out to the populace. Let the ward mayors decide on the details of how to distribute them.

▷ Post information about shopping and such to the website.

▷ We can use Self-Defense Forces helicopters. It's alright to use them for things like inspecting conditions on the ground.

▷ Medications for people with psychiatric conditions are running out. We're looking for psychiatrists through nationwide networks.

We have to prevent the medical system from collapsing.

▷ Speed in constructing temporary housing is crucial. The more they are delayed, the more of a struggle things will be for evacuees.

As to conditions at the evacuation sites, arranging for baths is quite a problem.

Line of Soma resident waiting to do shopping

I understood just how important getting temporary housing built is.

Acute Period Chapter 2

● **March 24th, 2011 (Thursday), 8:00 a.m. 30th and 6:00 p.m. 31st Disaster response headquarters meeting (HQ chief's instructions and discussion)**

▷ Work to get even more foodstuffs distributed.

▷ Soma's medical system is gradually returning to normal. However, the fact that Minamisoma's psychiatric hospital is no longer around is serious.

▷ It would be great to have a lot of volunteer physicians. Work to set things up so that these people do not have to camp somewhere. They will immediately add a lot of power to managing the evacuation sites.

▷ The issue of how much education will be sacrificed is an extremely thorny one. If the number of evacuees goes down, we would be able to move them to Hamanasu Hall and the arena, but right now that's impossible.

More people are likely to come to Soma from Minamisoma. Get the temporary housing built quickly!

▷ Fukushima Medical University has said they would send people, so I asked to send them to Minamisoma. I'd like the people in psychiatry to go to Minamisoma.

Tokyo Medical University spoke about dispatching physicians on a long-term basis.

▷ Community associations are being set up at each evacuation site. For example, each classroom has a leader and the principal is putting them together. The atmosphere is really upbeat.

▷ General practice physicians and dispensing pharmacies in the city are for the most part back in business. The physicians who have come to help from outside the city should be managed collectively at the health center.

Ask these outside physicians to handle the evacuation sites.

▷ Have the water obtained as relief supplies distributed to residents to be stored at each household.

The author disembarking from an Self-Defense Forces helicopter

●**March 25th, 2011 (Friday), 8:00 a.m. 32nd and 6:00 p.m. 33rd Disaster response headquarters meeting (HQ chief's instructions and discussion)**

▷It is important that we speak compassionately to people who have come back after evacuating due to the nuclear station, etc.

▷I want to ascertain the state of community associations among residents by distributing daily commodities and rice. I want to make it known as widely as possible about rice distributions and so forth, including people in apartments and people not in our administrative district.

▷Time to do radio calisthenics! Get everyone in the city up for their physical and mental health twice a day.

▷Figure out the minimum amount of oil and similar supplies that Soma needs, and come up with projections for how much will be supplied. The fuel situation has improved.

▷Report to the headquarters meeting the number of households moved into private apartments. Provide rental assistance even to people who went directly to realtors and found apartments on their own on the premise that they would have entered temporary housing once it was built.

With people coming from Minamisoma also, we are short about 1,000 temporary housing units.

▷Regarding the outstanding issue of psychiatric care, specialists in the field have been dispatched from Fukushima Medical University.

Also, in response to a request I made to the president of Tokyo Medical University, two physicians will be coming from there.

General practice physicians are steadily reopening their doors, but the surgical theaters at Soma public hospital cannot be used due to the earthquake.

▷The mayor of Nagareyama City said he wants to help our municipal workers, so we'll have the vice-mayors discuss the matter.

People doing radio calisthenics at an evacuation site

Acute Period — Chapter 2

(7) Medical care

When the disaster first occurred, we had no concerns about a collapse in medical care thanks to the total cooperation from the Soma Branch of the Soma District Medical Association and good back up from the two hospitals in the city. However, the arrival of evacuees from Minamisoma City was destabilizing, and as the days went by people in Soma's evacuation sites also began complaining of feeling unwell. As a result, shortages in medical personnel became a new problem.

Furthermore, given that life as evacuees in the evacuation sites was getting longer, we could not rely only volunteer physicians available for only a day or two as the medical care system.

I made request for the long-term dispatch of physicians to the Japan Medical Association (JMA) through that group's vice-chair Takashi Hanyuda (then and now a member of the House of Councillors), and also to the All Japan Hospital Association (AJHA), with which I had been affiliated as director of Soma Central Hospital. I also contacted Tokyo Medical University President Masahiko Usui—a personal acquaintance—about the dismal state of affairs in Soma and asked to send a medical team on an ongoing basis.

The JMA decided to launch its emergency response JMA Team with the dispatch of teams from Ishikawa and Shizuoka prefectures. Tokyo Medical University and the AJHA also dispatched teams with physicians at their core, and in a relay format linked together on the ground in Soma. The support team that President Usui sent from the university in particular was a topflight group led by its ace in this field, Professor Junji Otaki from the

Physician

Dental examination

General Medicine Faculty. The medical teams based themselves at the Soma municipal health center. They held a medical aid team liaison conference with the members of the Soma district medical association, Soma branch, every morning at 8:00 a.m., and looked after health management for the disaster victims.

Medical aid team liaison meeting

For example, there was an outbreak of influenza at an evacuation site with several hundred people. In conditions that lowered the physical strength of disaster victims and in particular their immune strength, we were concerned about major outbreak of infectious diseases. In fact, the number of sick people rose in a flash. As a request from the aforementioned liaison conference, the physicians asked me to open new evacuation sites.

Accordingly, I opened an influenza quarantine evacuation site at the Nittaki community center. We established a system wherein physicians would test people for influenza at this medical quarantine site. Those who tested negative would be sent back to the evacuation sites where people from their community awaited them.

Thinking about it seems obvious now, but the thing that made this system with all those steps—analyze symptoms, examine for influenza, treat at Nittaki community center, make final check to see if the sufferers can return to the evacuation site they came from—worked smoothly. It was outstanding leadership displayed by leaders of the improvised teams gathered together at the health center, former Soma Medical Association Chair Katsutoshi Kashimura, Ishikawa Prefecture Medical Association Chair Dr. Takashi Komori, Shizuoka Prefecture Medical Association Chair Dr. Katsuhiko Suzuki, and of course the advice from the aforementioned Professor Otaki among others.

The next serious problem was the gasoline shortage. We relied on every intermediary we could find to get gasoline from around Japan, but demand for official uses such as ambulances took precedence over sales to the general public. We dealt with this by setting up special gas stations for official use and arranging for the use of gas coupons to keep them separate from public sales. This method allowed us to also supply ambulances and other such vehicles from Minamisoma City, which had temporarily run out of

Acute Period Chapter 2

gasoline. Distribution of gasoline to medical personnel was handled the same way as gasoline for official use. Fuel for ambulances and the means for clinical nurses to commute to work were seen as equivalent. Gasoline for making homecare visits was also regarded similarly.

On March 22nd, to address another big issue—shortages of medications arising from pharmaceutical wholesalers having evacuated—I made a phone call to prod a wholesaler headquartered in Tokyo. The company's managing director came on the phone. "The very fact that we are truly in trouble here means you ought to be getting to work. If your employees say they refuse to go to Soma, have the president bring them by himself."

"Mayor, I understand. We absolutely will resume business in Soma, so please give us some time."

"The medical solutions used in artificial dialysis will run out in three days. Please hurry."

Michitane Soma, scion of the locally prominent Soma family, heard the exchange and said to me, "Mayor, if that's the case, I'll go to Tokyo to get them by myself. Please make a list of the medicines needed, and also give me a highway travel permit."

We quickly got in touch with all the hospitals in Soma and Minamisoma, made up a list of all the medicines that were needed, and handed it off to Michitane and his companions.

The following day, he came back with a truck loaded with all of the medicines needed. Thanks to this scion's quick decision, we were able to avoid a severe crisis. Eventually, two pharmaceutical wholesalers—Kowa Yakuhin K.K. and Toho Pharmaceutical Co., Ltd.—would open temporary business offices in Soma.

The gasoline shortage was also severe. The gasoline that we had secured with great difficulty was stopped in Niigata as the tanker truck drivers did not want to go to Soma. We thought it was all over. It was at this moment that Yuichi Ara, a squad assistant leader (today a squad leader) of a fire brigade in the Ono district, said that he would go to Niigata to get the gasoline and set off in a tanker truck to bring it back. I want to tell the people of Soma once again how—at these moments when I was heartbroken over how cold the world could be—the warmth of these two gentlemen made me so very happy.

65

(8) Volunteer activities

On March 21st, we opened a Volunteer Center on the second floor of the Soma Chamber of Commerce building. I was grateful to have so many volunteers gathered together from around the country. Among them there were a lot of people I knew, but they didn't want to bother me so they quietly registered at the Center and did the work they were assigned.

I firstly realized just how truly grateful I was for the volunteers when we got them to work systematically. When it came to the work of the volunteers to deal with the tsunami damage, if they didn't put together teams at the very least they might not be effective and if they didn't do the work systematically then it might engender feelings of unfairness among the disaster victims.

The approach we adopted at headquarters was to first register the volunteers, enroll them in insurance, check the state of urgent medical care (we had concerns about tetanus and such arising from injuries while working), match the optimal tasks for the nature of the volunteer activity, and send teams out to work sites.

We got an enormous amount of help and thanks to the goodwill of so many. It went beyond medical are to include volunteers removing wreckage and washing out mud from houses, the removal of sludge and cleaning up around homes, and getting public health worker send from JICHIRO to deal with health management at evacuation sites.

We mail an interim report every year with gratitude to the homes of all the volunteers we have registered. Some of the mail sent to university students who have since graduated and moved away gets returned, but about 60% of the mail gets through.

Volunteer Center opened

Removing mud from inside a house

Acute Period — Chapter 2

(9) Encouragement from Taro Aso and Junko Mihara

With the uproar over the nuclear power station, people had the impression that the contamination due to exposure and radioactivity was relatively severe in Soma, too. In particular, no matter how many times you explained things to people we knew in Tokyo, they believed we were in a dangerous area. This was the biggest reason for the halt in the distribution of goods.

Thereupon, I asked two people I had gotten know—former Prime Minister Taro Aso (his younger sister is wife of the 33rd head of the Soma family) and actress turned Diet member Junko Mihara (she has long had a close relationship to the city, and in 2010 visited for the Soma Nomaoi wild horse chase festival)—if they would come on an inspection trip and offer some words of encouragement.

The two willingly agreed to come, and in particular went to the evacuation sites to encourage people. I remember how the faces of everyone brightened up in an instant.

Junko Mihara getting an explanation from the author

Taro Aso offering words of encouragement to evacuees

67

Mayor's e-mail newsletter - March 24th, 2011 Issue

(10) Castle under siege (First email magazine after the disaster. Distributed to all city households.)

I want to begin by offering my sincerest prayers for the repose of the souls of the many people who lost their lives in the earthquake and tsunami.

Immediately after the earthquake's shaking had ended, we assembled in Soma City a Disaster Management Headquarters and instructed that people be called upon to flee from a tsunami and be guided away. The homes of 5,027 people in coastal areas were swept away and left in rubble, but about one-tenth of those people died. I must offer heartfelt appreciation, respect, and apologies to the members of the fire brigades who got so many people to evacuate. Seven firefighters who were delayed in making their escape because they were giving instructions on evacuation or leading people away died in the line of duty. I believe that in atonement the very least I can do is to make an all-out effort to rebuild the lives of so many people and their hometown for which these individuals exchanged their own precious lives to protect.

Immediately after quake struck, we poured all of our energies into gathering information and rescuing the survivors. Only one person died from the destruction of the earthquake. Fifty minutes later an unbelievable report came into the Disaster Management Headquarters. It said that a tsunami had overrun the Route 6 bypass. I couldn't believe it, but in fact the housing clusters in Haragama and Isobe had been wiped out. Everything other than high ground in Obama and Matsukawa was engulfed in waves, while no house remained recognizable. I was filled with worry and anxiety, but the next job for the Disaster Management Headquarters was to protect the survivors and manage the health of those who had been rescued. We spent the evening getting disaster victims who had been left isolated among the ocean waters that had

Acute Period — Chapter 2

swallowed up everything along the coast to come take refuge at one of the many evacuation sites and concentrated on warming them up and getting them to have water and a meal.

As time went by reports began coming in of family members and friends who were missing, but no one at the Headquarters showed any emotions on their faces. Everyone knew that in this state of emergency the city would have to come together and tackle the tasks at hand. At the 4th disaster response headquarters meeting held 10 hours after the disaster, we vowed together to move step-by-step forward toward recovery and broken down the courses of action to be pursued into short-term and medium-to-long-term responses. I thought that tomorrow we would have an overall picture of the disaster, and we would have more detailed information about the victims. However, I also had it in mind that whatever the situation, we would not hesitate with steadfastly carrying out our plans.

I knew that after two days the evacuation sites would become overcrowded due to the mix of disaster victims and people who were taking refuge because they no longer had essential utilities. However, thanks to the assistance of some of the women firefighters and the Self-Defense Forces we were able to distribute at least a minimum amount of boiled rice and relief supplies that had already arrived.

We followed the mid-to-long-term plan—including transitioning

people who had lost their homes away from evacuation site living to autonomous living in apartments or temporary housing, sorting things out as much as possible at disaster-struck sites, and arrange for health management and psychiatric cares for those people who had long been disabled for one of those reasons or the other—pulled ourselves together as a team, and took our first steps forward.

But.

A second demon struck from Futaba district 45 kilometers away. This was the anxiety produced by the fear of radioactivity. The ever-growing nuclear accident combined with a day of nervous news reports to stir up terror not only in neighboring regions but throughout Japan. From the moment that a region with a 20-kilometer radius became a designated evacuation zone, the feeling had been spreading even in Soma that we needed to flee far away.

At the same time, people in the transport and distribution business around Japan became sensitive, and avoided going into the Soma region and Iwaki City. Gas tanker trucks only went as far as Koriyama, and drivers had to go from here to get them or we would not get our hands on any fuel. The few convenience stores and supermarkets that were open after the earthquake closed because no goods were coming in. In addition to the inconveniences in daily life arising from not having gasoline or daily goods, fears about radiation spreading from the nuclear power station struck the Soma region.

The populace had their eyes glued to their televisions all day long, and commentators worked themselves up in explaining the dangers. Certainly, the evacuation zone at Chernobyl had reached out to 30 kilometers, but despite the fact that Soma is 45 kilometers away and is

Acute Period

Chapter 2

not asked to evacuate, you could see people were filled with anxiety.

If the radiation levels rose, wouldn't that mean that the evacuation had come too late? Is the national government staying quiet to not stir panic among the people in spite of conditions in fact being so dangerous that they will present a health hazard? Just maybe, isn't now the time to make an escape? Hadn't the U.S. government actually set an 80-kilometer evacuation zone for their citizens?

In fact, a mass escape had begun from Minamisoma City, where people were taking refuge indoors. Fearing that since it was like they were on an isolated island offshore that was not going to get any gasoline, food, or medical supplies, they would be slow in escaping a Hiroshima-like explosion. That fear accordingly drove the Minamisoma people into Soma City. These people thronged the evacuation sites in Soma. Consequently, we turned the defunct Soma Girls High School into a new evacuation site for the people of Minamisoma. The capacity was about 1,000 people. Of course, we had an obligation to also provide them with foodstuffs, but we realized they were in more trouble than we were and so took them in. I saw some people at the Disaster Management Headquarters stiffen up at this news for an instant, but no one voiced any objections.

However, the people of Soma could palpably sense the worries and desire to escape of their Minamisoma counterparts, and this stirred up a crisis mentality and feelings of impatience. Anxiety ran rampant that if they did not flee quickly, they might well suffer from disorders due to radiation. For the Disaster Management Headquarters, it was inconceivable for us to decide on our own to evacuate

The Haragama district seen from helicopter (author photo)

71

before an order to do so had come from the national government. We affirmed this justifiable position at a disaster response headquarters meeting, and then I went around to deliver a speech on it at three evacuation sites.

At the next disaster response headquarters meeting, we set down the policies to be steadily pursued en route to recovery. We broke them up into short-term responses, mid-term response, and a long-term plan, with idea of pushing steadily forward on them with adjustments made for actual conditions in the city. If during that process instructions came from the national government to temporarily evacuate, then out of concern for residents' health and their very lives we would have to carry out a systematic mass evacuation. However, if we were driven by vague anxieties and delayed a reconstruction plan, it would be unjustifiable to those who died. First and foremost, for people vulnerable to disaster like the elderly living at evacuation sites removed from Soma would most likely be difficult. For that reason, at this stage where no instructions had been received from the national government to evacuate, we had no

Distributed to all households as extra edition
(March 25, 2011)

Acute Period

Chapter 2

intention whatsoever to remove any people from Soma City.

However, the worries throughout Japan about radiation from the nuclear station meant the distribution of goods to Soma had come to a decisive stop. The effects of this were particularly serious when it came to medicines. I spoke with a top executive from a supplier and got him to understand the reasons why they simply could not disengage from Soma. Having gotten them to understand and secured a supply of medicines, the treatment institutions in Soma were able to remain open. However, the problem was supermarkets and convenience stores were unable to procure daily necessities and foodstuffs.

This put restrictions on the lives of Soma's populace, but if we gave in now to inconveniences in living and fears about the nuclear station it was certain that the Soma region would never be able to recover in the future. The day before, I assembled the ward mayors who comprise the city's administrative organization and got them to understand that Soma City was now living under siege conditions. Neither the nuclear uproar nor the damaging rumors affecting the distribution of goods could be expected to go on forever. If we gave in to them, we would be doing something inexcusable to the fire-fighters and squad leaders who had fallen in the line of duty trying to protect the lives of people in disaster-struck districts from the tsunami.

At minimum, you can live if you have rice, a bowl of miso soup, and a pickled plum. The Great Tenmei famine (1782-88) was far worse. That's why we behave like we're a castle under siege and do our best to push ahead. Happily, we have received support from mayors around the country, so we have no worries when it comes to provisions.

Chapter 3: Evacuation Shelters

(A record from March 26 to June 17, 2011)

(1) Opening of psychiatric outpatient facilities (March 29)

As we entered the third week of the crisis, distribution systems and medical care systems were in place in the evacuation shelters. The next problem we confronted was the stress and poor physical health brought on by living at the sites for extended periods. Mental health care was a particularly urgent issue.

At the request of Shinichi Niwa, a professor of psychiatry at Fukushima Medical University, we put together a "Mental Health Care Team" comprising doctors and nurses assembled from all over Japan. All activities in the psychiatric domain were overseen by Professor Niwa in a system that dispatched doctors and nurses based at health centers to each evacuation shelter.

Two weeks after the earthquake, both psychiatric clinics in Minamisoma city had closed their doors, resulting in a situation in which there was no way to provide psychiatric patients with their medication. The evacuation shelters, where hundreds of people were living together without any boundaries, were extremely difficult environments for psychiatric patients to deal with. The fact was that grave situations were occurring because people were running out of their medication.

It was under these circumstances that Soma General Hospital hurriedly set up a psychiatric outpatient clinic on March 29, allowing us to at least offer prescriptions, but since all of the medical wholesalers in the Soma area had evacuated, we were also confronted by the problem that dispensaries were unable to operate. However, supply of medication to pharmacies in the city resumed thanks to the assistance of Yasuo Takita, president of Kowa Pharmaceuticals, to whom I appealed directly.

Although improvements in psychiatric care were achieved thanks to the help of a great many people, the closure of the psychiatric clinics remained a grave problem. Incidents of emergency hospitalization had to be referred to psychiatric hospitals in Fukushima city, a situation that continues.

Soma General Hospital
Temporary psychiatric outpatient care

Evacuation Shelters

(2) The "Saigai FM" station starts (March 30)

The FM station inaugurated to hail missing people and to communicate data on radioactivity measured in dozens of locations around the city began broadcasting on March 30, 2011.

It was created at the suggestion of city hall staff, who went ahead with preparations one after the other, looking at me sidelong as I stood bewildered that such a small city as this could achieve such a thing. I was surprised at the staff, who, unused to the task though they were, stepped up to the microphone and began the broadcasts, living up to their declaration that "staff members will do all the broadcasts, so that information is delivered in real time."

There was the calm voice of Sayuri Horishita, a singer originally born in Soma who was volunteering. Women from the Commerce Association, who volunteered as personalities because they thought that the city staff must be finding things difficult.

Soma city had far deeper reserves of strength than I had thought.

Opening with city staff

City residents who volunteered as station personalities

(3) Starting construction of temporary housing (March 26)

The first phase of construction of the temporary housing in the east ground, on which we had been frantically seeking to acquire materials and land since the day of the earthquake started on March 26.

At that time, the primary issue for us was to give people the capacity to live their lives with the luxury of privacy that temporary housing would afford them, and thus we were delighted at the news that construction had started.

At this stage construction of 1,500 homes was planned, 1,000 of which we had requested that the prefecture build, with Soma city acting as agent for the construction of the remaining 500. Although about 1,500 homes had been destroyed in Soma, apartments requisitioned during the construction process were designated as "designated temporary housing" for which the prefecture paid the rent, leaving us with a surplus of 500 dwellings. However, since arrangements for the construction had already been made, this surplus was allocated to earthquake victims in other municipalities.

(4) Restarting schools and dividing partitions

The earthquake occurred in March, which is graduation season in Japan, but the elementary and middle schools were being monopolized as evacuation shelters, and thus were unable to hold graduation ceremonies. Since this was also the spring vacation period, few classes were actually missed, but in April we had to reopen the schools.

First, we asked evacuees to change locations and adjust things so that we could vacate the classrooms that were being used as evacuation shelters, allowing them to be used as classrooms for the children.

Evacuation Shelters

Chapter 3

Dividing areas with partitions

Most people were cooperative about moving, making comments such as "We'll go if it helps the children's schools to reopen..." so this operation proceeded smoothly, so I thought it a good opportunity to use partitions to divide the gymnasium into separate areas.

When I asked Yoshino Gypsum Co., Ltd., a company located in the eastern area of the industrial park, for help, they donated a large amount of drywall to us. In order to use this drywall as partitions, our staff constructed wooden stands to divide the evacuation shelters into smaller areas, providing each person with "1 tsubo (about 3.3 square meters)" of private space. We also placed a single tatami mat in each 3.3 square meter space, creating independent family areas possessing a floor and tatami.

One of the significant merits of dividing the gym with partitions to create private spaces for families was that we were able to give the evacuees temporary addresses for each family.

Actually, we were working to create a database that contained information on each and every person, but having a current address, no matter how temporary, was fundamental to providing administrative services.

When the Kumamoto earthquake occurred in 2016, we still had 150 sheets of the

Sending drywall to the town of Takamori in Kumamoto prefecture
(May 6, 2016)

79

drywall that we used for these partitions stored, so after cleaning off any mold, we sent it to the town of Takamori in the earthquake-affected region of Kumamoto prefecture. At the directive of town mayor Daisei Kusamura it was distributed to the towns and villages who needed it, where it again proved useful.

(5) Free legal consultations (April 11 onwards)

The crisis headquarters was worried that some of the people who had had the misfortune of having their assets swept away might commit suicide for economic reasons.

We took swift, strategic, and unified action, with "no more deaths" as the paramount theme of our disaster response measures. In the early stages of the crisis, we rescued people pinned under buildings by the earthquake and called for people to evacuate from the tsunami. Next, we provided aid and medical care to those who had escaped through evacuation, working to ensure that no more people died— in other words, to prevent any more deaths directly related to the disaster.

As life in the evacuation shelters seemed to settle down somewhat, from early April worries began to emerge of people committing suicide due to their economic circumstances, but at this stage there was as yet nothing decided about any special measures from the country such as resettlement or guarantees of security. In particular, many fishermen had lost their boats in the tsunami, and before them stretched a lifetime of debt.

Since these were people with a strong sense of responsibility, I felt that unless we were proactive in offering advice on debt and dual loans, it was possible that something unexpected might happen, thus I enlisted the help of the Fukushima Bar Association through a lawyer who had been dispatched to the Soma region, seeking advice on establishing a legal advice office. At the time, the deputy chairman of the Japan Federation of Bar Associations was a lawyer named Tadashi Ara, who was originally from Soma. He put the city in touch with the Japan Legal Support Center, and

Free legal consultations

Evacuation Shelters

made every effort to bring my hopes to reality. Thanks to him, a system of human support through lawyers dispatched by the Federation and the Center was decided.

We also received endorsement from the Shiho-Shoshi Lawyers' Association, the Tax Accountants' Association, and the Association of Notary Publics, and with the addition of land and housing inspectors, a free legal advice office offering one-stop service was established in the city hall branch of the government office on April 11, 2011.

More than 3,500 people have received advice from this office in the period through to July 2017, when I am writing my manuscript. As of today, none of the survivors of the tsunami have committed suicide.

I would like to express my gratitude to all the lawyers who have participated in the consultations, including everyone at the Japan Legal Support Center.

column

(6) If not for the power plant
(The real tragedy of K that neither the newspapers)
(nor the mass media reported)

Although radiation levels were not high enough to warrant an evacuation directive in the Tamano district, which lies adjacent to Iitate
village—an area that was completely evacuated—it was subject to
restrictions on its agricultural produce. Shipments of dairy products
in particular were immediately suspended.

When we thought about the risks of radioiodine these were emi-
nently sensible measures, but I think the measures that followed
thereafter were insufficient. At the very least, I think that we should
have told the producers at an early stage that their earnings would
be fully compensated.

K, who was 54 at the time, ran a dairy farm in the mountainous area
of Tamano. He was married to a 32-year old woman from the
Philippines, and had two children, aged five and six.

He was blessed with children late in life, and was looking forward to
enrolling them at Tamano elementary school that April. However,
the Philippine government had issued a recommendation that all
Philippine nationals resident in Fukushima return to their country,
judging that the nuclear power plant accident posed too great a risk.
Following this recommendation, his wife had taken their two children back to the Philippines. K, having lost his purpose in life, sold
his cattle and followed his wife and children to the Philippines,

but was unable to bring them back. Returning alone to Japan, K
reluctantly applied to Japan Agricultural Cooperatives for a loan to
purchase the livestock needed to restart his dairy farm, but was told
that they couldn't lend him any money due to his existing debt. He
then visited the free legal advice office in Soma in the evening.

The lawyer there noticed K's abnormal state of mind, and determined that he needed psychiatric care more than help with loan
application procedures. City employees gained him an appointment
for an outpatient assessment from the psychiatric unit temporarily
established at Soma General Hospital.

Evacuation Shelters — Chapter 3

However, the following morning, K took his own life, leaving a message written on the wall in chalk: "If not for the power plant..."

K was the only person in Soma whose death was related to the nuclear power plant. The mass media were in a fever over the words he wrote on the wall,

with many reporters coming to me for comment. I explained the situation, stating that the circumstances behind his death were complex, and that despite the budgetary provisions the country was making for dual loan measures, the fact was that this information had not promulgated everywhere, and that there might also be problems in the nature of international marriages, but none of the television stations or newspaper companies reported this. Only the local newspaper printed my comment that "We are concerned about his children in the Philippines."

(7) The nutrition control menu at evacuation shelters (After implementation of the meal service - April 18 onwards)

As a general rule, hot meals were on offer at evacuation shelters. Volunteers and Self-Defense Force personnel made rice balls, to which were added canned goods from aid supplies and supplementary food donated by friends and acquaintances. Since long-term health management is difficult under such conditions, I wondered if it would be possible to use the school meal preparation facilities to offer set meals for breakfast and dinner.

However, at the time the distribution of goods was in disarray, and it would be difficult gather ingredients; moreover, getting cooks and nutritionists would have been impossible. This problem remained unresolved in March, but then Shidax Corporation, a large company in the school meal domain, offered a proposal to gather both ingredients and personnel from around Japan. Thinking that if they were really able to do this then we absolutely had to ask them to help, I spoke with company president Kinichi Shida. After our conversation I believed that he was someone I could trust, and decided to take his company up on their offer.

The capacity of the school meal facilities were nowhere near enough to prepare 4,000 meals, but thankfully we were able to borrow the food preparation facilities of the staff canteen of the Alps Electric Co., Ltd.'s Soma Factory, which was not operating at the time. We also added hiring 35 preparation staff from among the disaster victims to the contract with Shidax, and hurried to create an evacuation shelter meal provision system. It was decided to use box lunches as a midday meal.

Although this system started as a transient measure to carry people through until they shifted into temporary housing, we later continued to provide side dishes for dinner as a way of preventing people from dying alone.

Shidax Corporation donated a mobile kitchen for use in preparing side dishes for those in temporary housing thereafter. With the completion of construction of all disaster public temporary housing in March 2015, provision of side dishes was halted, and the facilities went to a silent standby. One year later, however,

Providing meal services at the evacuation shelters

Evacuation Shelters

in April 2016, the mobile kitchen was loaned from Soma city to the town of Takamori in Kumamoto prefecture after the Kumamoto earthquake, and its operation entrusted to mayor Daisei Kusamura. After we had finished our task and come back, and were all getting ready to wash it together, the kitchen was loaned out again to provide support for the areas afflicted by the torrential rain that fell on the northern Kyushu region on July 5, 2017. Beginning on July 13, it was loaned out sequentially to Hita city in Oita prefecture and Asakura city in Fukuoka prefecture, thanks to the help of volunteer operators from the Shidax Corporation. This marked the third occasion on which it had proved helpful.

We would also greatly aided in many areas by Masataka Kataoka, president of Alps Electric Co., Ltd., who allowed us to use the kitchen in their company's old staff canteen free of charge. Not only did he allow us to use part of the factory as a morgue, he also let us use many of the factory areas as materials warehouses. Without the Alps Electric Co., Ltd. Soma factory, we would surely have been left in chaos, and were thus extremely grateful to have its use.

(8) Restarting the schools (April 18) and measures to counter PTSD (Post Traumatic Stress Disorder)

The schools reopened on April 18. Even at Isobe Elementary School, which had been severely damaged, welcomed ten new entrants. Every one of these children had family or relatives who were affected by the disaster, and their simple determination to push ahead despite this was touching. However, in school classes we noted some strange responses that could clearly be attributed to the effects of the earthquake.

For example, children would begin to cry when words associated with the sea were used, or would fidget and be unable to settle down, and the regular reports we received from superintendent of education Norio Ara at the daily crisis meetings were grave. Although we had expected this to a certain degree, we felt strongly that systematic, ongoing care

Isobe Elementary School entrance ceremony (April 18, 2011)

from a clinical psychologist was needed, and rushed to put together a team to handle PTSD.

Yasuo Miyazawa, head of the SEISA Group who had come to provide support in the aftermath of the earthquake, was of the same mind, and used his influence to help the children, sending three clinical psychologists from the group.

Together with Soma Central Hospital, he requisitioned an eight-room residence in the central area of the city for use as accommodations for people from the SEISA Group and other doctors and students who were volunteering help, naming it the "SEISA Dormitory," and keeping a member of the group staff there at all times. The facility welcome many medical volunteers.

Ryutaro Takahashi, assistant director of the Tokyo Metropolitan Institute of Gerontology (now the Tokyo Metropolitan Geriatric Hospital and Institute of Gerontology) also sent us a public health nurse. I think this was what allowed us to work smoothly with the doctors.

The PTSD counteraction team, and thereafter the NPO "Soma Follower Team" worked independently, coordinating with the city's Board of Education.

The activities of the Follower Team were supported by many organizations. These activities sparked the empathy of everyone at Poole Gakuin in Osaka, with each of the students donating 100 yen per month to the Follower Team. 1,400 students attend the school, so this amounted to 140,000 yen every month, sufficient to purchase office and teaching supplies.

Tetsuo Okubo, vice president of Nippon Kodo Co., Ltd., sponsor of the well

Chairman Yasuo Miyazawa (left)
(April 20, 2011)

Evacuation Shelters

known "Mainichi-koh (incense)" commercial and the popular "Shoten" TV program, visited my office. He made a donation out of sympathy after hearing my story. Every year, Nippon Kodo deposits the sales of their products sold on site at regional performances of "Shoten" into the city's bank account, as a donation to the Follower Team.

Noted luxury brand Louis Vuitton Japan built a base for the team's activities.

I must also bow my head in gratitude to Louis Vuitton, who constructed the "LVMH Kodomo Art Maison," and information education facility intended to stimulate children's sensitivities toward art, and to give them hope for their futures, stating that they hoped to aid in the rebuilding of Soma and to contribute to allowing our children to grow up in ease.

The Soma Follower Team
General meeting for establishment of an NPO.
(June 2, 2011)

Soma Follower Team members

▽ Yasuhiro Sudo (Leader: Clinical psychologist)
▽ Ran Takasaki (Clinical psychologist)
▽ Yoshiko Shiomitu (Public health nurse)
▽ Katsuhiko Yoshida (Psychiatric social worker/
  Family advisor)
▽ Ken Nishinaga (Counselor)
▽ Masaaki Abe (Education counselor,
  career consultant)

Mayor's e-mail newsletter - April 24, 2011 Issue

(9) The Earthquake Disaster Orphan Scholarship Fund ordinance

40 days after the disaster the full extent of the damage to Soma city had become clear.

1,512 households faced a life-threatening risk due to the water rising above floor level, or in other words, before the inundation by the tsunami, and the basic resident register was revised to 5,249 people. Of these, a total of 475 people either lost their lives or went missing at this stage today. Although it is not known how many of these people were in the stricken area when the tsunami hit, I cannot suppress my wonder and gratitude that less than ten percent of the people there were taken by the disaster. Such was the size of this tsunami that there were almost no houses remaining that had kept their original shape, and it was the fire brigade who evacuated 90 percent of the people living there. However, the number of victims had increased by three over the time of the previous e-mail newsletter, reaching 10 people.

In the "Hamanasu-kan" evacuation shelter, where the people of Isobe district were living as a group, I met the mother of a firefighter who had died while doing his duty, and hung my head. What could I say to someone grieving for a lost son? How could I convey my own feelings of apology? There before me, as I raised my eyes, lost in my own doubts, she stood firm, dignified with her head held high.

"I tried to stop him, but he went to help with the evacuation, saying it was his job. He was a good, kind boy. I have to live right for the sake of my grandchildren."

The ten firemen who had died at their posts left behind 11 children, nine of whom were less than 18 years of age. Thinking of how those people felt dying leaving

Evacuation Shelters

Chapter 3

Soma City Earthquake Disaster Orphan Scholarship Fund ceremony (July 2, 2011)

children who were not yet independent members of society, my chest grows tight. They must have felt terrible regret. As reparation for the assistance they offered so many citizens of Soma, it was almost too difficult to bear. As long as Soma city exists, its citizens must never forget those firemen.

While those of us left behind could in no way take the place of their lost fathers, we created a livelihood support fund ordinance in the hope that it might serve as some form of recompense. Under this ordinance, the children receive 30,000 yen per month until they turn 18. There are a total 44 children less than 18 years old who are orphans, having lost one or both parents. I wish to decide by consensus to assume part of the economic responsibility until the children come of age. If I receive approval at this month's council meeting, I would like to begin this support.

The funding will be from a savings account created for the donations for the orphans. I hope to receive donations from around the world, with the city providing general funding if the donations are not sufficient. The total amount is approximately 200 million yen.

If donations exceed this amount, the balance will be set aside as scholarships to aid in the passage of these young people through university. If that occurs we will have to revise the ordinance, but one more condition is that the fund works to strengthen the academic abilities of the orphans to help them live better in future.

Although the elementary and middle schools of Soma started the new term late, on April 18, as we had feared the children from the disaster-stricken areas had emotional scars that were an impediment to their studies. We assembled the "Soma Follower Team" from six clinical psychologists and public health nurses, positioning it as a separate organization from the Board of Education, offering support for students who were victims of the crisis. The current plan is for the program to run for two years, and I would like the team to continue to provide nuanced guidance in order to improve the students' academic abilities, even if they appear to have stabilized mentally.

The other day television crews from Finland and the United Kingdom who had read my e-mail newsletter visited for an interview, and I appealed to them to offer the friendship of their countries to these children. Thereafter, we also prepared an English-language version of the badge for the account for donations to be displayed on the city website.

I would beseech all of you now reading my manuscript for your endorsement.

Evacuation Shelters

(10) The first induction into the temporary housing (April 30) and crisis headquarters support

The first phase of construction of the temporary housing in the east ground, which started on March 26, was at last complete at the end of April.

However, it was no easy task for the evacuees to set up a new home. Although the Japanese Red Cross Society provided a seven-item set of major home appliances (including a refrigerator, television, washing machine, etc.), people still needed small items to go about their lives. Yukie Osa, president of the Association for Aid and Relief, Japan, an international NGO, presented each household in the temporary accommodation with a "pots and pans set" containing pots, a kettle, a chopping board, knives, and other essential items to support them in their new lives.

Added to that, I provided them with 30 kilograms of rice per person and a set of blankets each from the rice and bedding gathered from fellow mayors throughout Japan for just this purpose.

Each household was also given 100,000 yen on moving into temporary housing to cover the cost of restarting. I was glad to hand over these kindnesses collected from all over the country for these people starting out on their journeys.

So that distribution of the meal services and boxed lunches at evacuation shelters did not become unfair, we thought it necessary to check whether people were having problems as well as offer nutrition-related support while they were getting used to their new lives in the temporary housing.

Handing over the keys at a ceremony for the
Kitaiibuchi emergency temporary housing
(April 30, 2011)

We thus had city employees hand over boxed meals for their dinner while helping people with their new start.

Completion of the temporary housing for the 1,000 evacuee households moving into these facilities from Soma took 40 more days. In the initial stages of the transfer to the new housing, it was necessary to assemble a support system for life there, which might continue for a considerable length of time, so we evaluated a support system through dialog with evacuees while handing over their boxed dinners.

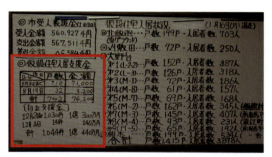

100,000 yen per household supplied to cover the cost of setting up

30 kilograms of rice per person

Bedding for each person

The "pots and pans" set Support from the "Association for Aid and Relief"

Evacuation Shelters **Chapter 3**

column

(11) The feelings of the Emperor and Empress

On May 11, 2011, their Majesties the Emperor and Empress of Japan visited Soma to offer encouragement to the area afflicted by the disaster.

I welcomed their Majesties as they alighted from a helicopter in the parking lot of the Soma Koyo Soccer Field, which had been washed away by the tsunami. This was a fulfilling moment for me, and possibly one of the proudest in my life. I guided them around, offering explanations, and for two and a half hours I was the time-keeper for the imperial visit. What astonished me more than anything was the happy expressions of the city residents who had assembled on the roadsides to catch a glance of the Emperor and Empress.

In the principal's office of Nakamura Daini Elementary School, I offered a summary of the earthquake. "Many of the people who were saved escaped to the Tsunomitsu Shrine located in one of the higher areas of the Haragama district, following stories that had been handed down from their ancestors. There is a tale of a giant tsunami that hit 400 years ago which has been passed down through the generations. I feel extremely grateful to their ancestors." His Majesty the Emperor nodded very gently at my words, and asked me if it was possible to visit the shrine. "I am very sorry, but the itinerary for our inspection today has already been decided."

At length, as the bus passed through the Haragama district, His Majesty inquired if the Tsu shrine was visible from where we were.

"Your Majesty, the shrine building is not visible, but it is located in the woods on the high ground you can see over there."

"Oh the woods....Yes, I see."

In an inspiring moment, the Emperor looked in the direction I was pointing, and nodded.

It felt like His Majesty had spoken not just to us, but to our ancestors as well.

Evacuation Shelters

Chapter 3

Mayor's e-mail newsletter - May 20, 2011 Issue

essay

(12) A new village

70 days after the earthquake. Although the move to temporary housing was proceeding according to plan, there were still 800 people living in the evacuation shelters. Until the transfer of all evacuees to temporary housing was complete in mid-June, the crisis headquarters continued to hold daily meetings. Although we had issued instructions to take breaks in turns for health reasons, when I thought about it, other than the one time I had missed a headquarters meeting due to business in Tokyo, everyone above department chief had attended every day. With the closure of the evacuation shelters, we will longer hold headquarters meetings on Sundays, so I would like to declare Sundays a holiday, but since we have three weeks left, I want people to try to keep going as they have been without taking a break.

Looking at the evacuation shelters that grew to house more than 4,400 people in the aftermath of the earthquake aroused a desire within me to complete the temporary housing as quickly as possible, and to ensure that not a single person died while living in the shelters. I believe that with the fortitude displayed by the city medical institutions, and the medical support activities of the Japan Medical Association, the All Japan Hospital Association, Tokyo Medical University, and the Tokyo Metropolitan Team, along with the volunteer activities of so many Soma residents and cooperating organizations, it will be possible to achieve my initial primary objectives. Of the evacuation shelters, the Emperor and Empress elected to visit the gymnasium of Nakamura Daini Elementary School, and offered a greeting to every person there individually. Further, when I explained, in response to a request for information on the area where the disaster occurred, that the survivors owed their lives to the firemen who had sacrificed their own, the imperial couple stood there in the drizzling rain, holding umbrellas as they offered a silent bow in honor of the deceased. Thanks to their Majesties, I felt, ever so slightly, that I had been forgiven.

I wrote previously of my feelings with regard to the children that the dead firemen left behind. However, the message that the firemen also left was that we should provide proper support for the futures of the survivors of the tsunami. Although we are creating a database of the living circumstances of all of the evacuees, we decided to first make a list of those households consisting of just a single person—in other words, those households where only one member of the family had survived. That was because the next thing we had to keep in mind after medical care as a secondary disaster was people committing suicide for economic reasons, and people dying alone. When we checked, there were 110 households consisting of just a single person, with a 93 year old man at the head of the list. Some of these people appeared to be struggling to cope with the fact that they were the only ones in their families to survive.

Although moving to the temporary housing was a goal for our mid-term plan, I believe that long-term support for such people is needed to allow them to be able to live by themselves in the new facilities. More than anything, we need to offer encouragement and a counter to loneliness. Although one suggestion was to have these people live together, they all expressed a wish to live by themselves. Given that, we hit upon the idea of having everyone eat a meal together in the assembly area, so that people would communicate with each other at least once a day, and decided to offer dinner through a system of rations. Thus, although dinner will be supplied for a year to everyone living in the temporary housing, sole householders will eat their evening meal together in the assembly area. We will also be proactive in creating opportunities for them to talk face-to-face, including health checks.

Diagram of group leader/household leader system

In order for all those living in temporary housing, including

Evacuation Shelters

Chapter 3

single-person households, to offer mutual support for each other in their lives, we want to create colonies for each district in every assembly area. One assembly area encompasses approximately 80 households, each of which will chose a representative, with a group leader chosen from among these to represent the assembly area at meetings of group leaders. Although group leaders will also serve as leaders of administrative divisions in some cases, the leaders' council will be positioned above the group leaders' meeting, with administrative services provided based on this system of organization. Accordingly, services such as residents' health checks, rationing of aid materials, and distribution of hot meal supplies will be arranged by the leaders' council and group leaders' meeting.

For Soma city, which took in refugees from Minamisoma city, the Futaba area, and Iitate village, who were forced to evacuate by the accident at the nuclear power plant, creating colonies for each municipality of the refugees' home towns and setting up a framework for administrative services are key points to allow these people to live in a region that is new to them.

Soma city appointed representatives of the city to each assembly area, but I also want to have the household of at least one employee of the government office living in the colonies from other municipalities. I made an appointment with the mayor of Iitate, which it had been decided would host 71 households, to discuss the residence of village staff. Currently we were receiving many applications from outside the city, but for the reasons explained above, we want the head of the village to make the final adjustments and decide whether to take them in. In addition, we want all of the citizens of other municipalities to do everything they can to look after the people entering the temporary housing from other municipalities, just as the citizens of Soma city do.

(13) Radioactivity countermeasures and briefings (from May 22 onwards)

The airborne radiation in Soma continued to fall from the levels experienced immediately after the accident at the nuclear power plant, and while it was possible throughout the city that personal exposure might exceed 20 millisieverts per year, we predicted that there would probably be no cases over five millisieverts. Either way, we had to obtain actual measurements from each person to get accurate results.

However, there was no clear opinion from the central government regarding long-term low-level radiation, and so we decided to let those families living in the Tamano district—the children of whom exhibited a comparatively high level of airborne radioactivity, even in Soma—move to the nearby Onodai temporary housing, which had almost zero levels of radioactivity, if the families wished.

When dealing with radioactivity, the most important thing is to be knowledgeable about it, and "fear it correctly, and avoid it wisely."

I had Professor Kami and department staff from the University of Tokyo Institute of Medical Science who were appointed radioactivity countermeasure advisers give briefings to Soma residents at 12 locations throughout the city.

A regional briefing by Professor Kami
(May 22, 2011)

Evacuation Shelters — Chapter 3

(14) Measures against sludge and dust (effects on worker health and residents' lives due to dust scattering)

As cleanup of the disaster afflicted regions, and removal and process of rubble in each area proceeded, serious cases of tetanus began to emerge in Ishinomaki city in Miyagi prefecture.

At this stage there were no clear research results regarding toxic sludge, but there were concerns that asbestos might be carried into the city from the detritus of the earthquake, so we constructed gates between the areas where city residents were living and those where sludge and dust were present, and instituted measures so that workers showered and then changed clothes before exiting the gates.

With regard to implementing these rules, we asked Kenji Shibuya, a professor of policy studies at the School of International Health at the University of Tokyo's Graduate School of Medicine to give a lecture for those affected, including construction company employees, seeking their understanding. These measures were intended to prevent the sludge and dust causing illness, under a standardized set of on-site rules.

1) Workers should all carry disinfectant sets, and use them in their work.
2) When returning to their normal lives from work sites, workers should shower to wash off sludge and dust, and change clothes.
3) Businesses hiring employees should appoint safety and health supervisors and enforce the creation of emergency systems.

Kenji Shibuya lecturing workers
(June 4, 2011)

Gate system equipment
(Shower/Iwanoko)

Mayor's e-mail newsletter - June 6, 2011 Issue

(15) For the futures of the children affected by the disaster

We are blessed and have been receiving financial aid for children orphaned by the earthquake from Japan and around the world. Some of this is from people with whom I have spoken, and who, inspired by my words, have embarked on broad-reaching fund raising activities on their return home. Other people came up to me with small amounts, saying as much. Where possible we wanted to sent a letter of thanks, and so when we receive bank remittances we would like to also receive an email with the name and postal address of the person making the donation. One more reason is that if I am still alive when these children grow to adulthood, I would like to compile a book of the names of people who have helped them, and present it to the children as a celebratory gift when they go out into the world, a reminder of everyone that came to their aid.

I myself also learned a great deal as I continue to oversee the recovery and rebuilding in the aftermath of the earthquake.
In my mind's eye, I can recall heartwarming scenes of the area around my home in Haragama where I grew up, but I am unable to accept that everything there is gone, and that the situation there now is completely different. Although three months have passed I have not been able to truly accept reality. However in front of people who have completely lost the lives they built up, I could not afford the luxury of wallowing in sadness and sentimentality, so I learned to carry out my official business without giving in to my emotions, and to read the future calmly for developments and take measures well in advance. More than anything, I realized that I was most relaxed when I was working, and I came to understand how much of a blessing it was to receive support when things were really difficult. I had not done enough to acknowledge others in the past to warrant receiving so much help, and I think that I will have to make up for that in life from now on.

Evacuation Shelters — Chapter 3

My honest feelings are that just as I am not able to accept the enormous damage inflicted by this disaster in its entirety, the children who were beset by that monster tsunami are unable to break away from the horrific experience. Added to

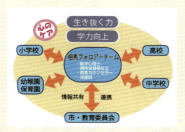

that, the despondency brought on by losing family and friends is eating away at the feelings of these children, who would normally be cheerful and sensitive. After the schools reopened on April 18, we have been receiving reports at every crisis meeting from the superintendent of education on the situation at the disaster-affected schools, and it appears that there are grave difficulties with PTSD.

To counter this we assembled the "Soma Follower Team" with a view to providing care from clinical psychologists. Although we began offering detailed mental health care from the end of April, once we started, the workload and how to ensure that care was ongoing became issues. Since students from kindergarten through to senior high school were eligible, if we were to provide comprehensive care for each and record their development, following their development for up to 15 years, we would have to manage personnel and financial resources for the long term.

On June 2, a general meeting to establish an NPO was held in order to ensure that these activities were carried out properly in an ongoing manner with transparency, in line with our philosophy. Koichiro Yamada, a member of the Soma Board of Education was appointed as director, while the post of deputy director was filled by Yukie Osa, president of the Association for Aid and Relief and a professor at Rikkyo University. Other knowledgeable people from Soma filled posts on the board, along with Nanako Kondo, a lawyer from Fukushima. The new corporate status made it easier for Soma city to provide support, and simplified the collection of donations.

Above all, we were able to objectively verify the difference between our goals and the budget. We hope to provide proper long term support for the children affected by the disaster, and act as advisers throughout the process of their growth.

Incidentally, the activities of this NPO go hand in hand with the support system for orphans.

I think that mere financial support is insufficient as a response to the parents who passed away leaving orphan children, and so we are calling for support from around the world for use in scholarships for their higher education after these children graduate from high school. However, we must not forget to offer sufficient support to allow them to acquire sufficient emotional wherewithal and academic strength. That is why when we are able to organize the systems, I would like to add an academic improvement category to the menu of NPO activities. We would then like the good intentions of the people who are kind enough to provide support to reach not just the orphans, but all of the children of Soma who were affected by the disaster, and at the same time, we are thinking as hard as we can about how to make the most effective use of them.

■Follower Team activities

●Daily

Stationed at Isobe Kindergarten, Isobe Elementary School, Isobe Middle School, Nakamura Daini Elementary School, and Nakamura Daini Middle School, offering consulting to students, teaching staff, and guardians.

●Summer vacation, etc.

Providing school counseling at each school for students, teaching staff, and guardians as requested. The staff also visit assembly areas in the temporary housing with the "Mental Health Care Team" from Fukushima Medical University, offering consulting services.

Evacuation Shelters — Chapter 3

(16) Completion of temporary housing (1,000 units for Soma city) and closure of evacuation shelters

On June 10, 2011, all of the temporary housing facilities for the Soma residents affected by the disaster were complete, and we informed all evacuees of our intention to close the evacuation shelters by June 17.

Unlike life in the shelters, where three meals a day were provided, those living in temporary housing would have to support themselves from their own income. Although some of the evacuees pleaded that they were unsure if they could live in the temporary housing, we explained as far as the city was concerned, in addition to the initial support for the move to these facilities (support funds of 100,000 yen per household, bedding and 30 kilograms of rice per person, and the "pots and pans" set), for the time being we would provide two side dishes of food for dinner and continue providing rice during 2011, and everyone agreed to move.

Later, evacuation shelters that did not close became an issue, but in Soma we were able to close every shelter within a week of the completion of temporary housing. It was because every evacuee understood that they would have to move to the temporary housing eventually, even if closure was prolonged.

At this point, measures taken by the city for evacuees included support for life in the temporary housing, and our new major goal, which was a major change, was the construction of disaster public temporary housing to move to higher ground. Obtaining final residences on high land will be a major milestone in rebuilding. At the same time, we embarked on the creation of an entirely new area, based on our recovery plan.

The closing of the evacuation shelter at Nakamura Daini Elementary School (June 17, 2011)

Life in temporary housing

(17) Hiroaki Ômoto

On June 12, 2011, a unit of the Ground Self-Defense Forces dispatched to Soma from Hiroshima finished their three-month deployment and were to leave the city.I and the executive of Soma city bade a tearful to Hiroaki Ômoto, commander of the 46th Infantry Regiment, sad to see him go.

The power of the Self-Defense Forces and their spirited support in the disaster-affected area proved to be an immense strength, not only in the cleanup and recovery of the region, but in supporting life in the evacuation shelters.

Ômoto, their leader, participated in the morning and evening sessions of our crisis meetings as a member. He took our requests at every meeting, acting and reporting on them. His steady character and frank manner with the Soma members led us all to think of him as a member of the Soma family, and we came to depend on him.

"I'll definitely be back."

The day of the 2016 Nomaoi festival. True to his word, Ômoto, after retiring from the Self-Defense Forces and become Director of Emergency Response in Kyoto, came to Soma again.

Gripping each other's hands and mutually delighted at our reunion, we were filled with emotion as we thought of our six-year separation, and about what had happened during this time.

Ômoto reporting on the completion of activities

Chapter 4

Temporary Housing
(June 18, 2011 to March 26, 2015)

(1) Temporary housing basic operating policy

An important issue at emergency headquarters when beginning the move to temporary housing was to build village community along with a system that enabled us to help one another as a collective. Failing to build a solid sense of community could result in mental which could lead to suicides and dying alone, and we were determined to keep others from dying.

Each temporary housing building would house five residences. There would also be a meeting place available for each group of approximately 16 to 20 buildings. One-thousand temporary homes would be available for victims in the city of Soma along with 10 meeting places. Later, 500 residences were completed by the city of Soma upon request from the prefectural government, which became home to victims affected by the nuclear power plant disaster in Iitate Village and Minamisoma City. Because the residences were delayed one to two months, Soma created a model pattern which was adopted in other towns and cities.

First we choose a leader out of an average of 20 temporary housing groups surrounding the meeting place. This person is selected by residents.

Because the resident colony centered around the meeting place mainly consists of the same original residents as the disaster-struck areas, it is possible to select someone who is trusted by the community. This person is called the Group Leader, and is hired to work at emergency headquarters on a temporary basis for four hours a day at 900 yen per hour. A Sub Leader is also selected and hired on a temporary basis.

Next, one representative of five households in a building is selected to keep

Temporary Housing

in touch with emergency headquarters and report on the health of residents and sanitary conditions of the living quarters. This person carries out this task for two hours a day, is named the Building Leader. The person is elected for this position in the same way as the Group Leader.

Several times a month a Building Leader meeting is held at the meeting place, where the Group Leader and Sub Leader take the bulk of the responsibility for discussing problems in temporary housing. The Group Leader and Sub Leader then gather at the City Hall a month to hold a Group Leader Council. This branched structure not only serves to distributes relief supplies and quickly communicate necessary information, but is also instrumental in helping form a community in temporary housing.

The 100 building complex, housing 500 households that were completed on July, 8, 2011, was overwhelmed with applicants from victims of the nuclear power plant disaster in Minamisoma City, Namie Town, and IIitate Village. Soma city accepted reservants right away only with signature of the victims.

In my opinion, they were residents of their respective municipalities, and I thought it is not my place to decide whether or not they should be accepted.

The list of applicants was forwarded to the heads of their respective municipalities, with the head of the local government requesting that we take care of their residents. Therefore, the basic responsibility for managing this process was placed on each local government head, clarifying the basic position of the city of Soma in accepting residents upon request.

I did not want to create a system of management that enticed victims seeking temporary refuge from the nuclear power plant accident to become Soma residents.

Therefore, after assigning temporary housing to the household of each municipal official, I requested that each head of respective municipalities

Household Leader meeting

107

Group Leader meeting

where they were evacuated from take care of the residents of their towns while living in Soma. In line with this policy, Norio Kanno, the mayor of Iitate Village hired the staffs on a temporary basis and placed them in temporary housing in the Iitate Village Block. However, there were not enough people to cover the position from other municipalities.

We were unable to provide an allowance or bedding to people who later came from other towns, although they were provided with pots and pans sets from "Association for Aid and Relief, Japan" as with residents of Soma. After obtaining the approval of victims in Soma, we believed it was necessary to distribute relief supplies gathered in Soma to residents of other towns. After taking care of the victims of Soma, 10 kilograms of rice were distributed as temporary food supplies to these people.

(2) Distribution of dinner dishes to all households (from June 18, 2011)

The Shidax Corporation dispatched staff to the evacuation shelter along with food supplies, providing a three-meal service. After all households had moved into temporary housing on June 17, they began distribution of two dinner dishes for all residents.

It goes without saying that, this service was aimed to prevent solitary death and provide nutrition to diet. In particular, elderly people who were left alone due to the disaster were invited to eat a full meal at the meeting place with the Group Leader. This system was made possible by the previously described Group Leader and Building Leader system.

The same service was provided to residents from other towns who came to

Temporary Housing

Distribution of dinner dishes

Meal at the meeting place

live with us later on. Subsequently, providing dinner dishes to residents of other municipalities on budget of city poses a tax burden, however, we obtained approval from emergency headquarters to do so. This is due to that fact that I thought it was not fair to discriminate against others while the city of Soma had the means to help.

This system was applicable to all residents at temporary housing who would live there; one year for the age groups of residents who is18 and under and 65 and over, and two years for disabled residents. This service continued until June 2015.

(3) City of Soma Reconstruction Meeting and expert Reconstruction Advisory Board Meeting (from June 3, 2011)

On June 3, 2011, the first reconstruction meeting was held. It was attended by the same members as the emergency headquarters. With the impending start of moving into temporary housing and long-term healthy living in temporary housing in mind, we began discussing the establishment of a reconstruction plan, along with its significance, goals, and the determination to move forward. In order to obtain objective advice and advance verification from experts on the thinking behind reconstruction and how to move forward, we established the Reconstruction Advisory Board Meeting consisting of experts that the city of Soma had previous connections with.

When establishing this plan, I drew a diagram at the first Reconstruction Advisory Board Meeting. Looking back to that moment six years in the past, the plan proceeded almost exactly as imagined due to the unbreakable tenacity of the city employees and the support of the Japanese government and friendly groups. Above all I was again humbled and surprised by the bonds of solidarity between the residents of our city.

First City of Soma Reconstruction Meeting
(June 3, 2011)

Temporary Housing **Chapter 4**

Mayor's e-mail newsletter - June 12, 2011 Issue

essay

(4) City of Soma Reconstruction Plan

On June 3, the "City of Soma Reconstruction Meeting" was held to discuss the future direction of reconstruction efforts in Soma, where I arranged the various topics that need to be covered. It was nearly impossible to imagine the future of disaster area in next three to five years as well as the ideal lifestyle for victims from the disaster. It was impossible to move forward in some areas without changing the government-run system, and the inability to establish the proper funds made many plans pure fantasy.

Over those three months, the emergency headquarters placed top priority on minimizing damage to physical and mental health due to the disaster, and on preventing the community from falling apart due to secondary disasters such as the nuclear power plant accident. Difficult problems occurred one after the other, and city hall staff along with citizens worked together to deal carefully and quickly with each one, which helped prevent any further deaths. I'm very thankful to the staff at the emergency headquarters in particular who worked tirelessly.

Truefully speaking, I remember feeling uncomfortable when the government launched the first reconstruction meeting not long after the disaster. For the month-long period directly after the earthquake we were completely focused on solving short-term problems, and the government's discussions focused on what felt like a far-off country to the rest of us.

Because this disaster was so unusually large in scale, the situation of each municipality that suffered was completely different. One of the major aspect of the whole problem was that, it does not mean the cities are "restored" even if everlastings went back as it used to be. This is because each areas of Fukushima had different views of "reconstruction" due to the distinguished characteristics of each resions.

More of less, the reconstruction process would be completely different in all the towns of Fukushima which suffered from the effects of the nuclear power plant disaster, Iwate, and Miyagi. Also, the damages and thoughts on reconstruction differ in each and every town in Fukushima. Because the situation in Soma can only be understood by its residents, we needed to think and work hard on formulating a reconstruction plan. I believe that the government's reconstruction council must work closely with each town and village to discuss reconstruction plans that take the actual situation into consideration.

One major feature of the massive damage due to the large tsunami was that reconstruction could never restore things to the way they were. After applying some residence restrictions even in disaster areas of Soma we needed to rebuild living and industrial areas, however, the future problem of how to handle the debris caused by the tsunami was out of our hands to solve. The general policy is to keep living and working spaces separate, however, attempting to build production bases for work areas and solar power without using public lands would result in impinging on resident property rights. Nevertheless, taking on the 25% land purchase fee as stipulated in the Act on Promoting Group Relocation (S47) was a burden for disaster-struck towns. A minimum subsidy of 10% or less is necessary, but preferably 5%.

First City of Soma Reconstruction Advisory Board Meeting

Temporary Housing — Chapter 4

If available, it can help support those affected by the disaster.
Naturally, relocating residences to higher ground is preferable, however, even if we can make such plans at that stage, it is impossible to plan for the future after relocation. The public disaster housing built on high ground cannot be sold at a low price in the future (5 to 7 years later). On this point I'd like to request that the government break down the system of barriers in serious earthquake special rebuilding zones.

One more important point is managing the long road to recovery. Regardless of how good a reconstruction plan is, losing lives to solitary death or suicides during the execution of the plan is a terrible thing. This is the reason why it is necessary to include a detailed management plan towards the goal in the reconstruction plan. It is a given that countermeasures for many anticipated problems be included in the reconstruction plan, such as health management, preventing solitary deaths, and dealing with PTSD in children while in temporary housing, as well as managing the health of workers as they clear away debris, revitalizing the local economy, and formulating radiation countermeasures. If we think of beginning reconstruction after overcoming these problems, the central theme was rebuilding the lives of citizens who have suffered in the disaster. This may seem a bit of exaggerating, though, I define "reconstruction" as the sate of which all of the generations of victims to be

Health checkup for disaster victims

being able to have a life plan.

We must build a full educational structure for the future of our children, and help support and raise orphaned children. We must provide stability and a medical care system for single-person households such as the elderly in particular.

For the younger generation we must provide a revitalized industry and secure employment.

To solve such large problems it is necessary to clear the rubble, plan for land usage, provide safe and affordable housing, and restore fishing ports and farmlands. When paying close attention to production businesses and thinking of how to develop these, the significance of the reconstruction plan becomes clear for what is needed when tying down knowledge of land usage, considering realistic housing acquisition methods, creating new ways to manage and new business formats for fishing and agricultural industries, as well as considering a vision of the future for all age ranges.

The reconstruction plan should also change and adapt to accommodate any future problems, as well as the scale, range, depth, and detail of government measures.

Soma city has fulfilled my manifest by functioning the PDCA based on our ASO9001 certified by municipal office. Next year we should be able to create a more effective plan in version 2 due to the PDCA cycle. There is no doubt that the ideas and methods of our ISO14001 certification will be of use in minimizing environmental impact. One of the most important aspects of utilizing ISO methods is a strong axis (principles). The axis that recovery hinges on is "soft industries that can help plan the lives of various age ranges and the production industries that help properly execute these plans." Because the city of Soma is well-versed in analyzing and handling new problems, checking progress, and reviewing methods, we simply need to keep moving toward our goal with confidence.

We established the Reconstruction Advisory Board Meeting and

Temporary Housing — Chapter 4

enlisted the help of experts in various fields in order to obtain objective evaluation and further knowledge in formulating our plan. The board was chaired by Professor Masayasu Kitagawa from Waseda University Research Institute of Manifesto, Kanju Osawa, the dean of Tokyo University of Agriculture, Hisakazu Oishi, former chief engineer at the Ministry of Land, Infrastructure, Transport and Tourism and current chairman of JICE, Jiro Makino, former National Tax Administration Agency director and current vice president of the General Insurance Association of Japan, Masahiro Kami, specially-appointed professor from Institute of Medical Science, University of Tokyo, Takeshi Niinami, president of Lawson, and Yukie Osa, chairperson of the Association for Aid and Relief, Japan and professor at Rikkyo University. Out of the people who came to Soma, seven of the experts I most admire cheerfully agreed to attend. We were hopeful that they would discuss options from our standpoint.

From here on out, we will go into the detailed methodology for each issue, and a further investigation of our financial resources. We are hoping to receive some guidance from the advisory board on version 1-1 of the plan during July, which we will then present to the citizens and supporters of Soma. The plan will then be posted to the website so that we can receive a wide range of advice from people who have supported the city of Soma after this earthquake and those from far away who have expressed their goodwill indirectly by providing donations for the rebuilding work.

Professor Masayasu Kitagawa

(5) Haragama Morning Market Club

The fishermen were not the only ones to lose their jobs due to losing the fishing port and fishing vessels in the tsunami and the radioactive contamination of fish due to the nuclear power plant accident. Fish wholesalers and processors were also driven out of work.

Volunteer wholesalers visited the mayor's office to ask for a location where they could hold an early-morning market every Sunday to sell seafood provided by people in the fishing industry all across Japan. I then propesed them to form and NPO for the future reference. They later received NPO status and not only sold seafood at the morning market, but ran a restaurant that served seafood dishes to help those in the area recover from the disaster.

Because living in temporary housing makes it difficult for disaster vulnerable people such as the elderly to shop for food and other daily necessities, members of the Haragama Morning Market Club were asked to sell items to them from a cart. We eventually recruited sellers separately, though, we received many supports from wives of fishermen.

One other major objective of cart sales was to take part in face-to-face sales in order to prevent solitary deaths.

Although now most of the temporary housing in Soma has been demolished, the Iitate Village and Minamisoma City blocks remain where one can still see cart sales today.

Haragama Morning Market

Temporary Housing — Chapter 4

Mayor's e-mail newsletter - August 8, 2011 Issue

(6) Carts

My mother lived on a farm in the suburbs of Soma. My grandmother Yae was a hard worker.

Because the farm was in the suburbs, she pulled a cart filled with fresh vegetables from the back yard and went out to sell their produce. I was a little embarrassed by going through the villages setting on the back of the cart and gasing the view which is different from Hamagaya, the fishing village I was raised. My grandmother loved to talk, and she made endless small talk with the customers who waited for us in the shopping district. Her customers included the Horai Restaurant in between Nakamuratamachi and Udagawa Town, and she stopped the cart to treat me to udon noodles with meat topping on days when her produce sold well. Even after I had finished slurping down my soup, my grandmother couldn't stop talking.

Actually, there was a person who sold natto beans in triangle packages by bicycle in Haragama, and I think the tofu seller used a cart. The woman pulling the cart praised me for helping out my mother by going out to buy tofu as I took my mixing bowl along with me. Fifty years ago, time flowed a little bit slower on the streets and beaches of Soma, and it was a place filled with conversations and smiles. I never locked the doors of my soy sauce factory or store, and all of the other houses left their doors open as well.

117

Right after the tsunami came, Haragama was a source for all kinds of debris. After it was cleared away and I looked at the flat, featureless land, all I can think of is memories of my childhood. But right up until the disaster, it remained the same as it was in the past, filled with conversation and laughter, and even now no one locks their doors. The houses along the beach were all filled with families, and pretty much everyone knew what they were doing.

Nowadays in cities it is said the people are isolated from one another, and that our focus on individual lives brought forth from an age of economic growth has brought with it social problems such as solitary deaths. With that in mind, I realize that areas such as Haragama, Obama, and Isobe, which were the source of rubble from the disaster, were rich in communication. The thing that most impressed me about these disaster countermeasures and the aspect that made the most sense was the attention paid to maintaining order in the evacuation shelters. The partnership of living all together without having people arguing or fighting only accomplished due to the wisdom of refugee even though some of them had to stay up to three months. We made use of evacuation shelters organized by village as a way to show compassion and encourage each other. The village unit was maintained when people moved into temporary housing, and the Group Leaders and Sub Leaders appointed as administrative support staff by meeting place where residents showed compassion to all.

Problem that arose was how to incorporate non-Soma residents into the circle of communication who were also living in temporary housing. For example, on the request of the mayor of Iitate Village, 164 households were put into a single block, and we obtained their understanding after explaining my vision to the Group Leader and Sub Leader. We, of course, provided the same services for them as the citizens of Soma, including provisions of daily supplies and evacuation shelter support service through the Group Leader Council. There were no concerns over incorporating residents from

Temporary Housing — Chapter 4

local communities such as Itate Village from the beginning, while, it was inevitable that some blocks house temporary villages with residents from various towns. How would we communicate with people we didn't know?

At a minimum, we must give consideration to supporting disaster vulnerable persons, in other words, those with physical or mental disabilities, and households with elderly who need special care, as well as supporting those who were left alone due to the disaster. At the least, during 2011 we intended to distribute dinners to all of these types of people living in Temporary housing who wished to receive this service, however, we also want to help support other disaster vulnerable people in the same way as Soma citizens. However, we must also make arrangements with their hometown municipalities.

In Soma, we plan on treating all people from 1,500 households as a single group and providing the same level of service until moving out of temporary housing, regardless of where they are from. For example, all persons will be able to receive a general health check without charge in order to maintain their health. We also need to take everyone into consideration in order to provide assistance in shopping and to prevent solitary deaths.

On this point, I even thought of door-to-door sales using carts as I mentioned in my childhood memory at the beginning. We could hire administrative support staff to serve as cart salespeople on a temporary basis with one person per each of the 16 meeting places, selling items door-to-door at each one of the temporary housing buildings. Because this is also an employment opportunity they would work eight hours a day, five days per week, and outside of sales times, they could provide everyday living support to disabled persons, helping with the laundry, etc.

When recruiting for this position, a number of women who lived by the beach and love to talk like my grandmother Yae applied. We searched high and low for the type of metal and board carts I used to ride as a child, but couldn't find a single one at any farm, so we settled on a stylish stainless steel folding model. It has been one month since this service began, with two persons making the rounds instead of one as noted in the initial plan. This way probably makes conversation more lively.

Temporary Housing Chapter 4

(7) 2011 Soma Nomaoi (wild horse chase)

The Soma Nomaoi festival is both a military training exercise and Shinto festival that has been held for over 700 years in the former Soma clan domain. The commanding general would depart from the Soma Nakamura Shrine, and the next day would conduct a series of events with his entire army at the Hibarigahara Athletic Field, and conclude the subsequent day with the "Nomakake" (wild horse chase) Shinto ceremony at Odaka Shrine.

Because in 2011 the Hibarigahara Athletic Field was designated as an emergency evacuation preparation zone, and the Odaka Shrine was an area under evacuation order, the entire event was canceled. Due to the strong desire of the city of Soma and cavalry of former Kashima to carry on the tradition despite the setbacks of the earthquake, and on the request of the 33rd head of the Soma clan, Kazutane Soma, a cavalcade was held in Soma only.

When thinking of the fact that the entire army participated in the Nomaoi festival on the following year, this was a meaningful event for Soma horsemen, as it means that the tradition has continued on uninterrupted.

The Nomaoi festival that year was broadcast across the entire nation as a way to show our efforts to rebuild, and I believe that it gave hope to all of the former Soma clan (from the city of Soma to part of Tomiokacho) who had fled all throughout Japan due to the nuclear power plant accident.

Commanding General departing from Otemon

121

Mayor's e-mail newsletter - October 25, 2011 Issue

(8) Ayane's determination

These events happened on September 10. At the memorial service to mourn those lost in the tsunami, second year Isobe Junior High School student Ayane Abe's words pierced the hearts of the entire audience as she spoke from the platform, representing her surviving family members. Ayane is the daughter of former assistant fire chief Kenichi. Although I talked about the courageous, dignified determination of Kenichi's mother whom I met at an evacuation shelter not long after the earthquake, I learned something important from the words of his daughter.

"I'm very proud of my father, who lost his life in the line of duty while trying to save the people of our village. Because I want to become an adult like my father, someone who helped others, I'll continue studying so I can go onto college and become a nursery school teacher."

Among the many thousands of eulogies I have heard, I don't think I have ever encountered such strong feelings of sympathy for the deceased. This fourteen-year-old girl taught us the goal that Kenichi, who is no longer with us, and all adults must struggle for in rebuilding.

Temporary Housing

Chapter 4

Fukushima is now in dire straits. Despite surviving the tsunami, all of Fukushima faces damage to their reputation and health concerns due to the nuclear power plant accident, and there is no end in sight to their struggles. Soma also faces issues such as rebuilding after the disaster and radiation fears, and we are prepared for a long fight as part of Fukushima, however, thanks to Ayane's words, I feel like I can see a white cloud floating in the sky just beyond the long slope on the other side of a ridge. Our hope rests not only with the children of Kenichi and our other firefighters, but with all of the children of Soma in whose hands our future rests.

It ttok only until the following month after the disaster to create regulations to call upon the world for the financial support of children orphaned in the earthquake, my first thought at the time was to ensure that those children who lost their parents receive monetary support. Support entailed funds for their daily lives and a full scholarship to continue schooling. Thankfully, the support funds exceeded 310 million yen. With 400 million yen we could supply each orphaned child with 30,000 yen per month, and enrollment fees for college, and full tuition scholarships that do not need to be returned. Some contributors are planning to continue their donations, so we are very thankful for these periodic funds. On behalf of their parents who are no longer with us, we'd like to thank those who donated from the bottom of our hearts.

I learned from Ayane that my thanks are not enough to those in Japan and around the world. We must continue to educate children so that they have the ability to continue on to college when the time comes. Because the children are our future hope for Soma, the most important aspect of rebuilding we can undertake is thoroughly educating those children.

I'd like to apologize for the sudden proposal to all attendees on the final day of the conference in September, however, the new

123

education fund "City of Soma Educational Rebuilding Children's Fund Ordinance" passed unanimously. All of these funds will be used to improve the academic ability of the children. For example, if an outstanding university student comes to Soma to help educate children after seeing them studying, we should set aside funds for their travel and lodging expenses. Kids have infinite possibilities. Because of this, there are a multitude of ways we can use this fund. There are only four years left till Ayane to take university entrance exam. Our regional reconstruction is going to be evaluated depending on where it leads to.

Temporary Housing — Chapter 4

Mayor's e-mail newsletter - February 28, 2012 Issue

essay

(9) Soma Idobata Nagaya

Despite tremendous efforts which failed to maintain privacy in the evacuation shelter directly after the earthquake, people did watch out for each other to the best of their abilities, even when conditions were such that one could hear the breathing of other people in the same room. Leaders volunteered at each evacuation shelter, with surprisingly almost no arguments during the three months living there. Staff from city hall were assigned to each evacuation shelter with plans to prevent problems, but the reason everyone was able to live together without any major problems was the sensibility to spontaneously form a community. When all evacuation shelters were closed on June 17 upon completion of temporary housing, we were afraid that splitting shelters into households would result in losing this function of watching over one another that had formed. We viewed this as a way to prevent solitary deaths among the elderly that had become single-person households due to losing family members in the earthquake.

The evacuation shelters became miniature societies, and the knowledge and sociability of evacuees presided over by leaders was amazing. To apply this sense of order in life at temporary housing, we decided to form each of the 1,500 buildings into blocks organized by meeting place. With 15 meeting places, there were

Soma Idobata Nagaya
(Completed May 2, 2012)

125

approximately 100 households per block, forming small villages, and the leader of each block became known as the Group Leader. Next, a Group Leader assistant was chosen. The Group Leader and assistant handled a mountain of necessary tasks, such as keeping in touch with the government, arranging distribution of supplies, managing sanitary conditions of each small village, and ultimately directing requests to the emergency headquarters. However, because it was impossible to visit single elderly households, and provide fresh foods to all of the 200 to 300 people in each village, a representative was chosen from each building (five households), which became known as the Building Leader. Because the Group Leader, assistant, and Building Leader all handled some tasks from the emergency headquarters, they were hired on a temporary basis as administrative support staff, although the pay was unfortunately low.

Their management style was indicative of the city of Soma, and we came up with the idea of having each of the elderly single households who were isolated due to the tsunami gather at the meeting

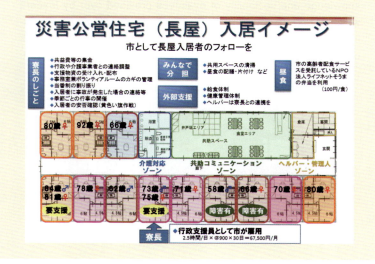

Temporary Housing

Chapter 4

place once a day for a communal meal. The Group Leader kept an eye on these individuals. The once a day meal (dinner) was the same food service system as used at the evacuation shelters. We also supplied two dinner dishes to each of the residents in temporary housing. This was mainly the work of the Building Leader. Eating together or delivering foods was a way to ensure that everyone was safe.

Dinner supply was costly and therefore it was one of our major suffer. Costs totaled approximately 200 million yen per year. Nearly all the members of the Diet who visited Soma praised our efforts in this regard, however, the system unfortunately did not entitle us to any assistance from the government. With the goal of promoting independence, this system will continue only for solitary individuals, children, the elderly, and others who are disaster vulnerable in 2012. At that time, the Group Leader and Building Leader system were useful. This personnel cost is used to connect people to one another, and because it was finally decided to continue this system in 2012, the Group Leader and Building Leader system will also be continued.

On a hot day last September, a long-standing kamaboko shop in Odawara sent enough kamaboko for 4,000 people. It was Grannie "Suzuhiro" who sent the kamaboko. She asked me, "Our kamabokos are fresh, so we're worried that they might spoil before it's delivered." I replied "Grannie, it'll be fine. We can deliver it within two hours." Actually it was delivered to all households before the end of the day due to the coordinated efforts of the Group Leader, assistant, and Building Leader. At times when there were not enough relief supplies for all

Common area (Dining hall)

127

households, the Group Leader Council decides on how to distribute supplies. Lately I've been attending the Group Leader Council with the Group Leader and Sub Leader as often as possible in order for them to understand our mindset on how to revitalize the area in the future, and to ask about how things are going. Of course communication between residents in temporary housing is important, but mutual understanding between the emergency headquarters and the housing sites is equally important.

Common area (Laundry area)

In 2012, when looking back at the past year's experiences after the earthquake I think of how we should strengthen support for the health management and future plans of victims of the disaster, and how we need to gradually move away from temporary housing at the same time. We made efforts to rebuld mutipledwelling complexes and even smaller single houses, still it was necessary to crease new villages in social communication that follows the Group Leader and Building Leader system.

The Soma Idobata Nagaya, completed in March with people moving in start of April was the first of these multiple-dwelling complexes, and the first step in moving out of temporary housing. Nevertheless, this system is designed to bring elderly out of those 99 people who are isolated due to loss of their family, to come close together. Thus in this sense it could be said that this system is an example of the model for challenging the general problem in elderly population rather than stepping forward into new society.

This row house is home to 12 households, with 39.6 m² per

Temporary Housing — Chapter 4

household. Each home has its own toilet, bath, and kitchen, but no space saved for a washing machine. Just as row houses in the past shared a common well, this complex has three washing machines in a common area for use by all residents. Nearby there is a slightly raised tatami room where residents can enjoy conversation. There is also a large shared dining hall where all residents can join once a day for a meal. We set the price of lunch at 150 yen however, and the "NPO Lifenet Soma" would handle meal preparation and delivery. Masayasu Kitagawa, chairman of the Reconstruction Advisory Board Meeting and professor at Waseda University, provided consultation on this project. Learning from the Group Leader system in temporary housing, a "Housemaster" was appointed to take the lead in eating together, cleaning common areas, and other joint tasks.

Eating together in the common area (March 12, 2015)

Taking into consideration the care that elderly residents would need at some point, disabled toilets and baths were built, and the entire building features a universal design. These features are also used by visitors, and the common areas can also be used for volunteer activities when the need arises (it was very difficult to secure lodging for disaster volunteers), so there was a need to use these from the very beginning. Because most residents were in the 70s to 80s age range, there was sufficient possibility that they may need minor assistance in ten years time, so we decided to do our best to make accommodations so that they would not have to be placed in an elderly care facility due to our inability to care for them here. To deal with this, we built a caregiver office near the entrance.

Based on this criterion, we selected residents and hired younger staff in their thirties and forties to form a project team simulation that could plan operations for ten years in the future when residents' health began to decline. Although these are long-term earthquake measures, we must think not only ten years, but also 20 and 30 years ahead.

During the simulation, the team came up with new ideas. Rather than trying to imagine different ways of taking care of each other when persons require long-term care ten years in the future, they proposed accepting elderly persons who already require long-term care from the beginning. After some research, we discovered that there were 18 two-person households that became single-person households due to the earthquake, and that there were 188 disabled persons.

Therefore, we decided to accept initial residents where two households have elderly residents that require care, and two households with disabled persons. In line with this, we decided to have a caregiver come from the beginning and residents were able to use the disabled-accessible toilet. I always felt that if we could manage at least to establish the system to keep eyes on one another, many people could maintain their life at home, even in the case of losing their partner. This resulted in the "NPO Lifenet Soma", which consists of both young and old members who visit and talk to residents. At the Soma Idobata Nagaya, the Housemasters are in charge of making sure this way of thinking is put into practice.

The City Hall staff is thinking of helping to make sure that daily living itself is a shared task, with the Housemaster taking charge of carrying out daily chores, and residents cooperating so that weekly, monthly, and yearly plans can be accomplished.

Dow Chemical, one of the world's leading petrochemical manufacturers, donated funds to help with the first row house which is

Temporary Housing

Chapter 4

planned for completion at the end of March. It is equipped with a solar power system, which is a prerequisite for public buildings in Soma, but it features a classic style that is reminiscent of the castle town of the Soma Clan. I would like to take this opportunity to express our sincere gratitude for Dow's kindness, and respond by doing our absolute best in rebuilding efforts.

(10) Beginning operation at the disaster waste intermediate processing facility (from October 28, 2011)

Clearing away debris is the most basic part of recovering from the earthquake. In addition to the massive amount of debris caused by the tsunami, dealing with collapsed and ruined houses as well as other structures was urgent.

However, cesium and other radioactive substances scattered into the air by the nuclear power plant accident directly after the earthquake had settled onto much of the rubble. Burning any of this rubble would result in secondary damage due to the smoke spreading contaminants. The Ministry of the Environment failed to decide on a policy for dealing with contaminated rubble at the beginning of the work, resulting in significant delays compared to Miyagi and Iwate prefectures.

However, because we could not sit idly by, we made a proposal on how to dispose of the debris, but went ahead with formulating a way to decide on the process using a selection committee consisting of experts from administrative heads and the chairman of the chamber of commerce and industry.

We considered the Isobe area as a location for rubble disposal as the tsunami wiped the area clean, however, because this spot raises concerns of damaged reputations in Matsukawaura, we formulated a disposal policy based on borrowing 10 hectares of land owned by SME Support Japan in the east area of the industrial park. In addition to the understanding of the residents in the area, the Hakuzo Medical Corporation, The Dow Chemical Company Japan, M.Setek Co., Ltd., Tanizawa Seisakusho, Ltd., Tohoku Sannohashi Corp., Yoshino Gypsum Co., Ltd., and Chiyoda Ute Co. Ltd. kindly cooperated with our efforts.

Temporary Housing — Chapter 4

On June 10, 2011, we made a public proposal for the disaster waste intermediate processing project. Then on June 30 and July 8 at the vendor selection meeting we evaluated and scored each company, resulting in granting priority negotiation rights to the Fujita Corporation. Later, waiting on approval from the Ministry of the Environment, we began construction on the intermediate processing site.

On October 28, the two-year intermediate processing project began. Soon after, construction and operation of the temporary incinerator began, but the most important factor in going forward was the cooperation of the people in the neighboring village and nearby companies.

Mayor's e-mail newsletter - November 11, 2011 Issue

(11) Portraits of families standing together

Along with others, Noriyuki Asahi, the executive director of the All-Japan Association of Photographic Societies, was seen in July consulting with city hall on lending support.

I just so happened to be a twenty-year member of the association, so I wondered what kind of support he was planning on for the disaster-struck area and I asked for the knowledge of the association in helping us.

The first thing Asahi proposed was providing several buses for transporting the elderly on their shopping trips . Although I respectfully declined his offer as we had already begun door-to-door cart sales in Soma, and that the bus service would not make a difference without counting it. Our mutual love for photography led us to open up to each other while talking about shooting photos.

While talking, we came up with a number of ideas. "Because so many of our members are seniors, we can't ask them to do heavy labor such as carrying rubble or mud. But you know, I think everyone wants to be useful." "Well, why not have them take photos, since they're already good at that?" "They won't be journalism photos, and it'd be rude to stick a lens in evacuees' faces." "Why not commemorative photos? Why not give people photos as presents? They would be more like studio portraits, and better than

Temporary Housing — Chapter 4

those taken by amateurs. I think it would give victims of the disaster hope. How about photos of families standing together?? "We'd like to help support the disaster-struck areas through photos, but is there a place where we can set up a studio?" "I think we could use the meeting places and make a tour of each one."

At this point, Asahi's expression gradually grew brighter. "If that's the case, we can get camera manufacturers to work with us... there's lighting equipment, and also we could talk to printer manufacturers..."

During the course of our conversation, we began planning a studio photo shoot at the meeting places in temporary housing sponsored by the All-Japan Photo Association, and the "Portraits of Families Standing Together" project began. Asahi and his companions from the association approaching us to work together resulted in various photo equipment companies joining the project, including Nikon, Epson, and Yamada Shokai, as well as famous studio businesses such as Profoto, Gin-Ichi, and Takahashi Camera. Hakuba Photo Industry and Sedia offered to provide albums. Every time there is a photo shoot, cosmetics pros from Shiseido will visit Soma to give beautiful finishing touches to female subjects before photo shoots. Although the photographers are generally members of the All-Japan Photo Association, pro photographers Takeyoshi Tanuma and Etsuko Enami had volunteered to shoot portraits for the first two days.

On the first day of the project, November 5, at the Yunuki temporary housing meeting place, seven groups of models were surrounded by a crowd of staff from cooperating companies who rushed to the site from Tokyo, as well as officers from the Fukushima chapter of the All-Japan Photo Association, and assistants from the Soma Photo Association. Although those being photographed were a bit nervous at first, the professional manner of Tanuma and Enami skillfully drew smiles out of the ladies who became flourishing with the help of staff from Shiseido cosmetics. The smiles of the models brightened the meeting place.

Mr. and Mrs. Watanobe are 80 and 76 years old respectively. They were born in Isobe, which was damaged in the disaster, and spent most of their lives on a farm there. They were blessed with three children and even some great-grandchildren. Ten years ago they retired and Chikashi lost his home while enjoying a peaceful retirement with his cheerful wife. There was no trace whatsoever of their home or fields.

While glancing sidelong at his wife while her makeup was deftly being applied, the profile of Chikashi seemed to eloquently speak of the unjustness of the tsunami. There is more than enough sadness and loneliness when seeing the steady work of one's youth, and one's life wiped away in a single moment.

While looking sidelong at his wife whose makeup is finished, Chikashi, who had been fidgeting, still has a hard expression on his face even after he sits in the chair for their portrait. In such occasions, the wife is usually the unflappable one, but regardless, one cannot help but feel bad for how awkward Chikashi seems compared to his wife's nice smile.

With only eight months since the disaster struck, I start to think that maybe this project was a bit too early when all of a

Photo:
All-Japan Association of Photographic Societies Director Takeyoshi Tanuma

Temporary Housing

Chapter 4

sudden the photographer Tanuma asks for a pose. "Mr. Watanobe! Could you just put your arm around your wife's shoulder for a moment? Yes, just like that!"

The two, who up to now had been sitting a bit apart due to shyness, were suddenly brought together by Chikashi's natural gesture of putting his arm around his wife. On doing so, he said "I don't think I've ever seen him put his hand on his wife's shoulder!", resulting in laughter from all at the photo shoot, and smiles on the couple's faces. Tanuma, truly is a pro photographer. The shoot was a charming experience, but the happy feeling that the finished shot gave to all of us is something wonderful to behold. Be sure to check the photos on the website.

With plans to shoot 150 groups of families, the portrait project will continue until the beginning of the new year. In time, when the victims' lives are rebuilt, it is our hope that the memories of these families standing together against this disaster will be handed down across the years.

Mayor's e-mail newsletter - November 21, 2011 Issue

(12) His majesty, the king of Bhutan

November 18. His majesty Jigme Khesar Namgyel Wangchuck, the fifth king of the Kingdom of Bhutan and his wife visited Japan for the first time after their wedding, finding the time to visit Soma between official functions to encourage the disaster-struck region. Because the media had covered the visit extensively, we received many phone calls, not only from citizens of Soma, but from others as well who wanted to catch a glimpse of the royal couple. For 40 minutes of their planned 90-minute stay in Soma, the couple mingled with children from the Sakuragaoka Elementary School, and for the final 40 minutes they requested to observe the disaster areas under my responsibility. Traveling with a young, beautiful queen gave great hope not only to Japan and the city of Soma, but the visit to Sakuragaoka Elementary School proved to be a wonderful experience for the children. The king listened to the singing of the children, who had practiced day and night, and left them with his creed of "training the dragon in one's heart." I look forward to the future of these children as they keep the king's words in mind.

Bhutan has not had a peaceful history. Until the 19th century, religious opposition fueled conflicts between tribes, pressure from neighboring Tibet, and its status as a small country put Bhutan under constant strain. In 1907, the powerful Wangchuck family who held influence in the provincial areas established sovereignty and unified the kingdom for a century after implementing a hereditary dynasty. In order for this small country of only 700,000 people to survive the drastically changing landscape of Asia in the 20th century, it is surmised that previous kings suffered many hardships. Indeed, Tibet, who had many times attacked Bhutan, had not yet existed as a nation.

Five years ago, Jigme Khesar Namgyel Wangchuck was enthroned, and is still only 31 years of age. However, in that time he has already completed the enormous task of transitioning to a

Temporary Housing — Chapter 4

constitutional monarchy. Rather than frivolously Westernizing, the king wears traditional garb, and lives by the national ideals of his traditional faith, giving him an air that we in Japan who have been swayed by modern civilization find refreshing.

I met the king and queen at the ruins of Matsukawaura Fishing Port as they made their way from the elementary school. When I was introduced as the mayor of Soma, the king held out his hand which I shook while expressing thanks on the behalf of our citizens. At the risk of sounding a bit rude, however, the king seemed to me to be a refreshing young man. The queen appeared to be a friendly younger sister.

They watched a movie of the disaster recorded from high ground in Matsukawaura Fishing Port on an iPad. I explained to the king and queen that the concrete pillars are the only thing left of the union market, showed them video of the destruction that took place here, and that even though some debris had been removed and partial reconstruction was taking place that radiation has been detected from the minimal catches of fish so that fishing is no longer possible. Yet, despite all this, the wives of fishermen have not abandoned hope, and are waving at the king and queen from the temporary housing complex. I humbly asked if they would give those women some courage.

The king and queen then proceeded across the road and gave a speech near at hand. "Today we have been tremendously emboldened and uplifted by the people of Japan. I am deeply impressed by and have great respect for the courteous leadership of those affected by the disaster. Bhutan and Japan share strong bonds of friendship. I came here with the goal of encouraging each other. Please do not give up hope."

I thought that the king was speaking of Keiji Nishioka, who went to Bhutan in 1964 with the Japan International Cooperation Agency to help improve farming in Bhutan, and later passed away in the country. On Google Earth you can see that Bhutan is a mountainous country, consisting of beautiful, many-layered, terraced rice fields. I'm sure that the people of Bhutan have beautiful souls as well. I would also like to pay tribute to the achievements of Nishioka in the same kind way the king spoke to the citizens of Soma.

Next we moved to the Obama Beach parking lot. The rubble has been completely cleared from the site, with only the concrete foundation remaining, making for flat, featureless scenery. I used seven A4-sized panels to describe the damage to the Obama area. The queen's face held a sad expression when looking at the striking panels. She was very unobtrusive, always remaining one step behind the king, and attempting to stay behind me, and I got the impression that she is a very generous person. The king let out a

Temporary Housing Chapter 4

large sigh as I explained to him that on these flatlands 2,000 people had lived peacefully where homes had once stood, that 146 people from this area had lost their lives, that the homes of over 6,000 people in the city of Soma had been washed away by the tsunami, that 90% of our citizens had safely evacuated without losing precious lives, and that 10 brave members of the fire department sacrificed themselves to save others while they led others to safety. "As long as the city of Soma continues to exist, we will never forget those we lost. In May, the emperor and empress of Japan came to this very spot to offer a prayer for those lost in the disaster. If I may be so bold, could I ask that your majesties from Bhutan offer a silent prayer?"

Before the king and queen had arrived, three monks that had already finished praying had placed a small altar and spread a carpet where the king nodded and proceeded to the carpet and beckoned me to take my place beside him. Because I did not want to come between the king and queen, I wanted to tell them I'd refrain from joining them, however, the queen naturally drew away from the king, so I reluctantly took my place in the center and began a silent prayer.

The moment lasted for several minutes while the monks recited a sutra. As usual, I clasped my hands and thought of the faces of my deceased relatives and friends, but also I wished for the future happiness of this young king and queen.

When it was finally time for them to leave, I left them with a gift of "Soma Komayaki" teacups which are no longer available, and a copy of the "Interim Report" published by the Soma emergency headquarters, wishing them a happy life together.
Their earnestness gave me great courage. I believe that other citizens of our city, including the children, share these same strong feelings. Although it is our duty to rebuild the city of Soma, it is also my wish that the king and queen of Bhutan be brave leaders of the constitutional monarchy, and overcome all difficulties that they face.

Temporary Housing

(13) Poll on disaster prevention group transfer and conference with disaster-stricken residents (Thorough discussion covering 79 sessions)

Rebuilding homes was a core part of rebuilding the lives of those affected by the tsunami. When summering the basic policy of the reconstruction plan in June 2011, we, however, decided on a policy of not rebuilding houses in areas where homes were washed away.

The reason for this was the basic reasoning that if a tsunami came in the dead of night when it is dark and most were sleeping, many would lose their lives. On the other hand, when people are working during the day, the land destroyed by the tsunami could be used as long as people were called on to evacuate and evacuation roads were provided.

Use of the coastline as a fishing port, disposal of goods, and as a beach during summertime would be approved on the condition that no one would be sleeping there overnight. As a tsunami countermeasure, we began installation of a speaker system operated wirelessly from city hall that would notify citizens in times of danger.

On August 18, 2011, we conducted a briefing meeting on the ordinance that forbidding to build resistances in tsunami danger zones, asking for the understanding of residents. It was also necessary for us to understand the plan for rebuilding life of each resident who had suffered in the disaster in order to secure land to build disaster public temporary housing.

An assistant project of the Ministry of Land, Infrastructure, Transport and Tourism began a survey of each household on September 20, 2011. Although

Land use and reconstruction project briefing
(November 11, 2011)

143

The author visiting victims for a survey
(December 5, 2011)

this was conducted as specified by the Ministry of Land, Infrastructure, Transport and Tourism, but as expected, only 60% of surveys were collected, making it an ineffective source of information.

In the end, it seems that relying on a consultation company is not the best way to go when gathering opinions on helping victims plan their lives. We at City Hall were not collecting information on our own. We decided to sit down with citizens and talk with two staffers for each person. I went around to three houses and sat down with the householder and listened from their standpoint. Based on the individual visits made by all staffers in December, we were able to form an outline for helping victims rebuild their lives.

Later, We needed to secure land and make various adjustments with victims regarding the final look of residential developments. A total of 79 different talks were carried out by the end of March 2015.

Temporary Housing — Chapter 4

(14) Speech at the United Nations (UN performance of HIKOBAE stage play) (March 12, 2012)

March 12, 2012 marks one year since the earthquake. The stage play "HIKOBAE" was performed at the small UN theater. This stage drama is set in the Soma. It shows the all-out efforts of the firemen who lost their lives in the line of duty, the struggles of the hospital staff and citizens intertwined with a love story (although the love story is fiction, the disaster is based on records of true events) rich in poetic sentiment. The play was written and directed by Toshi Shioya, a director who is familiar with the city of Soma, and it was performed at the UN playhouse by the permission of Secretary-General of the United Nations Ban Ki-moon and UN ambassador Tsuneo Nishida. This was a superb opportunity for the city of Soma to express our thanks to the world for the support they have given us since the Great East Japan Earthquake. I memorized a speech translated into English for me, and read out the words of thanks in the Soma accent in English.

"I have found happiness in living among the casual warmth of the people who surround me. I believe that the newly rebuilt city of Soma is one filled with kindness." As a timid person, I don't think I have ever been so nervous as I was when standing in front of 150 diplomats from various countries.

However, the cast led by director Shioya and the leads played by Shuri and Ryohei Suzuki all delivered top notch performances. The lines were translated into English and projected onto the screen in the background, which made me realize that believable acting does not rely on words. Many in the audience were moved to tears.

The play enjoyed success on Broadway in New York after the UN performance.

After finishing performances at the Galaxy Theater in Tennozu Isle upon the return of the play to Japan, it was performed free of charge for Soma citizens at the "Hamanasu-kan".

Director Shioya arranged for all of the families of the firefighters who lost their lives in the line of duty to be in attendance.

The thing that struck me was seeing those family members clutching a photo of each one of the 10 deceased firefighters to their chest during the performance. The members of the troupe were even more nervous than their performance at the UN theater. At that time, I decided we needed to erect a monument in memory of these firefighters.

The success of the play led director Shioya to consider turning it into a movie, however, he unfortunately passed away suddenly one year later. "HIKOBAE" became his posthumous work, and I believe it is our responsibility to cherish the feelings of friendship toward Soma that he put into the play.

Director Shioya (left) playing the role of a doctor at the stage performance of "HIKOBAE" (March 31, 2012 performance in Soma)

Temporary Housing   Chapter 4

Mayor's e-mail newsletter - June 18, 2012 Issue

(15) Emergency supplies storehouse

One month ago we started holding public meetings at large temporary housing meeting places and community centers at each district in the city. We talked about various issues including how we all faced the devastation of the earthquake for the past one year and three months, evaluation of our initial response, thinking on radiation, future countermeasures, and specific plans for reaching our rebuilding goals. Using 40 PowerPoint slides we engaged in discussion and explanations, completing these sessions at six of ten locations. The serious attention given during my speeches and the expression on each individual's face gave me strength.

Thinking back, the first 24 hours were the most solemn and a time when many decisions were required. How the process was handled during this time was pivotal in determining the success or failure of future disaster countermeasures. Although I leave it up to future generations to evaluate the appropriateness of my decisions, I sometimes have flashbacks of those times. I remember feeling frustrated that I could not distribute clean water or provide warmth for those shivering in the cold night, and devastated when I learned that some of the firemen leading the evacuation would not be returning home. Because I work at headquarters as a chief, I kept telling myself that I could not complain or let the worry show on my face, and I regret that we were unprepared for such a large-scale disaster. I feel regret over those who were lost, and I never want future mayors or citizens to feel the same.

The emergency supplies storehouse measured approximately 600 square meters. The stores of blankets and emergency rations were woefully inadequate in the face of such a massive earthquake. Also, because our city is located in an area that is not readily accessible, the area for picking up relief supplies was also inconvenient. Although we could have handled typhoons and flooding due to torrential rains, we were reminded that our naive thinking that we

could deal with moderate earthquakes is dangerous. Actually, I was worried about cesium contamination immediately after the nuclear power plant accident, and distributed 10 liters of bottled water to each citizen from our stockpiles, but realized that we must keep a permanent supply on hand from here on. We also must have at a minimum, one blanket for each citizen. Additionally, we must keep an orderly stockpile of supplies necessary for situations such as experienced in this earthquake, as well as functional emergency supplies storehouses that can be used as stations to distribute relief supplies during times of disaster.

Last July we sent relief supplies such as water and instant noodles in response to the flooding in the Aizu region and on the Niigata border as a way to fulfill our obligation. This kind of reverse supply will become a large task for the city of Soma in order to help out towns that provided aid in our time of need.

With this in mind, we are currently formulating our basic plan with the approval of the Reconstruction Agency and related organizations. We are considering Takamatsu city land in the Yawata area (4,000 square meters). We have already obtained the approval of the local government, there is sufficient storage capacity, it is equipped with functionality for smooth transportation of relief

Temporary Housing Chapter 4

supplies, and we would like to build an emergency supplies storehouse that could serve as a landmark in this area.

I also realized that the fire department are the guardians of the city in the event of an emergency. As was proved in this earthquake, the fire department's knowledge of the area and information from them is the deciding factor in any first response. Therefore, we are considering adding the fire department headquarters office as well as a firefighter holding area and disaster preparedness training center at the new emergency supplies storehouse.

In addition to sister towns such as Nagareyama, Toyokoro, and Taiki, we are forever indebted to the generosity of Adachi in Tokyo and Susono who we have already concluded an agreement with. In addition to these municipalities, we would like to have firefighters and others from the departments who we have formed strong bonds with through their support after the earthquake come learn from our knowledge gleaned during the experiences of the 3/11 earthquake. These include the cities of Inagi, Odawara, and Saijo, with whom we have signed disaster prevention agreements, and other cities which we will sign agreements with in the future, such as Ono, Maibara, and Ryugasaki. Because our countermeasures and knowledges for the disaster are all listed in the interim report, we would also like to have municipalities and businesses who have helped us. So please do not hesitate to visit. Although the facilities will not be completed for one year, a number of staff from city hall are currently undergoing training to be able to deliver lectures when the facilities open.

As I mentioned in the introduction, we have decided to erect a monument to the 10 firefighters who bravely stood on the front lines

Water stockpiles at the storehouse

149

rescuing many people, but who tragically lost their own lives in the line of duty. This monument will stand at the side of the entrance to the emergency supplies storehouse as a reminder that these heroes are always remembered by our citizens. I hope that those who come to train at the emergency supplies storehouse will stop and pay their respects.

The "Fallen Firemen Monument Construction Committee" will be launched with the fire chief as the chairman, and the monument will be built by the kindness of the citizens and others throughout Japan praising the efforts of these brave souls. I sincerely hope for your support in this effort. I believe this effort will bring some relief to the surviving families and myself. Although the director will be placed in the Soma disaster prevention office, we believe it would be more appropriate to have the construction committee handle construction rather than treating it as a city project, with the city of Soma handling management.

Thanks to the smooth collection of the "Earthquake Orphans Charity" for the education of children orphaned in the earthquake, we have gathered nearly enough funds to cover the costs of university. We are also considering an ordinance at the June assembly to send 76,000 yen per month. We would like to thank those in Japan and around the world for their generosity on behalf of parents who are no longer with us.

Unveiling ceremony for the Soma fallen firemen monument
(August 25, 2013)

Temporary Housing

Mayor's e-mail newsletter - July 17, 2012 Issue

(16) Soma Terakoya School

Thanks to everyone's generosity, we raised over 400 million yen in contributions for earthquake orphans.

The support fund system for children orphaned in the earthquake began because we felt sorry for the firefighters who lost their lives in the line of duty, but due to the warm generosity of people from around the world, we were able to cover not only living costs, but even help out with tuition for higher learning such as university fees. If we imagine the feelings of the firefighters of Isobe and Haragama thinking about their families when they saw the approaching tsunami and resigned themselves to die, it is easy to know what we need to do. We must ensure that their children grow up healthy and strong, that their aging parents live a peaceful life, and that the villagers that they tried to protect live a contented, peaceful life.

This is the essence of the reconstruction plan.

When defining what reconstruction means for Soma, the primary objective was helping victims rebuild their lives appropriate to their ages. Helping children grow up healthy and giving them the strength to keep on living as adults. Creating an environment that lets the elderly live in peace and comfort. Providing the younger generation with a safe living environment and permanent homes, as well as rebuilding industry so that they can plan their lives. We must also formulate disaster countermeasures to the best of our ability based on this experience in order to build a safer local society.

While making sure the number one priority is overcoming obstacles to childrearing and education due to the disaster, we must strive to gather information for the welfare of elderly persons who are alone, rebuild residences, and restore the fishing and farming industries, as well as promote service and production industries in order to formulate health strategies and decontamination procedures against radiation as the core principles in our reconstruction efforts.

The completion of "Soma Idobata Nagaya" is just one part of the various projects noted in the above principles, whereas construction on single homes and offering of land for sale have yet to begin. Therefore, it cannot be said that reconstruction projects are proceeding optimally or very quickly, but we have put forth out best efforts.

Regarding production industries, we are doing our utmost to achieve the principles of reconstruction efforts thanks to the warm friendship of the mayors who have supported us so far, the support of the Ministry of Land, Infrastructure, Transport and Tourism, the Ministry of Public Management, and the Ministry of Agriculture, Forestry and Fisheries, and the dispatch of 21 engineers. Staff from the city of Soma are working together smoothly to tremendous effect. I'd like to express my sincere gratitude.

On the other hand, dealing with children mainly involves service industries in which we have achieved rock-steady results due to the efforts of many individuals. Details can be found in the report below along with an expression of thanks.

Although we decided to reopen the schools one month after the earthquake on April 18, the board of education reported to me that many children were still traumatized by their terrible experiences as

Temporary Housing

Chapter 4

well as losing blood relatives and close friends. To deal with the effects of PTSD (post-traumatic stress disorder), we recruited clinical psychologists and public health nurses from around Japan and started the "Soma Follower Team" volunteer organization as an external arm of the board of education on April 20. This organization later acquired NPO status and operates on donations from around the world. Their main activities include dispatching clinical psychologists and public health nurses to affected elementary schools and junior high schools, in-home counseling via consulting physicians in certain cases, as well as study assistance to help improve academic abilities as a way to combat PTSD on a suggestion from myself.

The idea of improving the academic abilities of affected children is related to my feelings of regret over the firefighters who lost their lives line of duty as mentioned at the outset. The disaster orphan support fund provides 30,000 yen in living expenses each month until the child reaches 18 years of age, as well as donations to cover nearly all costs for college (with no obligations to repay). Also, we are currently seeking assistance in providing a monthly allowance of 76,000 yen (nationwide average sent college students) in boarding fees for university students, an initiative that was approved by the conference last month. The kind support for Soma's efforts from around the world is both amazing and makes us keenly aware of our responsibility.

Responsibility includes dealing with children's PTSD, effectively using contributions to ensure that children have sufficient academic abilities to graduate high school and continue on to university. The challenge of improving academic abilities is not a matter for children orphaned in the earthquake only, but touches all students and all children in Soma affected by the earthquake. Even though we will do our utmost to protect the children from the ill effects of radiation, they will continue to live here while facing the damaging rumors of radiation.

Upon hearing the determination of brigade 9 (Isobe district) assistant fire chief Kenichi Abe's daughter Ayane, the "City of Soma Educational Rebuilding Children's Fund" ordinance was passed at the conference last September, and has received 70 million yen in donations. The first thing we used this fund for was to purchase iPads for affected junior high school students for use as an educational tool for learning drills and science studies. There were many problems such as accessing harmful sites, dealing with various updates, and securing educational content. Despite that, with the assistance of Takeshi Fujii, the star intructor at Yoyogi Seminar, as well as the enthusiasm of on-site teachers and the Soma Board of Education, everything worked out perfect in the end. Not only did this result in improving the academic abilities of the children, but it is also necessary for children to learn how to use information technology in order to thrive in the future.

During the summer break directly after the earthquake we asked graduate students from the Miyagi University of Education to provide supplemental lessons in school classrooms, however in autumn this initiative was canceled due to insufficient staff. For this initiative, because funds were sufficient to allot as much of the budget as possible to childrearing funds, and we made a request to the University of Tokyo Faculty of Education on the introduction

Temporary Housing

Chapter 4

from former Senior Vice Minister of Education, Culture, Sports, Science and Technology Kan Suzuki. On March 27, vice president of the University of Tokyo, Yoshiteru Muto responded very positively to our request to dispatch volunteer students on the weekends, so we begin preparations to receive them right away. The program was intended for students at the elementary and junior high schools, however, due to the volunteers coming on Saturdays and Sundays, we turned the temporary housing meeting places into study halls. The Soma Follower Team made arrangements for their time in Soma. We had them come to Fukushima by bullet train where they were transported by station wagon to Follower Team lodgings where they stayed and dined. Staff from the board of education set up the venues, gathered the children together, and presided over the study sessions.

The first study session began on June 16. The first volunteers were graduate students from the University of Tokyo Faculty of Education who did a wonderful job of captivating the children. Lessons began with games for elementary students, and points on studying for junior high school students. Children were smiling energetically and had serious expressions when studying. I began to call these study sessions the "Soma Terakoya School".

Although we had all been wondering how living in temporary housing affect the growth of these children, we realized that as long as the adults kept life in temporary housing orderly, the children would follow along as well, with sufficient possibilities for them to develop rich sensibilities and social skills. Along with expressing our heartfelt thanks to those at the University of Tokyo we will work diligently at our reconstruction efforts in order to make the "Soma Terakoya School" more meaningful.

Mayor's e-mail newsletter - August 31, 2012 Issue

(17) Your future is bright

The other day I visited the home of the late fire chief of the Isobe district, Masahiro Inayama to offer some incense after the Obon holidays.

At the altar I found myself under the intense, cool gaze of his portrait. In the corner of the room I saw the toys of Masahiro's first grandchild, whose birth he had been excitedly waiting for. Masahiro's daughter had a tough time being pregnant during the evacuation, and when the baby was born safely last summer I feel like it is because of his watchful eye from this funeral portrait. Masahiro's mother Yoshiko is 82 years old. Her husband, a fisherman like his many forbears, passed away four years ago, and she spent her peaceful remaining years surrounded by loved ones such as Masahiro and her grandchildren. Although she is a petite woman, her kind expression is exactly like that of Masahiro. Her face, from her eyes to the wrinkles in her cheek show a lifetime of joy and sorrow.

On my way home from her house, I looked behind me on hearing a barking dog. Is it waiting for Masahiro to come home?

The great earthquake struck on March 11. Masahiro, who had been working on contract work for precision machinery at his home called out to his mother Yoshiko and pregnant daughter, "Evacuate to Isobe Junior High School right now! I'm a firefighter so I have to help others evacuate. Wait for me there!" He said this as he put on his firefighters coat and rushed out the door. His wife was working at the hospital, taking care of victims in the aftermath of the earthquake and his eldest son Daiki was at Soma High School with his friends.

Yoshiko rushed to grab some of her favorite valuables and grabbed some dog food to feed Masahiro's beloved dog Ai, and left for the junior high school on high ground. When she heard from villagers one after the other that the massive tsunami had swallowed many

Temporary Housing — Chapter 4

homes and people, she began to worry about Masahiro. She figured that before long her son would show up and yell "Are you OK?" so she left the gymnasium and waited in the car all night long. She barely remembers eating the half rice ball and cup of water provided by the city. Late one night she heard from a friend of Masahiro that the last time he had been seen was leading others to safety near the Isobe Fishing Port. The district of Osu where the fishing port is located suffered the worst of the damage, where not a single building was left standing. He was on the very front lines of the disaster.

Once dawn broke and an evacuation route from Isobe Junior High School to the city was secured, she went with the rest of the villagers to the designated evacuation shelter, "Hamanasu-kan". Because she thought she couldn't bring the dog with her, she left it and some dog food with an acquaintance. Finally, Masahiro's eldest married sister who lived in the city came to pick her up, reluctantly leaving the "Hanamasu-kan" shelter behind. Later, worried over the accident at the nuclear power plant, another sister who was married and living in Saitama came to pick her up on March 14, leaving Yoshiko to wait for Masahiro away from Soma.

March 31. Masahiro in a firefighter coat made his silent return. Funeral homes were not yet reopened, so his body was cremated on April 2. Because I was swamped with work as we prepared to reopen the schools, the head of the general affairs attended, finding the venue overflowing with mourners including fellow firefighters and others. Many people shouted "We're with Masahiro to the end!", accompanying him to the crematory where Yoshiko clung to his coffin and screamed.

Fallen firemen monument
(On the grounds of the disaster prevention storehouse)

"Masahiro, you were a great man! A great man! A great man..."
Then, Masahiro's eldest sister, raised her hands to the sky when she heard her mothers cries, and wrung out a cry of
"Long live Masahiro!"
This was their final offering to Masahiro, who had bravely faced the tsunami and lost his life in the line of duty while saving many others. All attendees felt the sorrow his mother and sister as their own and cried.
Masahiro Inayama was the Soma brigade 9 fire chief, and he was 49 years old at the time of his passing.

Masahiro's son Daiki, who was in his first year of high school at the time of the earthquake, is now in his third year. His features are masculine, just like his father. Daiki told me with conviction, "I'm going to become a firefighter just like my father."
His spirit is truly admirable. Helping raise Daiki so that he can follow his heart's desire is a way to repay Masahiro for all he has done.

Go for it, Daiki! Your future is bright!

Temporary Housing

Chapter 4

Mayor's e-mail newsletter - December 10, 2012 Issue

(18) Fishery warehouse

December 9. On the land where the Soma Futaba Fishermen's Union was washed away in the tsunami, construction has begun on an 11-building complex that houses fishing gear storehouses with attached work spaces, with 12 subdivisions in each building (each vendor is allotted a 29.7 square meter subdivision and two subdivisions for each trawler). Along with childhood friends who are now fishermen, we worked and reworked the plan and obtained the approval of the Reconstruction Agency and Ministry of Land, Infrastructure, Transport and Tourism to begin rebuilding. The complex is scheduled for completion next year, and we enjoyed an exciting groundbreaking ceremony while expressing our wishes for recovery from the tsunami and nuclear power plant accident, and safety during construction.

When I was a child in Haragama, there were countless fishing rowboats in the shallows near the beach up until the mid-1950s. The beach which greeted fishermen after returning from fishing in the morning was always a place to play for children. Parents loaded nets onto carts to bring them home where they were spread out and mended. Finally, when motorized fishing boats became the norm they would leave from the nearby port at Matsukawa where we children would go to play and get small fish. The beach at Haragama was always bustling with playing children, and parents would pull carts full of fishing nets and tools back home where they would work. Then the 1990s arrived, and the beach at Haragama where I used to play became Port of Soma Quay No. 1, and my fondly remembered scenery was gone. Although the large

Haragama fishing gear warehouse (for trawlers)
(Completed June 28, 2013)

159

fishing vessels now put out to sea at ports in Ibaraki and Mt. Kinka in Miyagi, and the job of carts now belonged to lightweight trucks, preparations for fishing were still carried out at home, making one's life and job of fisherman one in the same.

Nearly everything was mercilessly wiped away by the tsunami last year, including all of the homes in Haragama, and all of the structures at the fishing union port aside from a concrete framework. After this event, four months later, we learned from the previous tsunami 400 years ago (After the great Keicho tsunami in 1611, during the rule of the 16th lord Yoshitane, no lives were lost in the tsunami five years later thanks to the order to move to higher ground), and established an ordinance that restricts residence in tsunami danger zones. We are currently engaged in building residential developments on high ground as reconstruction housing, however, when considering disposing of these developments in several years, we can only provide 165 square meters of residential rental sites, and reconstruction project land for sale is already set at 330 square meters. Fishermen say the space is too cramped to work in, however, the area of land for sale is determined by the government, and although we are trying to develop residential land on high ground, there are limits to the amount of land that can be developed.

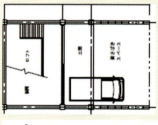

 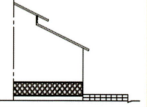

Temporary Housing

Chapter 4

On the other hand, it is permissible to build businesses and other areas for daytime use on land under residential restrictions. Making the port off-limits will make it impossible for fishing business to grow, and as long as the warning system and evacuation roads are well maintained, we believe the land can be used provided that no one stays overnight in the area. If we think of a tsunami arriving at midnight, residential restrictions cannot be avoided, however, we can do our best to ensure that the land is safe to use during the daytime.

I would like to restart the fishing business in Soma, and I firmly believe that the day will come when a lively fish market can be found here just as it was before.

Even when that day comes, we will not lift the residential restrictions for the Haragama area making it necessary to completely separate everyday life and fishing-related work such as net mending, etc., in order for the fishing industry to continue. Therefore, the plan is to allot to each vendor with a compact vessel a 29.7 square meter building, along with a workplace (row house style fishery warehouse) with attached 49.5 meter storehouse including open-air sections in an 11-building complex with 131 subdivisions. If we are going to the trouble of building this complex, we'd like to make something that looks nice, that can serve as a symbol for the rebuilding the fishing industry, and create added value for the fish caught in this port, which is why we have decided to adopt a design reminiscent of a Japanese-style, flat roof tile old-fashioned warehouse. The new concept of separating the seaside fishing industry from private life may present difficult efforts due to the circumstances of the great earthquake, but I would like everyone to think of this as a new era for the fishing industry.

Although operations will be in the hands of the fishing union, I sincerely hope that, as the buildings are connected together, that those who work there will remain connected, and that this project will bring back the lively Haragama of my youth.

Explaining the fishing port damages to Prime Minister Shinzo Abe
The late Hiroyuki Sato, head of the Soma Futaba Fishermen's Union

Temporary Housing — Chapter 4

(19) Completion of the new community center (October 7, 2013)

October 7 marks the two and a half year anniversary since the earthquake. We now welcome the completion of the new community center built to replace the previous one that proved dangerous in this earthquake. Because it had deteriorated, there were plans to renovate the exterior before the disaster, and many citizens requested a Japanese-style. Because the community center is located nearby the castle ruins of Baryo Park, the building was designed with a familiar castle town look. This was the first large building erected after the earthquake, and the people of Soma anxiously awaited its completion as a "symbol of reconstruction and the solidarity of the citizens."

At the completion ceremony, Minister of Land, Infrastructure, Transport and Tourism Akihiro Ota, who had visited Soma many times since the earthquake to encourage us, delivered a congratulatory speech. Later, IHI president Tamotsu Saito presented the hall with the gift of a Steinway grand piano, and representatives from the design company and the president of the architectural firm presented a letter of appreciation.

The entire hall gave three cheers, and I had a request for my predecessor and previous mayor, Shigeru Konno. The previous mayor, Konno was 86 years old at that time. He is an extremely energetic person and his powerful cheer served as a wish for the bright prospects of recovery in Soma. I

Three cheers
The late Shigeru Konno,
former mayor(center)

Minister of Land,
Infrastructure and
Transport Akihiro Ota

never thought it would be the last time I saw the previous mayor, yet he passed in February of the following year. Because I was able to see off the former mayor to his final destination at the new community center as a city funeral for his many years of hard work, I feel a connection to him. Later on, the bust of the former mayor erected by his relatives was relocated near the entranceway of the community center.

Soma Bon dance
(Community center plaza)

At the inauguration ceremony we invited all of the Soma city management who were the sponsors of the event, visitors who presented congratulatory speeches and letters of appreciation, and others to come onto the stage in formal Japanese attire. The president of the construction company also joined us in the role of master builder. We then had former mayor Konno along with his wife stand for a commemorative photo. We hope that the former mayor watches over the history of the city of Soma from his next life.

Temporary Housing — Chapter 4

Mayor's e-mail newsletter - December 12, 2012 Issue

(20) Soma City Folklore Museum

This earthquake has resulted in massive damage to Soma, mainly in the villages along the shore. Even it is well known that many precious lives were lost during the disaster, including the firemen leading others to safety, people who barely escaped with their lives also lost areas as a means of production and living. Thanks to the government's reconstruction budget and the generosity of people around the world in helping us rebuild our lives and industries, part of the reconstruction residences has been completed and site preparation has begun in order to move to higher ground. These efforts show that all citizens are working together to walk the long road to recovery. However, we have reaffirmed that getting victims into their final homes and rebuilding industry as it was before require considerable time and effort.

One thing we must not lose sight of in this situation is the fact that out of the homes lost in the tsunami, many were traditional Japanese-style houses and storehouses that had collections of folk materials detailing the way of life and work of recent times. Traditional Japanese-style homes washed away included farms in the Isobe area that had been operating for generations, as well as miso and soy sauce storehouses in the Haragama area from the late 1800s. In these old buildings were stored daily necessities and farming tools and instruments used in modern times, and these

165

pieces of cultural heritage were lost to the city of Soma. It is almost as if the memories of the people who lived on the shore were washed away by the tsunami.

On the other hand, there are groups of citizens who have worried about folk materials being lost, and have been collecting them. Recently, thanks to the kindness of these people, local folk items such as currently owned farming equipment and fixtures, and daily implements have been donated to the city of Soma so as not to lose these memories of daily life.

There was something that reminded me that if we are careless, we could lose these precious folk items.
Last summer we began door-to-door cart sales at temporary housing. This initiative had various objectives including making purchasing easier for those with bad feet or backs who had trouble shopping on their own, checking on elderly people living alone to prevent solitary deaths, as well as fostering communication between those gathering around the carts when they were shopping, etc. Of course there were no supermarkets in Haragama when I was a child, and older women wearing coverall aprons and selling tofu or natto from carts were a common sight. When I remembered those carts as we began to sell items door-to-door, we searched high and low but to my surprise, we couldn't find a single one in all of Soma. In this 21st century digital society, there isn't a single cart left over from those nostalgic filled days of my youth. We

Folklore Museum opening (July 26, 2014)

Temporary Housing — Chapter 4

had no other choice but to purchase stainless steel folding carts. Although it is compact, lightweight, and durable, it is completely devoid of character. Although useful, these stainless steel carts appear lacking. I miss the black iron frames of the old carts with their fat tires and wooden base.

I'll wager that if we went to another town we could find one of those old-fashioned carts.
But the most important factor was the connection between people that was created when pulling the carts in those days, which is undoubtedly the most powerful driving force behind rebuilding now, and everyone cooperating has accomplished a great deal. That is why I believe we must preserve farming, townhouses, and other aspects of the life of common people.

As a counterpoint to the cultural materials describing the introduction of the Soma Clan displayed at the historical cultural property museum, which is planned for renovation next year, we will use this donation of folk items to build the Folklore Museum of memories next to the museum, showcasing the local folk culture of how the common people live. It will be a wooden, two-floor structure with 264 square meters of space on both floors, and I'd like to recreate a living space on the first floor with a hearth and pothook. We're also

Making straw sandals at the Folklore Museum (June 15, 2015)

thinking of forming a committee to run the museum, borrowing the wisdom of citizens to determine what should be put on display. Although we currently have plenty of folk materials due to donations, opening this initiative to the public will likely result in collecting even rarer items.

Be sure to drop by the museum if you come to visit Soma. Since the beginning, those in the Haragama and Isobe areas who have helped each other in daily life at temporary housing have wished for an opportunity to pass on to future generations fragments of community memory on how the people of Soma live.

Temporary Housing

Chapter 4

Mayor's e-mail newsletter - January 19, 2013 Issue

essay

(21) Duty and sentiment (Friendship with supporting local governments)

Since the new year, I have been interviewed by more persons from the media than ever before. Most of the questions are "How are conditions one year and ten months after the earthquake?".

In addition to the broad range of projects in rebuilding after the earthquake, the completion schedule for these differs for the city of Soma, the prefecture, and the national government, making it very difficult to give a general answer. Also, there are various hurdles to setting objectives in service industries, making it difficult to gauge progress accurately, so I usually answer, "I guess were roughly around the third station of climbing Mount Fuji?".

I also give them my impression on the situation in the following way. 'What I learned from this disaster is that people cannot survive on their own, and that dealing with disaster relies on duty and sentiment.'

In other words, I've reaffirmed just how important the surrounding community is to one's life, and how I will never forget that the friendship of local leaders is what has helped me overcome times of crisis.

Directly after the tsunami, the people who fled to the evacuation shelters from the seashore were happy that they had made it out safely, and busy encouraging each other, however, we needed to continue providing enough food and provisions for 4,000 people. I was so worried that people who had been spared from this monster of a tsunami would become dehydrated or malnourished. Incidentally, the day after the earthquake, we received continued shipments of water and processed, pre-cooked rice as emergency rations. The day after the earthquake on March 12 we were incredibly relieved to receive aid in the form of water, emergency rations, and blankets from people in Nagareyama, Yonezawa, Adachi, and Joetsu, who braved the damaged roads in city hall cars to come

169

help us. On the third day after the quake, relief supplies were delivered not only from cities we had signed a disaster prevention agreement with, but from the mayors of other friendly cities, including Komoro, Nikko, Susono, Namerikawa, Susaki, Ono, Shinjo, and Sakata.

"Disaster Mutual Support Agreement" with Sanjo, Niigata (February 25, 2013)

One that I remember in particular is the mayor of Tsuruga, who packed a truck full of relief supplies himself, and delivered it to me to raise my spirits.

Damaging rumors due to the nuclear power plant accident resulted in deliveries being halted, with no way to obtain food supplies. Also, because the first relief supplies from the prefectural government did not arrive until late at night on March 17, the citizens of Soma only survived the first week after the disaster due to the friendship of these cities. The cities of Inagi and Nagareyama delivered water tankers by the morning of the 12th. Because the earthquake had disrupted the water supply all across the city, we were very thankful for this provision. The heads of local governments continued to send water and food supplies without letup. This aid was dispatched based on the individual orders of various mayors when seeing the horrible conditions in Soma before I could even ask for their help.

Tamio Mori, the mayor of Nagaoka and the chairman of the Japan Association of City Mayors, called me right after the earthquake to ask if Soma was OK, and I answered that we would manage somehow, as I did not want to trouble him. However, because he was so worried about us, he came to visit us in Soma on April 2nd. When telling me not to hold back from asking if there was anything he could do to help, I took him up on his offer, replying that we did not

Temporary Housing   Chapter 4

have enough manpower for reconstruction. I asked if he could send some engineers.

Despite this sudden request, engineers were sent from Nagaoka on three month rotations starting July 1. Assistance from mayor Mori continues to this day in regard to insufficient manpower for the massive tasks Soma faces.

When torrential rains centered on the Aizu area of Fukushima and Niigata from July 28th to the morning of the 31st were covered in a TV broadcast, I called the mayor of Minamiaizu and mayor Mori who had both helped right after the March 11th disaster. The mayor of Minamiaizu reported that they were fine, but that Tadami and Kaneyama were in trouble, asking if I could provide any assistance there. Mayor Mori told me that the city of Nagaoka had experienced too much damage to deal with on their own, but that the city of Sanjo also needed help. He requested that I help mayor Kunisada of Sanjo.

When calling each mayor, I learned that the three towns had suffered considerable damage, and that evacuation shelters were full and they requested water and food supplies. At that time the city of Soma had a stockpile of 240 tons of bottled water as well as a surplus of instant noodles and emergency rations due to the worsening situation because of the accident at the nuclear power plant, so we

Sending relief supplies to Tadami, Kaneyama, and Sanjo in Niigata
(July 31, 2011)

Sending relief supplies to Maibara, in Shiga
(September 16, 2013)

171

sent 20 tons of water to Tadami, 10 tons to Kaneyama, and 12 tons to Sanjo, along with several thousand portions of instant noodles to each town as a way to repay the debts to the mayor of Minamiaizu and mayor Mori.

Later I became closer with Isato Kunisada, the mayor of Sanjo, through the Japan Association of City Mayors and meetings with other mayors during the declaration of decentralization, realizing that he is a dependable young mayor at 40 years old. He is polite, and his administrative skills are faultless. Although we became acquainted after I offered my support during the torrential rains, he sent two Sanjo city hall staffers to help us out last October as he knew of our long-term needs in Soma for additional manpower. He is a young, but faithful person. Next month we will sign a disaster prevention agreement with Sanjo, thereby securing the close relationship between our two cities.

The city of soma spent nearly 50 billion yen this year alone on reconstruction projects. Compared to our usual budget of 14 billion yen per year, the projects are mind-numbingly massive. We also expect that work will only increase once the details of the projects have been confirmed. I have no idea how many years this will take when thinking of Soma city hall's ability to take on the projects. Thanks to the consideration of the Ministry of Internal Affairs and Communications, one engineer from each of five cities across the country have been dispatched to Soma, however, thanks to the

Temporary Housing

Chapter 4

generosity of the mayors in our disaster partnership cities and friendly cities, 15 staffers have been dispatched from 11 cities. Without exception, each and every one of these persons volunteered to come, making each one equal 10 of any other person.

Before the disaster the city of Soma had concluded disaster prevention agreements with Nagareyama, Adachi, and Susono, resulting in the mayors of these cities providing a powerful support system. After the earthquake we signed new disaster prevention agreements with Inagi, Odawara, Saijo, Maibara, Ryugasaki, Ono, and Nikko. Also, following in the footsteps of mayor Masataka Ishihara of Komono in Mie prefecture, other mayors also came to provide supplies and physical support many times. The assistance these cities provided us deepened the connection and warm friendship with the city of Soma, and by sending staff here helped them learn how to deal with earthquakes, and are led by mayors with impeccable leadership skills and a passion for developing their own solid disaster countermeasures.

Because we suffered a shortage of water, food, and blankets during the March 11th earthquake and tsunami, the disaster prevention storehouse that is currently under way in Soma will be fully stocked in order to ensure the safety of our citizens during the next disaster. One other objective in this aspect is to ensure that we can dispatch trucks full of relief supplies for other cities when necessary, as they were there for us in our time of need. Soma has been saved by the sympathy of countless other people since the day of the disaster until now. I believe that ensuring we move forward with reconstruction is our most important obligation in repaying their kindness, and I feel that it is our duty to prepare to help them when they experience such disasters so that we do not have to feel the regret of not being able to do anything.

(22) Operation of the temporary incinerator for disposing of disaster waste materials (February 20, 2013)

Although disposal of rubble is the most basic aspect of reconstruction after a disaster, incinerating the massive amount of rubble which exceeded 200,000 tons proved to be a major problem in intermediate processing.

When nationwide news reported that because the rubble could not be completely disposed of in Miyagi and Iwate that municipalities across Japan, beginning with Tokyo and Niigata, would assist in the incineration process, the media was shaken by many people opposing the initiative, saying that they did not want rubble from Tohoku in their prefectures as it could contain radioactive contaminants.

The governor of one prefecture replied to one mayor who declared that they would accept the rubble, "Are you trying to kill us?"

The funny thing is that I mistakenly thought of myself as a good leader if I showed the attitude that I would not allow even a particle of radioactive substances to be taken out of our prefecture, regardless of whether or not we were talking about having someone take on the burden of Fukushima's rubble.

If Iwate's rubble is dangerous, how would those of us in Fukushima keep on breathing?

Against this background I thought that building a temporary incinerator would be next to impossible, but the calm demeanor of the people in Soma won the day.

We formulated plans for building a temporary incinerator on the five

Lighting ceremony for the temporary government substitute incinerator
(February 20, 2013)

Temporary Housing Chapter 4

Temporary government substitute incinerator

hectares of land owned by the city that had not be sold off in the east area of Soma industrial land, and began explaining and negotiating with the neighboring villages and factories.

One requirement I had for gaining their understanding was having people of the neighboring villages and factories measure the air dose rate. Also, because one requirement is that the smoke does not emit radioactive substances such as cesium, we should measure the smoke exhaust daily to ensure there are no radioactive substances.

I also said that if the dose in the surrounding air shows considerable increase, or if there is cesium present in the smoke that we will immediately stop incineration.

Regarding this policy, the people showed their understanding and wanted to move forward with reconstruction, and construction began on the incinerator.

While burning the leaves and branches of trees trimmed in the Tamano area for decontamination, the residents took readings and proved that there was no cesium discharge in the smoke. Four years after the earthquake the temporary incinerator had fulfilled its role, and was dismantled under strict measures to prevent radioactive materials from spreading.

Mayor's e-mail newsletter - March 11, 2013 Issue

(23) Support from the Tokyo University of Agriculture

The day after the disaster I was at a loss for words when I saw the rice paddies of Iwanoko, Niida, Kashiwazaki, Nittaki, Isobe, Yunuki, Kitaharagama, and Niinuma that had been damaged by the tsunami. The roots of the pine trees that had been swept along from the Osu area were pointing toward the sky in such a way that it looked like the roots were growing thickly on top of the sludge. Among this, the rubble of destroyed houses was strewn about. I was crushed with sadness when I realized that it would be impossible to restore the area to fertile fields again.

But before that I needed to make sure that the thousands of people forced into the difficult environment of the evacuation shelters were kept safe. I realized I had no time to feel sorry, and turned back to the emergency headquarters. The farmers were also in complete shock. At the evacuation shelters I heard people say that they had lost their farming equipment in the waves. They were talking about how it was all over because there was no way they could grow anything in a field of sludge. Despite this, I know that everyone was trying their hardest just to survive right after the disaster. The next day, we received orders to evacuate within 20 km of the nuclear power plant, striking the citizens of Soma with another wave of fear.

The fear of radioactive contamination resulted in distribution channels being closed off, and we watched gasoline and food supplies quickly dwindle. Those of us from city hall and the evacuation shelter faced with surviving the immediate crisis instead of trying to plan for reconstruction in the future.

"East Japan Assistance Project" Full coordination with the Tokyo University of Agriculture (Beginning May 2, 2011)

Temporary Housing — Chapter 4

Finally, from the end of April when fears due to the nuclear power plant started to die down slightly and give way to coolheaded thinking, the farmers who had suffered in the disaster started thinking realistically. They said that even if they gave up farming, there was nothing else for them to do at this age. They wanted to continue farming. However, because it would be very difficult to purchase new farming equipment at this stage, farming would be impossible unless it was efficiently carried out as a village agricultural business.

Dean Kanju Osawa (left) carrying out a local survey

When I heard this, I wondered if there was any way that I could turn this seed of desire into hope. A village agricultural business is a transitional form of agricultural corporation. Instead of the massive investment to purchase agricultural equipment such as tractors etc. that a small-scale farm would require, the farmers could consolidate farmland for use in a corporation of their own making and aim to create a large-scale efficient farming industry, where even the farming industry is being globalized as a matter of course. Even with the city supporting victims of the disaster, a corporate organization is more consistent than door-to-door assistance.

We then raced to organize farms affected by the disaster, in other words, to establish an agricultural corporation. Even if the entire initiative did not succeed, partial success would mean that we could continue on later. We spoke heatedly with the head of the Tohoku Regional Agricultural Administration Office many times, and he provided technical assistance until we were able to establish an agricultural corporation, and he promised to provide further assistance as much as possible later on.

The next event occurred one day in May. Kanju Osawa, the dean of Tokyo University of Agriculture who had sent volunteer students to Soma, saw me visiting the office. Charmed by dean Osawa's honest personality, I began frankly asking for his advice on initiatives after the disaster and on future problems. The dean then kindly said that he would put the full power of the Tokyo University of Agriculture behind Soma's efforts to revitalize the farming industry.

At that time, our major challenges were as follows.
1. How would we restore affected farmland covered in driftwood and sludge, and how would we create income for the farmers who would make up the constituent parts of the agricultural corporation?
2. Decontaminating and restoring the Tamano area with its comparatively high levels of radiation (village next to Iitate Village)
3. How can we restore the Wada Strawberry Union, which has lost more than half of its production base?
4. If we use this opportunity to consolidate some farmland, can we remake it into new, large-scale rice paddies?
5. Farmland is difficult to recover due to significant rubble, and new land usage where owners are spread out and future utilization as farm land has not been established

I asked dean Osawa to provide technical guidance on the above difficult challenges and he became a member of the "City of Soma Reconstruction Advisory Board Meeting", which was inaugurated in June.

In the summer of 2011, Tokyo University of Agriculture vice president Takano provided logistics support, directing professors Monma, Goto, and Shibuya to provide local leadership and carry out local surveys. Progress was also being made on establishing an agricultural corporation, and we began explaining and persuading

Temporary Housing Chapter 4

the motivated farmers in preparation to get them organized. The city of Soma introduced the professors from the Tokyo University of Agriculture to the area, explained the purpose and tried to have them come into the circle of the village, and although they showed signs of confusion at first, the people in the area gradually came to trust them.

Professor Monma, who was in charge of radiation countermeasures in the Tamano area, ended up renting an apartment and settling in Soma. He took various measurements of radiation contaminated soil in farmlands, established standards for measuring the air dose rate in two locations, and the depth for soil samples in two locations, then explained the details of these results to area residents. His enthusiasm resulted in people of the Tamano area following professor Monma's lead, even when they would not listen to me.

The high amount of air dose rate and damaging rumors resulted in putting off planting in 2011, however, green manure crops were planted and reversal tillage plowing helped lower soil radiation levels so that planting could take place in 2012. He is also thinking hard on vegetable cultivation and dairy farming.

On the other hand, professor Goto, who is providing guidance in former Iitoyo (includes Iwanoko, Niida, and Kashiwazaki) is a soil expert. He reminds me of the author Kenji Miyazawa. Even after the scattered driftwood is disposed of, I think that the tens of centimeters deep sludge accumulating on top of the rice paddies will make restoring them impossibly difficult, but the professor told something incomprehensible at the very beginning. "Rain is the best way to desalinate.

Soil surveys by university students

Reversal tillage can turn the sludge into fertilizer." In short, the driftwood was carefully removed and as long as the rice paddies were plowed, they would naturally desalinate. He also mentioned that substances carried by the sludge would form sulfuric acid, which would need to be taken care of. We would need to add iron and steel slag to adjust the PH levels and supplement minerals in the soil. We were surprised to hear that iron by-product could be used as fertilizer, but the absolute confidence of the professor moved us and eventually everyone there was convinced. In response to this plan, Nippon Steel & Sumitomo Metal provided iron and steel slag. Chairman Aritomi of the Yamato Welfare Foundation kindly donated tractors and other farming equipment to replace the ones lost to the tsunami.

In the autumn of 2012, an amazingly abundant harvest of the "sludge tilling, iron and steel slag rice" crop was gathered not long after the efforts of the agricultural corporation began in the Iitoyo area. Despite a mere 1.7 hectares of rice paddies, this crop exceeded our wildest dreams as we had thought the situation completely hopeless after the disaster. I'm sure the flavor was colored by my emotions, but the iron and the steel slag rice was the best tasting rice I have ever eaten.

March 8, 2013. Vice president Takano was welcomed at the presentation ceremony where Nippon Steel & Sumitomo Metal donated a massive amount of steel and iron slag for our 50 hectare planting efforts this year, which was held at the city hall. The name I came up with wasn't even worth criticizing, therefore it ended up having

Measuring radiation levels in the Tamano area

Temporary Housing — Chapter 4

a label 'Reconstruction Rice' printed on a one kilogram bag. I, however, believe we still need a stylish name in enka-style to express the painstaking effort. We must inspect every bag of rice in respect manner, even though there would not be any problems in contamination of cesium considering the desalination process and the level of potassium concentration.

Professor Itsuo Goto (left) and the author harvesting rice (September 30, 2013)

The strawberry union has also produced tremendous results due to forming an agricultural corporation. I'd like to introduce further details at another time. However, in order to revitalize the farming industry based on the above results, we also need to consider overall efforts including other uses of farmland. If we don't carry out basic surveys and research, we cannot produce a decision on land use, so we need the continued cooperation of the Tokyo University of Agriculture.

I'd like to express my deep gratitude for the generosity shown toward Soma up to this day, and continue in our efforts to revitalize the farming industry in a way that is accepted by the world at large, and our descendants in the future.

Soma rice in school lunches

Mayor's e-mail newsletter - March 11, 2013 Issue

(24) "Wada Strawberry Farm" agricultural corporation

Until right before the disaster, the "Wada Sightseeing Strawberry Farm" was very prosperous. Thirteen members of the strawberry union greeted visitors with a smile on their faces at their greenhouses. It was popular with children, particularly with kindergarten students.

Since opening in 1988, the farms welcome 30,000 to 50,000 visitors every year from January to May, yet half of these vinyl strawberry greenhouses which are such an important part of the Soma scenery were instantly washed away in the tsunami. The sludge carried by the tsunami covered the nearby rice patties, erasing their original forms. The strawberry farmers, while dumbfounded by the damages, were then hit with the accident at the nuclear power plant. Because strawberries are cultivated inside greenhouses, they merely need to rebuild them after being washed away by the tsunami and replace cesium-contaminated soil to produce strawberries without any worries of radioactive contamination. However, how would they sell these among damaging rumors of radiation? With shipping companies avoiding the area due to fears of radiation, would customers still come?

Perhaps they saw through my worries, but even the elderly among the affected union members were determined to give up investing in rebuilding the farms. Strawberry cultivation is time consuming and difficult for older farmers, as they need to bend over and work close to the ground. I realized I could not irresponsibly cheer them on in this task.

But union leader Yamanaka did

The greenhouse the day after the earthquake

Temporary Housing — Chapter 4

not give up. The group of university students from the Tokyo University of Agriculture along with volunteers from all across the country helped to take the first steps toward rebuilding. The desire to rebuild directly after the disaster was a beacon of light. He was absolutely determined to reopen the strawberry farm at the few homes of farmers that were spared damages in the tsunami.

At that time, the young son-in-law of former head doctor Takashi Haneda came to visit me. His name was Hirasawa of the JGC Corporation, and he proposed hydroponic strawberry cultivation in a positive pressure dome-shaped greenhouse . I realized that hydroponic cultivation would do away with any bending over and resulting back pain, and that we could systematize fertilization and management. However, because this was part of the reconstruction effort, it could simply create a rift between affected farmers only. If that is the case, why not have all members of the union form an agricultural corporation, create a large hydroponics strawberry greenhouse as part of a Soma reconstruction project, and lend it to the corporation free of charge?

I had nothing to counter this argument, so I brought the idea to the members of the union. Proposing the forming of an agricultural corporation all of a sudden proved to be difficult for some people to understand, and not all were convinced, however, those who felt that they were too old to continue in strawberry farming would serve as stockholders with the head of the industrial division at city hall coming to help out a number of times.

After establishing the "Wada Strawberry Farm" corporation and building the first extra-large vinyl greenhouse, on January 13, 2013, Takumi Nemoto, the recently inaugurated Minister for Reconstruction was invited to the opening ceremony

of the new hydroponics strawberry farm. All involved had smiles on their faces. Reuniting with Minister Nemoto, who is a former acquaintance, was a happy occasion for us both, and I was very glad to be able to introduce a rebuilt facility that allows us to give our full attention to farming and sightseeing operations as an agricultural corporation without worrying about radiation.

That afternoon, Yoshimasa Hayashi, the Minister of Agriculture, Forestry and Fisheries visited the facilities. This was my first time seeing Minister Hayashi in eight years since I was called upon to explain local administrative reform as part of the LDP's subcommittee, and I was amazed that he was able to reproduce nearly that entire conversation. That day we spoke about the challenges of the Soma agricultural industry, and he discussed with us how to connect to a sixth sector industry as a new form of production, including an agricultural corporation. He has been an intelligent person as long as I've known him, and he is undoubtedly moving forward. The second of the greenhouses is currently under construction, and we have realized the necessity of the third building when taking into consideration expansion, such as forming a sixth sector industry.

Although we unfortunately did not build a dome-shaped greenhouse as proposed by Hirasawa, meeting him and hearing his idea was like turning on a bright light for me. Thank you.

Wada Sightseeing Strawberry Farm
Opening ceremony
(January 13, 2012)

Temporary Housing

Chapter 4

Mayor's e-mail newsletter - March 18, 2013 Issue

essay

(25) FIFA Football Center preparation

The following occurred in 2003.

An announcement has been made that of the 500 hectares of land in the Koyo district industrial park, 115 hectares of undeveloped land on the western side of the no. 6 bypass will be sold off by SME Support Japan due to canceled plans. When industrial waste disposal businesses sprang into action we instantly thought that there was no way we would allow this to become a disposal site for industrial waste from the metro Tokyo area, and we talked the price down to 1.3 billion yen and purchased it on a 20-year deferred payment plan. In spite of the severe financial straits of the time, we made this decision based on considering the future of this region. Just two kilometers down the road was the ocean that produced abundant catches of fish in Haragama where I had grown up.

Fifteen hectares of this space was already filled with coal ash discharged from thermal power plants, but we decided to fill in the coal ash in the remaining 4.6 million cubic meters volume of the hollow after Soma obtained the permission and funds for disposal of industrial wastes. Later, as a way to use the 15 hectares of reclaimed land, we turned it into east Japan's largest park golf course with nine courses and four softball fields. Enthusiasts of these two sports formed NPOs which manage the area on behalf of Soma.

June 2009.

The Soma Soccer Association proposed that we build a soccer field on the 10 hectare plot of land where a vegetation mat was planted to prevent ash scattering on the coal ash reclaimed land that was now available for use.

They even thought of the finances, and told us that they had no intention of making unreasonable demands. They merely wanted whatever land we could spare and a toilet. They also wanted to build one soccer field of natural grass where public games could be held.

185

We agreed with some conditions. We would begin construction immediately as long as they formed an NPO that promotes soccer and the health of youths, and that they take on everything, from lawn management to planning soccer matches.

October 2009. The NPO "Dream Soccer Soma" is finally formed.
Just as promised, the grounds open in May 2011 and maintenance begins on the Soma Koyo Soccer Field. One side contains a culvert for draining water and a natural grass court with sprinklers. The three other sides contain vegetation mat courts that where children can play without being modified, along with toilets that also include multi-purpose toilets for disabled persons, a parking lot, and a simple office.

FIFA/JFA supported Soma Koyo Soccer Field reopening after renovations

Temporary Housing

Chapter 4

Then,
on March 11, the tsunami came for the soccer field. The parking lot on the ocean side was flooded, and some of the natural grass was covered in seawater. Because the industrial park was built six meters above sea level as a tsunami countermeasure and the structures in the port helped weaken the waves, the damage was not as severe as one might have thought. The surrounding area was covered in debris, and the accumulation of seawater in the basin made it a poor choice for a soccer field. Because we were thinking only of survival at that time, we completely forgot about the soccer field. In those days the only things on our mind were making sure no one died, moving from evacuation shelters to temporary housing as soon as possible, and providing some kind of rest for victims. The challenges with the highest priority were limiting further destruction, and taking care of functions that had been lost, such as restoring the fishing port.

Then at the end of April, the emergency headquarters received news that suddenly changed the mood of Soma citizens.
The Emperor and Empress would come visit Soma to pay their respects.

Reconstruction Exchange and Support Center
Normally used as facilities for the Soma Koyo Soccer Field
(Completed September 15, 2014)

187

At that time, even vendors avoided Soma due to fears of radiation, so we wondered if it really was OK not to evacuate the citizens. It was in this state of affairs where no one wanted to visit when the news of the emperor and empress would come to Soma, lifting our spirits. Furthermore, the place where a helicopter landed was the parking lot of the Koyo Soccer Field, which was almost completed.

The imperial couple visited on May 11.
I stood stiffly at attention while waiting for the helicopter to arrive, and faced the Emperor and Empress with the most respectful bow I could muster. While showing them the affected areas, I was surprised at the looks of joy on faces of Soma citizens. There was no trace of the enormous burden of sadness I had seen only the day before, instead they were happy. After spending approximately three hours with us and seeing them off at the soccer field, I decided that I wanted to open Koyo Soccer Field to keep the children positive.

Planting natural grass turf

Temporary Housing

Chapter 4

When seeing my resolve, chairman Miyazawa of the SEISA Group, who were providing assistance in helping the children of Soma deal with PTSD began to set the plan in motion. They traveled all around the country asking for assistance in the Soccer soma project, asking coach Otaki of the famous Shimizu commercial High School to come, along with their current members and alumni of current J League soccer player to help with soccer practice for Soma High schools and conduct soccer classes for the children of Soma.

July 17. On a day when bright sunlight made the grass shine, the Koyo Soccer Field opening ceremony was carried out at a field filled with children. Although coach Otaki is a quiet person, you could sense his sincerity once he began speaking. We were thankful when he said, "I'll come again if you need me here. We can help Soma rebuild through soccer." 1,550 teams, totaling 24,400 people have used the field in the one year and eight months since that day. The NPO in charge of field maintenance and usage are doing an excellent job.

Then, there were requests to either replace all of the grass from the roots up or use artificial turf from the parents and guardians who were worried about the radiation. We posted real-time updates of radiation measurements at the Koyo Soccer Field, finding readings of approximately 0.4 microsieverts per hour. Although the exposure is minimal when spending time on the field, there is a big difference between safety and peace of mind when it comes to radiation. As long as people do not feel safe, playing while worrying about one's health is not a good way to enjoy the game.

However, even low estimates for artificial turf cost 100 million yen, and replacing all of the turf would cost about the same. Because it would not be appropriate to pour our entire budget into soccer alone out of all other sports, we needed to give priority to other reconstruction projects.

Just at that time, we received information on the "FIFA Football Center Emergency Support Project" from the Japan Football Association. This indicated that the FIFA (Fédération Internationale de Football Association) support project for the three affected prefectures could be held in the city of Soma. The details included the city of Soma lending land to the Japan Football Association free of charge and they would provide natural turf and an artificial turf field, allowing Soma to use these free of charge as a form of support for the city. A specialist will be dispatched for three years in order to maintain the turf. After that, Soma will be in charge of maintenance but, during that time we will learn maintenance techniques to ensure the level remains on par with FIFA soccer fields. Japan Football Association executive director Fukui visited the spot many times and requested that we do this as well. As a result, FIFA and the Japan Football Association agreed to provide one field with artificial turf and three with natural turf. Because it is being lent free of charge as public land, on receiving approval from the council on March 6, after long anticipation I visited Japan Football Association chairman Daini, vice chairman Tajima, and senior managing director Tanaka to thank them for the many discussions since last year and for providing the best possible outcome for Soma.

We plan on communicating our efforts after carefully managing the FIFA Football Center throughout Japan, and I requested their further support in our efforts to promote soccer in Soma as well as inviting teams to play here and holding soccer classes taught by

Temporary Housing

Chapter 4

famous soccer players. I was very glad to hear that they were sympathetic to us and pledged cooperation in the future.

We also thought of the parents when considering how to let children focus fully on soccer without worrying about radiation. Also, if many soccer enthusiasts come to visit Soma, the nonresident population will increase on behalf of Matsukawaura that changed drastically due to the tsunami.

The Matsukawaura Ryokan Union are also lending their knowledge. The NPO "Dream Soccer Soma" is full of enthusiasm. Organic coordination is necessary, such as working with three NPOs Koyo sports facilities and lodging facilities to arrange for accommodations during events. Although we have many things to do, we have been able to work together to set a new goal that brings us hope.

Speaking of such hope, I believe the name "Dream Soccer Soma" is particularly appropriate. When thinking back, each and every event in this area since 2003 has been like something from a dream, particularly the two years since the March 11 earthquake.

Mayor's e-mail newsletter - July 14, 2013 Issue

(26) PTSD countermeasures and Louis Vuitton

April 15, 2013. The ground-breaking ceremony for the "LVMH Kodomo Art Maison" is held in Nakamura 2-Chome, Soma to commemorate the donation of the facility by the world-famous LVMH Moët Hennessy - Louis Vuitton.

Starting April 18, 2011, just one month after the earthquake, elementary, junior high schools, and public kindergarten classes were reopened.

The first problem faced in running classes were the "psychological scars" the children bore due to the earthquake and tsunami. For example, when hearing the words 'ocean' or 'wave' during class, some children would start crying, grow restless, or become otherwise emotionally unstable. The reports from the superintendent of education at the daily meetings at emergency headquarters were all shocking to hear.

This highlighted the urgent need to consider PTSD countermeasures, resulting in recruiting clinical psychologists and public health nurses from across Japan. Yasuo Miyazawa, chairman of the SEISA Group, which specializes in developmental disabilities, dispatched school counselors, associated director Ryutaro Takahashi of the Tokyo Metropolitan Geriatric Hospital and Institute of Gerontology kindly sent public health nurses, clinical psychologists recruited from the city of Soma, and these

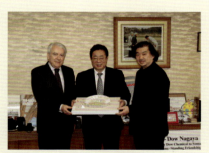

President Emmanuel Prat of LVMH Moët Hennessy - Louis Vuitton Inc. (left) and designer Shigeru Ban (right) (April 4, 2012)

Temporary Housing

Chapter 4

6 staff members formed an emergency PTSD consulting team, which began operations on April 20. At this initial stage, rather than defining the type of organization the team should be comprised of, it was necessary to formulate countermeasures as quickly as possible.

Later on, because we realized the importance of continuous follow-up for PTSD measures for approximately 10 years, the team was reorganized into an NPO with a formal structure and finances, and positioned as a related organization to the Soma Board of Education. The organization was established as a corporation on August 5, 2011. Operations are mainly funded by donations, and as long as reconstruction service industries have the budget to pay the personnel costs, and we can either make it a commissioned project from Soma to the NPO or squeeze the necessary funds by making it an individual project if it does not provide support measures.

The background behind making this implementing body an NPO and considering its systematic and continued operation was due to the generosity of president Masayoshi Konaka and vice president Okubo of "Nippon Kodo Co., Ltd.", a company who visited Soma in April and offered their support, along with the 1,400 current students from the "Poole Gakuin" Junior & Senior High School who promised to send 100 yen per month. In the case of "Nippon Kodo", the entire proceeds of a yearly charity concert would be donated to the project, with over 50 million yen total proceeds received over the past three years.

The efforts of the NPO Soma Follower Team staff were excellent from the very beginning. The team began coming to schools to help not only the children at the elementary, junior high schools, and kindergartens in the city affected by the disaster, but all children in the city gripped by fear of the nuclear power plant accident, etc., casually looking for problems, and in some cases making house calls with doctors at temporary housing. After gaining the trust of the

193

children, the team then consulted with teachers and listened to their concerns.

They offered effective solutions such as improving academic performance, and other ways to spend time in school with confidence. Also, the worldwide donations from the "Earthquake Orphans Charity" provided sufficient funds to help students financially as they moved on to college, but the effort to give the students enough academic ability to pass college entrance exams is important.

Therefore, "improving academic ability" was added to the projects of the NPO. We consulted with then Senior Vice Minister of Education and current member of the House of Councilors, Kan Suzuki, who introduced vice president of the University of Tokyo, Muto who I met and talked to about possibly sending volunteer university students to assist children affected by the disaster in Soma. Thanks to their understanding and kindness, the "Terakoya School" now operates at temporary housing and special classroom lessons are held for students who desire to take part.

Representative Kan Suzuki lent me his ear on many occasions in talking about the health risks to children due to radiation. All children under 18 years of age would be examined for internal and external exposure as a radiation countermeasure, with anyone over

Temporary Housing

the strict yearly limit of 1.6 millisieverts of exposure per year subject to decontamination as well as lifestyle guidance and thorough health management. We also discussed building a logical foundation with cool-headed formulation and implementation of countermeasures to avoid causing any secondary psychological damage. As a result, we did not have any child in Soma exceeded a dosage of 1.6 milisieverts per year up till now. The foremost problem is the many female students who were concerned that they may not be able to get married in future due to the risk of abnormal births. This is unmistakably a form of PTSD. These kinds of thoughtless, scientifically unfounded, irresponsible utterances merely serve to deepen the pain of the children in Fukushima. The NPO must make sure to thoroughly follow up on these issues as well.

In October 2011, the NPO began operating smoothly. Former Senior Vice Minister and current member of the House of Councilors, Kan Suzuki introduced us to the Louis Vuitton company, who were considering supporting the children affected by the Great East Japan Earthquake. When I visited their Japanese branch, I explained our attempt in dealing with PTSD of children in Soma as well as the approach to improve their learning ability. Emmanuel Prat, the president of the Japan branch, called our efforts creative, and said that we should think of how to support the city of Soma. I then asked him if the company could donate a "children's museum"

Opening ceremony(July 2, 2014)

195

to the city as a base from which to combat PTSD and as a way to cultivate their aesthetic sentiments. I believe representative Kan Suzuki's presentation moved the heart of the president. He replied that we should start thinking about the location and size of the facilities, and I and PR manager Mari Saito of Louis Vuitton began planning.

In the Nakamura 2-Chome of Soma there is a 1,650 square meter vacant lot where municipal housing once stood. After showing the area to Saito as the proposed spot and gaining her approval, planning began on the "LVMH Kodomo Art Maison" in December 2011 by volunteer international designer Shigeru Ban living in France.
As one would expect of a world-class architect, Shigeru Ban's designs and ideas were innovative. The building is planned for completion by the end of 2013. While this facility is intended to function as the headquarters for dealing with PTSD, it features a number of contrivances for cultivating the children's aesthetic sense. Looking at the arrangement of small rooms where LVMH aims to cultivate the children's "creative" sensibilities, such as the reading and listening room, the free drawing room, and the library with picture books, etc. on display, is so much fun I want to be a kid again.
Right after the earthquake, our efforts to tackle the problems that

Temporary Housing — Chapter 4

Musical composition classroom

arose one after the other helped us find new developments and supporters, and have changed into incredible opportunities for the children of Soma to grow and change. We sincerely look forward to the completion of the "LVMH Kodomo Art Maison" while expressing our thanks for their encouragement and for giving the children strength and dreams for the future.

Mayor's e-mail newsletter - July 14, 2013 Issue

(27) Soma Tourism Reconstruction Information Center and Thousands of Visitor Hall

The scenery of Matsukawaura lost in the disaster was a boon to area tourism, and something that attracted many people to Soma. This resulted in successful Japanese-style inns and guest houses in the area, alongside work for locals in the agricultural and fishing industries. I still remember the beaches overflowing with tourists in early summer digging for clams.

The beautiful pine forests of my youth were washed away by the tsunami, giving the area the feel of a featureless embankment, and now after the sadness is gone, only a feeling of emptiness remains. How many decades would it take to regrow the pine forest if we planted right now?

Even so, the inns and guest houses were filled with workers who had come to restore the damaged thermal power plant. But once the power plant was restored, the once vibrant tourist area was blanketed in silence. Although there is still demand for lodging from outside the city for reconstruction projects, this is absorbed by business hotels in the city, resulting in much fewer people who stay at tourist inns and guest houses. The final blow came when local fish was avoided due to the accident at the nuclear power plant, making it very difficult to attract customers.

The proposal to build the JFA Football Center by the Japan Football Association proved to be a ray of light for me during those times. They offered to build a total of four official fields as a way for FIFA to support

Thousands of Visitor Hall and Central Community Center
(Open February 15, 2015)

Temporary Housing Chapter 4

the affected areas, including three natural turf fields and one artificial turf field. Later on we received the support of Toto to build another artificial turf field for a total of five. Of course the children were happy upon hearing the news, but also the proprietresses of the various inns and guest houses were smiling as well. Until the pine forests of Matsukawaura are regrown, its location as a soccer mecca gives us hope.

On top of the land reclaimed from coal ash in the east area of the industrial park one can already find the largest nine-course park golf facility in all of Tohoku and softball fields where four games can be held simultaneously, which are managed by NPOs formed of enthusiasts in each sport. If the former soccer field managed by the NPO "Dream Soccer Soma" is transformed into the JFA Football Center, these three facilities will make it possible to develop powerful sports tourism strategies. In addition to holding various tournaments for each sport, we can increase the number of visitors and guests at lodging facilities according to event plans and operating style, including promoting training camps and holding sports classes taught by famous athletes, etc.

One other unexpected development was increasing the number of visitors to Soma by having them come see the progress of rebuilding efforts. Although many representatives of the Diet have come to visit Idobata Nagaya, including the Minister of Finance and the Minister of Land, Infrastructure, Transport and Tourism, more people are coming to observe the finished results of our rebuilding

efforts such as the detached residences completed one after the other, the community center in Isobe, the fishery warehouse in Haragama, and the emergency supplies storehouse in Takamatsu. I feel that visitors simply passing by our city and seeing only the destruction and temporary housing and remarking on how difficult we have it is rather annoying. Instead, I'd be happy to share information on the current efforts of Soma citizens and future disaster countermeasures, so we would welcome visitors who'd like to observe. If groups of 10 or more people come to stay in the city and observe our reconstruction efforts, staffers from city hall can provide simple tours. Smaller groups that wish to tour the city can be handled by the tourism association, but there is also a growing trend among this number.

For soccer matches we work in coordination with the Koyo area NPO to arrange lodging who have planned a facility for greeting visitors with tours and a description of reconstruction efforts. In order to stimulate the enthusiasm of inns and tourist businesses and communicate objectives in a way that is easy to understand, we discussed options with the Reconstruction Agency and named the facility the "Senkyaku Banrai-kan (Thousands of Visitor Hall)." In addition to offices and an accessible toilet for persons with physical disabilities, the Thousand Visitor Hall is equipped with the following facilities. There is an entrance hall for greeting guests. A training room includes a PowerPoint presentation

Hallway

Training space

Temporary Housing — Chapter 4

for including emergency headquarters efforts directly after the earthquake, rebuilding initiatives, and radiation countermeasures for those who have come to learn about disaster countermeasures. A Japanese-style room is available where visitors can remove their shoes to relax. There is also a kitchen where one can come enjoy local cuisine. Because the Thousands of Visitor Hall is being constructed in connection with the demolition of the old central community center and the construction of a new city hall main building, it will be possible to use two community centers with a space of 495 square meters if the schedule is adjusted.

Because we have obtained the approval of the Reconstruction Agency and will begin construction this year as a project to stimulate the city, we began discussing the creation of a specific organization between the chairman of the tourism association who is also the head of the chamber of commerce, the Matsukawa Inn Union, the City of Soma Inn Union, and the three NPOs in charge of managing the soccer fields, park golf course, and softball fields. We will begin by planning sporting events, taking care of visitors, including promotion, operation, dealing with athletes, etc. We will arrange lodging for those who wish to observe reconstruction, as well as provide explanations and tours at the Thousand Visitor Hall. We're currently asking volunteers to provide tours, which we'd like to increase to 10 people who work systematically on a rotating basis.

We will be asking the head of the chamber of commerce to lead the organization, with the "Soma Tourism Reconstruction Information Center" starting operations on October 1. Although it is called an information center, it is merely an organization under the umbrella of the chamber of commerce intended to increase the visiting population in coordination with city hall.

Next year we plan to begin construction on the "Memorial Hall for the Repose of Souls", in which will commemorate those lost in the tsunami, along with photo exhibitions that show what Haragama, Obama, and Isobe used to look like, as they are now completely unrecognizable. Once complete, we will invite many people to visit, including local residents and those who visit the city of Soma. We plan on running this facility under the direction of the Soma Tourism Reconstruction Information Center.

Temporary Housing — Chapter 4

Mayor's e-mail newsletter - August 19, 2014 Issue

(28) Strong Bones Park

During the time when many victims of the earthquake and tsunami were living in temporary housing our first priority was ensuring that there were no solitary deaths, and thanks to the efforts of the Building Leader representing five households per building and the Group Leader representing each meeting place, there have been no solitary deaths in Soma temporary housing to date. As often as possible, I attend the meeting where the Group Leaders of 15 blocks gather, and I am very grateful for their efforts. This disaster has shown us just how precious the connection with others in the community is to human life.

The second objective is maintaining resident health in long-term living in temporary housing. Fukushima prefecture in particular has the unique problem of radiation exposure, and in addition to exhaustive air dose rate measurements, we carry out external exposure tests and internal exposure tests using whole-body counting for children of all grades. This process is a radiation countermeasure that enables us to confirm that resident exposure across

multiple temporary housing complexes is extremely low.

The next step is keeping in good shape to prevent adult diseases. In order to avoid nutritional imbalances and prevent solitary deaths, two dinner dishes are provided for seniors 65 years of age and older, and children, however, living in the cramped confines of temporary housing must have accelerated their lifestyle diseases.

In the city of Soma, Professor Kami and his staff from the Tokyo University Institute Of Medical Science along with Kenji Shibuya, a professor of policy studies at the School of International Health at the University of Tokyo's Graduate School of Medicine, and doctors from the Soma Medical Association have cooperated with us to conduct special yearly health exams at temporary housing. The exams are made possible due to funding from the Novartis pharmaceutical companys.
We paid particular attention to blood glucose levels, hyperlipidemia, and osteoporosis. In addition to insufficient exercise due to the cramped living confines of temporary housing, there was cause for concern regarding vitamin D deficiency due to lack of fish in the diet resulting from radiation fears.

With these concerns in mind, reinforcements came to our aid in 2013 and 2014. This included physical therapists from the Hoeikai Hospital in Fukuoka and Dr. Takeaki Ishii of the Kyushu University Department of Orthopaedic Surgery. With their support, we were able to carry out bone density tests via ultrasound in addition to physical therapists conducting motor ability tests.
Although the results showed tendencies that confirmed our fears, we received advice from public health nurses to promote exercises as a form of overall health management, such as adding radio calisthenics, walking, and other exercises, as well as nutritional advice to add fish to dinner dishes whenever possible and modify the taste of meals.

Temporary Housing — Chapter 4

Thanks to the efforts of many people, residents are proceeding to move into public disaster housing, however in the autumn of 2013, Dr. Ishii of Kyushu University proposed an interesting plan. He asked if we would consider building a promenade in the park adjoining the public disaster housing complex so that residents could walk as a way to prevent osteoporosis.

There is a total of seven locations for public disaster housing complexes in the move to higher ground in Soma. The largest of these sites is the Karishikida area, with nearly seven hectares of space. This would give us 70 single homes, four multiple-dwelling complexes housing nine households, 43 lots of land for sale from 264 to 330 square meters, and a mini park at 3,300 square meters. It is scheduled to be completed this year, and with 144 households it will become a wonderful village after residents have transferred, so we are planning various measures to ensure the independence of residence, including a meeting place, park, street vendor trucks for those who have trouble going shopping, as well as a mini bus service for those who must travel to the central city area for doctor's visits or shopping.

As Dr. Ishii proposed a plan about a 3,300 square meter mini park before, we have begun considering the role of an urban park for the affected areas. General city parks are built for disaster prevention and environmental conservation purposes, but also as a location for all ages to enjoy communing with nature, recreational activities, healthy exercise, cultural activities, and a variety of other activities

Street vendor truck

(according to the Ministry of Land, Infrastructure, Transport and Tourism). Although the playground equipment commands attention, we think it may be a good idea to modify the park for our aging population. Demographics show a balanced trend between the aging population and other age ranges among the population in the affected areas in Japan after 10 to 20 years.

As we have continued to support life in temporary housing, the city of Soma has reached the conclusion that a promenade should be designed to maintain the motor ability functions of aging residents as a way to promote exchange between children and the elderly, and help build a community based on the health exam data and current experience. We will base designs on the advice and knowledge of the physical therapists from Hoeikai Hospital who have been providing assistance in health exams since last year.

Making one lap of the promenade will provide a measure of exercise stress, with height differences on the path included in order to help maintain muscle tone. There will be low rise stairs with a handrail and wheelchair slopes arranged side by side along with gazebos in two locations as a place to rest. There will also be walls near benches for assisting with stretching as well as other modifications that make it easy to enjoy a full body workout.

For the next five years I am planning to assign a special administrative district director in accordance with the previously described Group Leader system in order for the new public disaster housing village community to function Community leaders will help promote physical and social fitness, respecting the guidance designed by physical therapists.

Temporary Housing — Chapter 4

Dr. Ishii proposed naming the park the "Narrow Road to the Bones" as a way to honor the traditional "Tohoku Narrow Road to the Deep North" by poet Matsuo Basho . After complaints that calling a park dedicated to combating osteoporosis 'narrow bones' calls to mind broken bones, the staff all agreed that the name "Strong Bones Park" sounded much healthier. This kind plan came about due to a proposal from Dr. Ishii as an orthopedic surgeon. As I walk along the path thinking of Matsuo Basho composing his lines in the fields, I'm reminded of Dr. Ishii's endless humanity. Thank you.

Mayor's e-mail newsletter - November 21, 2014 Issue

(29) 2014 Manifesto Awards Grand Prize (November 14, 2014)

November 14. This year there was a Manifesto Awards announcement and award ceremony, and I received the grand prize from chief judge Masayasu Kitagawa. I'd like to express my thanks and give a report below.

Manifestos are originally submitted as a "public commitment" with the voters during an election, and used to evaluate the status of achieving such a commitment at a later date. This means that previously these commitments were merely flowery words such as 'I aim to improve our educational system' or 'I will work to promote the agricultural industry' and not used to evaluate one's promises.
Therefore, manifestos later contained requirements in order to evaluate the concreteness of such commitments after elections.
(A) Quantify whenever possible for later verification (For example: Ensuring that there are no children on waiting lists for nursery schools, etc.)
(B) Ensure that evaluation is possible at the competition even if quantification is difficult (For example: Whether or not improvements have been made to academic ability)
As detailed above, a policy subject to objective verification and evaluation, as well as additional reconsideration and execution that enables improvements and efficiency via the PDCA cycle is defined as a manifest.

This type of movement began in earnest in 2004, and administrative promises in the national election of political parties came to be called a manifesto. This is called a local manifesto in the case of regional elections. Verifiability means that the manifesto must be concrete, and demands that numerical objectives be set.
Although manifesto based elections are now commonplace, they have been carried on since long before verification of voting

Temporary Housing — Chapter 4

behavior results, and voters are sometimes misled by exaggerated promises. The manifesto of the regime change in 2009 was one of those times. Policies difficult to make good on financially later on such as childcare allowances, and toll-free expressways became the voters' means of judging promises.

However, because the thinking has shifted from manifesto-based elections founded on vague election promises such as enhancing welfare and endeavoring to promote agriculture to quantifiable and verifiable commitments, the administrative capacity and ability to establish policies of political candidates has been called into question.

I believe that the mindset behind manifesto-based elections is correct. However, voters must now possess the ability to determine whether the politician or the policies they present as a manifesto have the ability to put them in place or whether they are possible to achieve.

This year's Manifesto Awards evaluated a total of 2,200 entries in categories such as citizens, the Diet, and local politicians. The citizen and Diet manifestos include action plans and the status of Diet policies and citizen activities such as NPOs.

Criteria for the city of Soma differed from general election promises, including establishing a specific plan of action in the middle of the night on the day of the disaster, the entire staff of the emergency headquarters sharing the same ideas while implementing

countermeasures, steady implementation of the reconstruction plan as a team in Soma after being established in June 2011, etc., and our efforts were praised for calmly establishing policies in the face of unprecedented danger and the entire staff carrying out recon-struction based on a common goal.

Although it is the mayor who presents the "manifesto" which con-tains the action plan directly after the disaster, and the mid to long-term reconstruction plan, to city hall staff and the citizens in order to rebuild the hometown of Soma citizens, which is where the victims live, it is the city hall staff who put the plan into action without sleep or any days off, along with the cooperation of the citizens including the fire department who face difficult tasks. Staff were dispatched from two hospitals in the city and one elderly care facility. They con-tinued to care for the sick and elderly while fighting back fears of the worsening situation at the nuclear power plant. The victims of the disaster also maintained an orderly community in the difficult living conditions of the evacuation shelters and temporary housing. The reason why we have survived today without a single person affected by the tsunami dying a solitary death or committing suicide is the connection between individuals, the smooth communication with city hall, and the traditional castle town culture of Soma.

The members of the "Eastern Rebuilding Association" stood together to do what they could to help rebuild their hometown, and helped purchase the land on which to build public disaster housing on higher ground. Relying on connections with relatives, friends, and acquaintances, they visited many people asking for help. The pace of reconstruction truly accelerated thanks to the help of the citizens. I believe this is worthy of mentioning.

In other areas, we received water and food supplies from friendly cities directly after the earthquake and tsunami. Engineers were also dispatched to help our reconstruction projects. We learned just how important the daily connection between municipalities is. We also received sizable funds from various companies including Louis

Temporary Housing

Vuitton and Nippon Kodo. The Japan Football Association was instrumental in increasing the visiting population by providing four official soccer courts in a single bold move.

The honor of standing out in the Manifesto Awards is thanks to the solid execution of the above reconstruction plans, and also the tireless efforts of city hall staff working to the full extent of their abilities, along with the citizens of Soma and many others. I would like to express my sincere thanks to all.

(30) The "Soma Kids Dome" bringing smiles to the faces of kids through the power of sports (December 18, 2014)

On December 18, 2014, an event was held to celebrate the opening of the "Soma Kids Dome" indoor sports facility, a safe environment where children can play and enjoy exercising.

This facility was made possible due to donations from across the country by the "Indoor Sports Facility Fund-raising Group" established mainly by the Rakuten Baseball Club, who operates out of Miyagi.

Mayor's e-mail newsletter - March 31, 2015 Issue

essay

Temporary Housing

(31) Eastern Rebuilding Association (all units of public disaster housing complete)

Last March 26. The completion ceremony was held for the final public disaster housing in Soma city, the Kitakoya Residential Complex.

This completes all planned 410 household residences. The breakdown includes the 58 households in the five buildings of the Idobata Nagaya, the 36 households in four apartment buildings geared toward young married couples, and 316 single homes. Smooth moves from temporary housing will proceed according to the transfer program. In addition to public housing a section land for sale was developed for those who wanted to build a new home on their own, with residential developments in nine locations and a total land area of over 30 hectares. Although construction remains on some parks, meeting places, and exteriors, we were able to complete general housing construction within 2014 without any solitary deaths occurring.

We are deeply moved by the efforts of production industries including the goods handling facility and headquarters office at the fishing union in Matsukawaura, the seafood processing plant under construction in Isobe and fishery warehouse for 16 fishing businesses in Haragama, the new main building at city hall, the pumping station for preventing ground subsidence, evacuation roads and bridges for subsequent earthquakes, continued development of land on higher ground, and completing bases for living at public disaster housing.

The morning after the earthquake and tsunami and after all-night crisis response meetings and handling emergency situations, I have never felt such life-changing astonishment and despair as I did when heading to the affected areas with the fire chiefs. There was no trace whatsoever of my parent's home, and I didn't know if my brother and his family had survived. Dumbfounded, I stood stock still in the field of debris, wondering how I could process this new reality.

Not only the field of rubble before me, but I wondered if there was any way we could help rebuild the lives of the 4,500 people in evacuation shelters without losing any more.

I noticed that someone was holding onto my back and sobbing out loud. "Haragama is gone. The soy sauce brewery is gone." I turned to a relative that was worrying about me and said "It's OK. Don't cry, we'll figure something out." With that reflexive statement, I and the fire chiefs turned away from the disaster area.

Four years later.

We were able to incinerate the massive amount of rubble that had driven me to the brink of despair, including the leaves and branches cleared during radioactive decontamination efforts. The problem with radioactive contamination of rubble in Soma made it impossible to even touch the refuse in the initial stages, however, thanks to the understanding of citizens we were able to construct a temporary incinerator relatively quickly, and safely incinerate wood and decontaminated organic matter while local villagers cooperated by measuring and confirming that there were no cesium emissions.

One more important issue was the reconstruction of housing, however it was not easy to move settlements to higher ground in preparation for the next tsunami. The areas that disaster victims preferred were quite small for the most part and the large number of landowners made purchasing land hopeless in our minds. The landowner of the Karishikida and Hosoda areas slightly inland from the coastline expressed understanding for the need to rebuild after the earthquake, resulting in a relatively quick start on planning land development. However, the Minaminoiri and Arata upland areas close to the coast consisted of a mix of fields and forests, and had over 100 signatory landowners. Also, the residents working in the main industry of coastal fishing affected by the disaster in the Haragama and

Temporary Housing — Chapter 4

Obama areas did not want to relocate far from the fishing port.

Then, one day the residents in the affected areas of Haragama and Obama brought a petition to the office of the mayor. They had formed a group called the "Eastern Rebuilding Association", and demanded that I rush to build residences in order to rebuild the area. The people in the group were those I had known since childhood. Some were childhood friends, some were relatives, and one was the priest of the temple our family supported. I thought, 'give me a break! My house was destroyed in the tsunami too. If anyone wants to sign that petition, it's me!' But I realized that our goals were the same, so why couldn't we work together?

It was thought to be impossible for Soma to buy out nearly 200 signatory landowners of the Minaminoiri and Arata areas, the upland destinations for moving. However, I was simply amazed by their capability of the Eastern Rebuilding Association at the end. They set out on a plan of attack by looking for local connections and blood relatives, and showing up uninvited at the homes of landowners and pleading with them as a group. Landowners with local connections came to negotiate many times, and were finally moved by affection to agree. It was quite a different type of negotiation from the formal way of working at a government office. In some cases

The author, asking for the assistance of the Eastern Rebuilding Association

215

we could not reach a conclusion as the heirs to the land were scattered across the country, so the city hall took charge.

In 2013, two years after the Eastern Rebuilding Association helped purchase the land, we were finally able to begin land development in the Minaminoiri and Arata areas. Altogether the area will contain approximately 80 single homes and 40 plots of land for sale where owners will build their own houses, making it a wonderful residential complex. Because my family has lived in the Haragama area for generations, my 88 year old father decided to purchase land in the Arata area.

If we had not had the cooperation of the Eastern Rebuilding Association, we would have had to either subdivide the residential space in the Karishikida and Hosoda areas or increase the number of multiple-dwelling complexes. Considering the future of Soma, we have conducted a poll on selling off land to residents of public housing as much as possible, as well as arranging a move-in timetable. We believe that having one's own assets are useful for rebuilding one's life. Also, it would be easier on the administration if residents were also owners rather than having future mayors manage 410 units of municipal housing, and we'd prefer that resi-

Completion ceremony for the Kitakoya
Residential Complex
(March 26, 2015)

Temporary Housing

Chapter 4

dents take care of these homes that were so difficult to build.

There are still many reconstruction projects ahead of us. In particular, service industries must never let their guard down in helping revitalize industry, dealing with radiation, and alleviating children's PTSD.

The completion of the public disaster housing brings me a small joy, even though it is one mountain I was able to overcome with the help of my childhood companions.

At the completion ceremony, I presented a handwritten letter of thanks from myself to the 26 directors of the Eastern Rebuilding Association. I shook the hand of each person, calling out their names in a loud voice.

If there was a 27th person, it would have been myself.

Chapter 5

Rebuilding Period
(Starting March 27, 2015)

(1) Completion of public disaster housing (March 26, 2015 - All 410 units in 9 areas completed)

Hosoda Higashi Complex
Completed (March 28, 2014)
▽65 homes ▽12 Idobata Nagaya homes

Hodota Myojinmae Complex
Completed (March 30, 2013)
▽46 homes

Minaminoiri Complex
Completed (March 16, 2015)
▽28 homes

Karishikida Minami Complex
Completed (March 3, 2015)
▽70 homes ▽36 apartments

Kitakoya Complex
Completed (March 26, 2015)
▽51 homes

Yamashida Complex
Completed (March 26, 2015)
▽56 homes

Rebuilding Period — Chapter 5

Mayor's e-mail newsletter - January 3, 2016 Issue

essay

(2) Reconstruction and regional revitalization

In March it will be five years since the disaster. The rebuilding and revitalization period begins in April.

Looking back on the past years, I can't say that there is nothing I wouldn't have done different, and that I don't have things to be ashamed of, but the calm and wise cooperation of many citizens, as well as the generous support of Japan and the countries of the world have helped Soma City reconstruction proceed basically according to plan. In particular, the abilities of city hall staff have far exceeded my imagination, filling these past five years with happy surprises. Receiving the highest honor in Japan at the 2014 Manifesto Awards was a great source of encouragement.

However... When thinking of the sad loss of the 458 lives including firefighters in the line of duty, members of my family and some friends, we must rebuild the region perfectly and even make some improvements compared to the region before the disaster.

Although it is difficult to see the light at the end of the tunnel when it comes to the damaging rumors of fish and the bargaining against crops, the City of Soma must continue to do what it must do as a way to support their efforts.

In addition to the joint distribution center that was completed for the fishing industry at the end of last year, the processing plant and the 16 person fishery warehouse are planned for completion during the first

Soma regional revitalization comprehensive strategy meeting

half of this year. By the end of summer, the headquarters offices of the fishermen's cooperative and goods handling facility will be completed. We are planning to rebuild the fishermen's cooperative outlet that was washed away in the tsunami, and to make it a market for our citizens, a review board to gather the knowledge of the JA, the Chamber of Commerce and Industry, and the people began operating at the end of last year. Because a goal has been established for the use of 1,100 hectares of damaged rice paddies, orders for construction are being placed for the agricultural industry.

Then...

Since the beginning of last year, when all we could think of was rebuilding, discussions of regional revitalization for local municipalities 35 years in the future began sweeping across Japan. It would have been better if discussions began at least three years later, and for a disaster-struck region such as ours that has not yet recovered from the earthquake, being struck with the harsh reality of competition between municipalities in regional revitalization was enough to freeze the blood in my veins. First, failure to present a solid comprehensive regional revitalization strategy would affect grants from the government.

Project team meeting

Rebuilding Period   Chapter 5

Although it was possible to ask a consulting company to do this for us, the people who understand our situation the best are the individual citizens of Soma. Also, the initiatives must be tackled with an awareness of the issues unique to our hometown, so consolidating the wisdom of the citizens was the best possible option. With that in mind, city hall staff conducted a briefing session on the status of rebuilding at nine community centers and decided to ask all households to fill out a questionnaire. Five different themes were brought up for important issues in regional revitalization: industry/ employment, tourism/exchange, childrearing/education, dealing with an aging society/health promotion, and history/culture/love for one's hometown. Citizens then wrote what they considered most important, as well as other items they considered necessary, and any ideas required to achieve these goals. When these questionnaires were collected by the administrative heads, they were able to find out the opinions of 80% of all households.

The team from city hall organized and analyzed the responses, formed a Soma regional revitalization strategy meeting consisting of 47 people with representatives from groups and local areas, and carried out discussions on each theme at sectional meetings. Finally, they collected the suggestions gleaned from each sectional meeting, presented them to the entire committee and debated

Resident briefing session

considerably on the appropriateness of suggestions from sectional meetings they were not assigned to, and lastly I provided a summary as the chairman this past September.

The suggestion that caught my eye and made me groan as an area fully committing our resources to reconstruction was utilizing completed reconstruction projects as tourism resources, and becoming a region that uses its ability to overcome disaster as social capital in the future. Some also had the opinion that future reconstruction projects should be useful from the standpoint of regional revitalization.

Although the skills of the administration and the cooperation of the people are necessary to change tactics in order to achieve our goals, with this being the first year in the rebuilding and revitalization period, we need to think positively in rebuilding from the earthquake, and do our best for our descendants.

Rebuilding Period Chapter 5

(3) Residential complex meeting place - Completed in 5 areas

Hosoda Higashi Residential Complex meeting place
Completed (March 23, 2015)

Karishikida Minami Residential Complex meeting place
Completed (October 19, 2015)

Minaminoiri Residential Complex meeting place
Completed (October 19, 2015)

Kitakoya Residential Complex meeting place
Completed (October 19, 2015)

Washiyama Residential Complex meeting place
Completed (October 19, 2015)

(4) Tobu Children's Community Center (Opened on October 31, 2015)

A Childrearing Salon and After School Kids Club were opened in collaboration with the local community so that children and their guardians, local elderly residents, and others can enjoy a place to mingle with other age groups.

The Tobu Children's Community Center Festival was held on June 17, 2017 with many parents and children visiting together and enjoying a variety of entertainment while mingling with local elderly residents.

Rebuilding Period

(5) Coastal rain drainage measures

Matsukawa Pump Station completed
(December 11, 2015)

Hosoda Pump Station completed
(September 28, 2016)

The ground subsidence caused by the earthquake in the Matsukawa and Hosoda areas resulted in land across a wide area appearing at a lower altitude than Matsukawaura where rainwater generally drains.
The rainwater must be drained from these two areas to Matsukawaura, using pumps just as is done in Holland.
Japanese-style pumping stations have been completed one after the other.

Matsukawaura Kankyo Park - A massive amount of driftwood was carried to the park by the tsunami.
(Photographed March 31, 2011)

Recovery work completed by NPOs and residents and reopened
(July 22, 2012)

227

(6) Haragama Joint Distribution Center (Completed December 17, 2015)

Haragama Joint Distribution Center
This facility is managed by the Soma Futaba Fishermen's Union where each wholesaler installs their own cold storage, bids on catches, and divides purchased fish for packaging.

A private viewing of the facilities was held, with 100 visitors gathering including members of the Soma Futaba Fishermen's Union and buyers.

Rebuilding Period

Mayor's e-mail newsletter - February 12, 2016 Issue

essay

(7) Neighborhood watch

Large magnetic stickers with a slogan was made to attach to the left and right doors of cars. An illustration of a lantern was included on the side of the sticker. A total of 50 cars per day patrol the neighborhoods right as school is let out for the day.

This volunteer self-defense group consisting of citizens 60 years of age and older was formed to protect women and children from the suspicious persons who have been seen more and more in Soma as of late. Beginning on March 1, the group will be patrolling their assigned routes from 3:00 p.m. to 7:00 p.m. in their own cars, with backup support from the Soma police department.

Today, the group called the Soma Neighborhood Watch Council, consists of volunteers from the city, administrative district associations, the fire department, the police department and crime prevention association began implementing the program.

All citizens participating in the program are volunteers. Because this act of goodwill is unpaid and carried out for the safety of the citizens, we will pay their gasoline costs and a fee for the use of their vehicles. We will also provide vests in place of uniforms.

Because we are requesting volunteers for this neighborhood watch program, we will need 100 people to register to cover the one shift every two days. This is just one part of community development achieved by the city working together with its citizens, and we believe it will help strengthen the bonds between citizens of different

Neighborhood watch patrol mobilization ceremony (March 1, 2016)

229

ages if it is carried out effectively. I must also make the rounds asking for volunteers.

Decontamination crews in the range of approximately 30,000 to 40,000 individuals have gathered in Fukushima from all across Japan. Decontamination is at its peak in Iitate Village, which was in the path of SPEEDI, and towns and villages where the nuclear power plant is located. Vendors in the City of Soma formed a decontamination union which has nearly completed decontamination tasks by workers in the city, doing away with fears of radiation, however, decontaminating areas with high dosage rates are likely to face a massive task. Because the workers come from all across the country, there seem to be a significant number of problem people, even though most are fine. One worker lodging in Nihonmatsu who moved to Osaka was arrested for murder last year, shocking the residents of the towns where workers are housed.

In Soma as well, an incident was reported in the newspaper that someone tried to drag a high school girl into a car, and made all parents seriously worried. When other rumors are included, we must consider that women are in considerable danger now. Although many municipalities now face this problem, the sense of unease grows each day among the residents of Soma when they see the large-scale housing for 300 to 500 of decontamination workers is built in our city.

At the end of last month, a citizen sent a letter stating their desire to start a neighborhood watch program, and requesting assistance from city hall. When meeting the person and listening to their story, I thought that the city and its citizens needed

Rebuilding Period — Chapter 5

to take action immediately before discussing the extent of decontamination work. Because we could not wait to begin until April of the following year, we called on the above group at the very beginning of February, and the council began operations today after obtaining their agreement. We must deal with this crisis using the power of the citizens who overcame the earthquake and tsunami.

(8) Isobe Seafood Processing Facilities (Completed February 18, 2016)

Although three villages in the Isobe area suffered severe damages in the tsunami, the fishing industry was rebuilt on the strong hope of the locals. A processing plant for catches of fish has finally been completed.

Through the Soma Futaba Fishermen's Union, this facility will be lent to the processing union formed by local processing vendors free of charge as a way to revitalize the fishing industry.

Here the vendors process local specialties such as sand eels, whitebait, whelk, and Sakhalin surf clams.

Isobe Seafood Processing Facilities

Seafood processing equipment

Radiation measurement

Direct sales of Sakhalin surf clams
(June 5, 2016)

Rebuilding Period

Chapter 5

Mayor's e-mail newsletter - April 19, 2016 Issue

essay

(9) Bringing the best wishes of the people in the food truck

Five days ago, on April 14, the Kumamoto earthquake occurred at night, with a magnitude of 6.5 at the epicenter in Kumamoto. This shocking news brought back the memories of the Great East Japan Earthquake five years ago. As per Soma's rules regarding earthquakes in other regions, we searched our records to find municipalities that had helped us in our own disaster five years ago. We found that the cities of Tamana and Yamato sent us relief supplies right after the disaster occurred, so we sent bottled water to both cities on the night of the 14th. Because Kyushu is so far from us we had to rely on a shipping company, however, we let the citizens know of our need to repay the debt in a newspaper article, informing them that we would be sending bottled water from our emergency supplies storehouse.

Incidentally, 28 hours after the first 6.5 magnitude earthquake, on the dawn of the 16th, an even larger quake at magnitude 7.3 hit the Kumamoto area. One major difference from the Great East Japan Earthquake was that both tremors occurred at night, and that the medium-sized aftershocks intermittently shook residents at a frequency of a number of times an hour. Although the scale of damage and death toll is incomparable to that of the Great East Japan Earthquake, residents were certainly gripped with great fear over the strong intermittent nighttime quakes at a seismic intensity of five and six. This brought back terrible memories of the merciless aftershocks of the quake five years ago.

On Saturday the 16th, the Disaster Countermeasures Team at City Hall called the Kumamoto Earthquake Countermeasures Council including members of the Diet, and began comparing on-site information collected ahead of time along with earthquake information from municipalities even minimally connected to Soma. There are relevant 12 municipalities in applicable areas close to an active fault

233

with a seismic intensity of five or higher. There are 10 relevant municipalities that include groups where I as the mayor of Soma am a member, such as the Association of Chiefs for Considering Social Capital Improvement and the Community Protection Association. There are 12 municipalities that we must support, including Kikuchi, where the Soma invited Hakuzo Medical Corporation sister plant is located, as well as Tamana which provided assistance to Soma during our time of need.

The current stockpiles at the disaster prevention storehouse built in preparation in 2013 for the next earthquake in Soma contain 27,000 two-liter bottles of water and 7,000 blankets. Although we purchase additional water each year in case the situation at the nuclear power plant worsens, the blankets are those donated by other municipalities during the earthquake. Soma will not suffer even if 10 percent of our stock is sent to Kyushu and when considering the fact that the number of municipalities that provided aid far exceeded those that Soma had a relationship with, we must think of this assistance as an initial step in a similar process. Although it was not possible to ascertain the details of the damages in all 12 relevant municipalities, we sent blankets and bottled water via shipping companies on the 16th, figuring that the supplies could be shared if they were not needed. We also called upon Soma citizens to

Sending relief supplies to Tamana and Yamato
(April 15, 2016)

Rebuilding Period Chapter 5

Food truck
Three staff drivers
(April 20, 2016)

donate to the victims in an extra edition of the city newsletter while reporting the second shipment of relief supplies.

However, the damages later kept spreading, and we learned in a broadcast on the 18th that they did not have enough water and food. Because many residents in Kumamoto were afraid to spend the night in their own homes, they flocked to evacuation shelters which were overwhelmed, with people spilling out onto the streets where they waited an hour in line to receive rice balls from the Self-Defense Forces. In addition to delivery delays due to damaged roads, the large scale of the disaster made it difficult to sort and transport relief supplies.

Certainly, Soma could provide only a tiny fraction of the required assistance, however, it was our wish to be as efficient as possible in aiding the victims, so we realized that a mid to long-term plan was necessary when thinking of our own long road to recovery. In this regard, we discussed matters at a second aid meeting on the 18th, proposing that we lend the food truck provided by the Shidax Corporation five years ago along with all 12 large gas furnace equipped cooking pots as part of an effective mid to long-term plan.

I then called Osamu Maekawa, a member of the prefectural assembly I knew from Kikuchi City, and asked whether or not it would be a good idea to send the food truck and large cooking pots. Mr. Maekawa was surprised when hearing this suggestion, saying that they would be grateful to receive the food truck right away, and that

235

he would ask the leaders of affected municipalities and have them contact the mayor of Soma as the large cooking pots should be useful for a long-term stay at the evacuation shelters.

Several hours later a fax arrived from the mayor of Takamori in Kumamoto, requesting to borrow the food truck and large cooking pots. We decided to keep two of the 12 large cooking pots in Soma in case of emergency, sending the remaining 10 to Takamori, requesting that the Kumamoto prefectural assembly make effective use of them across a wide area.

Mr. Maekawa apologized for not being able to retrieve them by car, but there wasn't a single person who asked us to pick up supplies when we suffered from the earthquake. Despite the nationwide shortage of gasoline during that disaster, volunteers struggled to deliver supplies to Soma. So of course we filled the food truck with bottled water and drove to Kumamoto.

When recruiting city hall staff, Information Policy Division Director Endo and Mr. Mori, the mayor's driver, and Mr. Sakamoto, a driver for the assembly, all who had a driver's license for large vehicles offered to help.

Although I felt bad about it, we asked the three of them to help for a full day to take the donation box containing the preliminary donations and deliver it to Tamana and Yamato along with the wishes of the citizens of Soma in the food truck.

Daisei Kusamura, mayor of Takamori
(2nd from the right)

Rebuilding Period **Chapter 5**

Mayor's e-mail newsletter - June 30, 2016 Issue

essay

(10) News from a far-off town

Last month I received news from Mrs. Kobayashi in Izumi city in Osaka.

As I read the neatly-written penmanship in ballpoint pen on stationery I became overwhelmed with emotion and grief, and immediately wrote a letter of thanks and a request to Hiromichi Tsuji, the mayor of Izumi, to offer up incense.

In the letter from mayor Tsuji which arrived after several days, he mentioned that he immediately visited the Kobayashi household only to find that no one was home. He left a business card and expressed thanks on behalf of the mayor of Soma when received a phone call from Mrs. Kobayashi.

I was very glad to find that Mr. Tsuji is a mayor who understands how we feel.

This reaffirmed that we have survived these past five years thanks to the support of many people.

With kind persons such as this and a lighthearted mayor, I'm sure that Izumi is a wonderful city.

I hope to visit Izumi someday. Also, the opportunity to connect with the community will help us respond in kind to Mr. X.

With the permission of Mrs. Kobayashi, I'd like to share with you the letter from her and my response.

237

From Mrs. Kobayashi

The light breezes of summer are finally here.
I'd like to take this opportunity to thank you for taking the trouble to send the Great East Japan Earthquake Interim Report along with the five-year record of Soma.
I sincerely appreciate receiving the latest interim report every time it becomes available.
When seeing the unbelievable footage of that day on TV, we wondered how you would fare in the future. I remember that at that moment, my mind started racing, having no idea how things would play out.
When you showed us the five-year record of Soma City, which amazingly rebuilt after the horrendous events of March 11, I realized just how much unrecognized effort went into rebuilding and I could not stop crying.
I spoke of these events to my deceased son, thinking of how happy he would be.

Last year, my son suddenly passed away due to a heart attack.
He was only 44 years old and in the prime of his life.

Since he participated for a month in after-school care for children as a volunteer college student during the Great Hanshin Earthquake, he was particularly worried about the children.
I remember him wanting to see for himself and packing the car with character sweets that he thought the children would like.
I don't think he has done something big, but I appreciate you very much for writing my son's name.
Later on, he was able to visit through the Izumi City Social Welfare Council.
I'm sure there will be more reports in the future, and I do not want to

Rebuilding Period — Chapter 5

take up your time for my son, so I am writing this letter.

Although my son's life was too short in this day and age, I want to express my deep thanks for allowing him to be a part of things even in such a minor way.

It is my sincere wish that the City of Soma and its residents continue to develop and live a healthy life.

Best regards,

May 16, 2016
XX Kobayashi (deceased)
XX Kobayashi (mother)

Issues of the interim report published so far

My reply to Mrs. Kobayashi

I hope this finds you well. Thank you so much for your kind letter.
I would like to express my sincere condolences on the passing of your son, and I hope that he has found peace.
The citizens of Soma are working together toward reconstruction and I believe this is thanks to the support provided by people such as your son directly after the earthquake.
I would like to continue sending the interim report to your son.
I look forward to your continued support in rebuilding Soma from far away.
Yours sincerely,

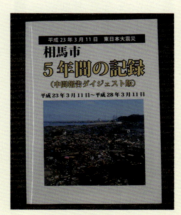

Five-Year Record
(Digest of the interim report) published

Rebuilding Period — Chapter 5

column

(11) Five years of life at Idobata Nagaya and strong-willed young doctors

The Idobata Nagaya built for elderly residents who were left alone due to the disaster was a total of five buildings and 58 households including Babano Nagaya completed in May 2012, and Hosoda Higashi Nagaya completed in December 2013, and resulting in 50 households with a total of 60 people moving in over a period of five years. Because the residents are elderly, a total of 19 residents left out of 13 households, including six persons who passed away, and the rest either going to live with family or moving to a care facility. As of July 2017, currently 44 persons in 37 households live in the row houses. Eventually we will be able to accept the general public in addition to persons affected by the disaster, as it sees many citizens have been expressing interest in the dwellings.

Although this project was originally conceived of mainly to prevent solitary deaths among low-income, single-person elderly households (see graph 1, however, there is no income restriction), five years of operation began to hint at problems with an advanced aging population in the near future such as will occur in Japan. Some residents who were healthy when they moved in five years ago have become weak or ill, highlighting cases that require care. However, thanks to the strong will to watch over and help one another, seniors from care level 1 to 3 were able to live independently in the row houses with the support from 3 caregivers.

Graph 2 shows current residents and the latest care level

Dr. Tomohiro Morita chatting with a resident

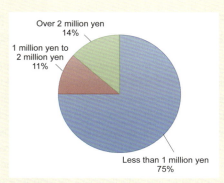

Graph 1: Status of resident income
60 residents up to the current time
(including those who have left)

of residents who left. Those who need care each have a care manager and primary physician, so it was not possible to establish a medical and care plan for overall management. With this in mind, Dr. Tomohiro Morita of Soma Central Hospital visited once a month for one-on-one health consultations with each resident, as well as taking a photograph with each person. Although I personally considered this one of the most serious areas affected by the disaster, and a project that I wondered on how far it could be taken as a public service, Dr. Morita not only kept records, but served a significant role in encouraging and putting at ease each and every resident.

Directly after the disaster, when he was a senior student at the Tokyo University Institute Of Medical Science, he came to provide medical assistance in Soma along with professor Masahiro Kami. He was most likely thinking of medical treatment in the disaster area. Later, after completing his initial training, eventually began living in Soma with his wife Mariko Morita, a fellow classmate who also came as a volunteer (current anesthesiologist at Minamisoma City Hospital), and is engaged in work as a local physician and

Rebuilding Period Chapter 5

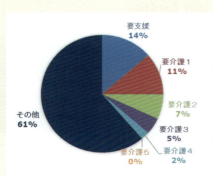

Graph 2: Status of residents who require care
60 residents up to the current time
(including those who have left)

raising children in the rich natural environment of Soma. I expect him to turn records of life at the row houses into a thesis to communicate the details to the world as a model case for an aging society. However, the happiest thing for me was seeing a young, strong-willed husband and wife team of doctors living and working in the disaster area.

The five row house buildings feature universal design with common spaces and disabled-accessible toilets, and have been designated as evacuation shelters as of April 2015 (able to accept a total of 99 people) on the permission of residents. Bedding is stored above the ceiling for such an occasion.

(12) Haragama goods handling facility/seawater purification facility (Completed September 18, 2016)

Seawater purification facility
Seawater intake, supply, and purification (filtration)

Haragama goods handling facility
Auction hall, tanks of live fish, radiation testing room, etc.

Fish Festival
The Fish Festival was held at the Haragama goods handling facility and attracted a lively crowd of nearly 8,000 people from in and outside the city. (October 1, 2016)

Soma-Haragama Wholesale Market damaged by the tsunami
(March 31, 2011)

Haragama goods handling facility - Winner of the Zenken Award
(June 27, 2017)

Rebuilding Period — Chapter 5

(13) New main building at Soma City Hall (Completed October 5, 2016)

Stockpiles are stored on the 4th floor

Soma City Hall
(Completion ceremony on October 5, 2016)

The move to the new main building was completed in
three days thanks to the efforts of all city hall staff.
(October 7 to October 9, 2016)

New main building opening ceremony
(October 11, 2016)

First floor community hall   Plants and trees help visitors relax
concert   at the rest space
(June 16, 2017)   (First floor community hall)

Rebuilding Period — Chapter 5

(14) Tohoku-Chuo Expressway - Abukuma Higashi Road open for traffic (March 26, 2017)

Tohoku-Chuo Expressway - Abukuma Higashi Road opening ceremony
The Tohoku-Chuo Expressway (Soma Fukushima Road) Abukuma Higashi Road opening ceremony was held on March 26 at the Higashi Tamano area Soma Tamano Interchange.

Mayor's e-mail newsletter - March 28, 2017 Issue

(15) My grandfather and a bicycle laden with vegetables

My 88-year-old mother is the second daughter of a farming family in the Kitaiibuchi area of Soma.

Ever since she married into the Tachiya family who ran a soy sauce and miso brewery on the coastline of Soma in 1949, she lived in a home only 100 meters from the ocean, but 10 years ago she moved to the Midorigaoka Complex in a hilly area to enjoy her retirement. Right after the earthquake, my father was worried about a tsunami so he wanted to go see the house of main branch of the family, but turned back when he got caught in the traffic jams of people trying to evacuate, and thankfully escaped the tsunami by turning back.

The older my mother becomes, the more nostalgic thoughts she has of farming as a child. In the small 33 square meter garden of her retirement home, she plants a few vegetables and enjoys working in the garden. As a farmer's daughter, my mother's memories bring her back to her girlhood.

1942. My maternal grandfather married off his eldest daughter in the former Hobaramachi (current Hobara area of Date City) area. Because there were no means of public transportation then, passing over the Abukuma mountainous area to get married was likely a difficult ordeal. But because my grandfather adored his daughter, every season he would pile vegetables on his bicycle and deliver them to her home in Hobaramachi. At that time, the Nakamura Highway (Currently, the National Route 115, designated as a class 2 national route in 1963) was a winding road with narrow turns and so little traffic that cars sometimes fell to the valley floor. Although such a situation is unthinkable now, my grandfather must have been looking forward to seeing his daughter's smiling face to brave such a road. He pushed his bicycle for an entire day, stayed at his daughter's home for several days, then made the trip back to Soma over the Abukuma mountains.

Rebuilding Period

Chapter 5

Tohoku-Chuo Expressway - Abukuma
Higashi Road open for traffic
(March 26, 2017)

1967. During the summer of my first year in high school, when I was 16 years old, I left Sendai on a bicycle, riding from Hobaramachi to National Route 115 and passed over the Abukuma mountains. Although some parts of National Route 115 were paved at that time, most of the uphill sections from Ryozenmachi Kaketa were gravel roads.

Because it was a hot day in August, I remember being very thirsty so I stopped by Ishida Elementary School for a drink of water where a day shift teacher also gave me some chilled cucumber and miso for a snack. Washing my dusty face with cool water and munching the juicy cucumber along with the salty taste of the reddish brown miso made me feel like I had been brought back to life. Even now, 50 years later, I still bow my head in thanks every time I pass by Ishida Elementary School.

But climbing the hill afterward was still difficult. My bike had drop handlebars and a transmission, something completely new at that time. On both sides of the rear wheel I had packed a tent and other items, but riding on pavement was still smooth and comfortable. Because National Route 4 from Sendai to Datemachi and the area between Date and Hobara were completely paved I was able to easily climb the hills in low gear, but I got stuck in the gravel roads in the Abukuma mountains, making it difficult to ride. I had no choice but to get off and push my bike, and the summit of Ryozen seemed so far off.

The sun had completely set when I finally began my descent from Tamano, and because I couldn't ride fast enough due to the gravel road, my bike light was dim. A wheel became stuck in the gravel on one of the sharp turns and I fell, injuring my foot. Although the pain and feeling of loneliness made me want to cry, I encouraged myself, saying that "My grandfather made this same trip on his bicycle to Soma". I finally reached my parent's home in Haragama at 10:00 p.m. Upon seeing his son who was supposed to be taking a summer course at a high school in Sendai washing his feet in the soy sauce factory at night, my father was very angry.

Later when I entered Fukushima Medical University, the humid heat of the Fukushima basin was torture. The Haragama area of Soma on the far side of the Abukuma mountains was close to the ocean, with a cool sea breeze making summers comfortable. I thought that if we cut a V-shaped pass through the mountains that maybe we could feel the Haragama sea breeze even in the basin.

1995. My first well-prepared question as an elected member of the

Tohoku-Chuo Expressway - Abukuma Higashi Road

Rebuilding Period

Chapter 5

prefectural assembly in the June meeting was to ask whether or not we could straighten the sharp curves of Route 115 to make an arterial high-standard highway. Unlike when I was in high school, the road was now completely paved, and because this was during the bubble economy, many people drove fancy cars, and there was still plenty of gasoline. However, despite being improved, the sharp curves were still difficult for traffic, particularly for ambulances where centrifugal force would cause patient's body to be tilted for the entire ride, and the intravenous bag would be on its side.

The Haragama coast where I would play as a child was already a concrete quay wall as part of the Soma Port Wharf No. 1. However, cargo shift on the curves in Soma Port and container trucks being unable to pass by one another on curved sections made this road useless for promoting industry in the northern areas of Fukushima.

No one was asking for something outrageous such as "hurry up and build the Tohoku-Chuo Expressway". However, in order to deal with emergency medical treatment and develop local industry in Soma and Fukushima at large, I wanted the prefectural government to seriously consider connecting the difficult areas along the route from Soma to the summit of the Abukuma mountains via an arterial high-standard highway at the very least. That was the gist of my question, and I waited two years for an answer. It seems that my ideas had gotten through at least somewhat, as inspection fees for creating the Abukuma Higashi Road on the ascending stretch of Route 115 to the summit of the Soma mountains were included in the budget.

Twenty years later.

Although the Great East Japan Earthquake was the greatest difficulty of my life, which has not yet ended, it also changed me and brought me great consolation. The opening ceremony on March 26 of the Abukuma Higashi Road as a reconstruction support road brought great happiness that years of prayer have been fulfilled.

251

According to Minister of Land, Infrastructure and Transport Ishii, the sea breezes of Haragama will reach the rest of Fukushima by 2020. I was asked to give a speech, and abashedly recounted a personal story about my grandfather's feelings for his daughter 75 years ago. I pictured my grandfather and grandmother's smiling faces in my mind, and I suddenly thought I might cry, but I thought of those who had perished in the earthquake and I gripped the microphone tightly.

But the whole experience was like a dream.

Rebuilding Period

Chapter 5

Mayor's e-mail newsletter - March 13, 2017 Issue

essay

(16) Flowers Will Bloom (City Hall community gallery)

On March 10, the day before the sixth memorial service for the victims of the earthquake and tsunami, a large canvas of Route 150 was hung on the wall of the citizen's hall at city hall.
Although it was drawn 20 years ago, it depicts the beautiful water's edge on the Osu coastline of that time, stretching from Matsukawa to Isobe, with an innocent young girl walking toward the viewer.
Is she walking toward us? Or is she walking toward the future? Standing before the piece, I felt weak in the knees.

If you listen carefully to the rebuilding song "Flowers Will Bloom," you will realize that it is a litany for the future of the disaster area being recited by a young woman lost in the disaster.

Six years ago today.
Twenty-eight-year-old Keiko who was worried about the tsunami perished while on her way to her home in the Isobe Ohama area six kilometers away from her office in the offshore area of town. She was on her way to help her grandmother, who was nearly 100 years old, evacuate.
She was the head of a cram school and a member of the political school I presided over once a month. She was a very intelligent

253

woman with interests in educational policies and welfare, always sitting in the very front row of my lectures, asking pointed questions and making clear statements. I thought it would be perfect for her to start off from working as a city councilor.

During the election in the year following the earthquake, three young students at my political school ran as candidates and were elected for the municipal assembly. Although it was not easy running the political school during the six years after the disaster, every time I pass by the Isobe Ohama area I think of that woman, how she would now likely be married with children, and polishing her political skills if she had survived.

The lyrics to Flowers Will Bloom gives the illusion that Keiko is singing to us from some far away land.

The piece of art mentioned at the introduction truly seems like a young Keiko is walking toward us from the lapping waves on the shore.

Last October 5th we celebrated the completion ceremony of the new main building after waiting so long in the old main building of city hall with many cracks caused by the earthquake. The exterior features a Japanese-style design that has worked its way into the grammar of Soma earthquake architecture. Because it is near the castle in Soma, we kept the building to a three-storied structure, making sure it was lower than the castle keep out of respect for the history of the Soma Nakamura clan.

One of my only specifications in the design was a six-meter hallway in preparation for earthquakes, with staffers and assembly staff considering the design of the office space. However, we used a creamy white color on the inner and outer walls, and a nearly black dark brown on the pillars in order to match the walls of the civic hall and other post-disaster reconstruction buildings.

Incidentally, we discovered upon moving that the white walls of the six-meter hallway had a rather solemn look, and that the walls were

Rebuilding Period

Chapter 5

much larger than we had imagined, something that was not obvious from the floor plan.

We considered adding ornamental plants to create a more homey atmosphere. We requested a total of over 50 ornamental plants to groups who approached us about donating an inaugural memento, but as the went by, we were overwhelmed as we felt that hallway is oppressive.

To solve this issue, we thought of the community gallery.

Decorating the featureless walls with pictures created by citizens would surely stimulate the senses of both staff and visitors alike. We thought that there was no better place to showcase the artwork of our citizens than on a wall whose presence we could not fully understand from design drawings alone.

In the first place, there wasn't enough in stock to mount pictures, and there was no budget to purchase them even though we wanted to decorate the walls.

When thinking of showcasing community artwork on the wide white walls of the new main building, we thought that maybe it does not have to be a picture drawn by a professional artist. We thought it would be wise to rely on the confidence of our citizens.

We approached some painting clubs and art instructors in the city and revealed this idea to them at the end of November. They all agreed heartily with our plan. We then had the school superintended and other staff at city hall join to form the City Hall Gallery Review Committee. We established guidelines on how to select pieces and how long they would be hung for, and received over 50 entries when including a notice in the January city newsletter that we

Community gallery (3rd floor)

would be accepting entries via photos. Nearly all of the photos were selected by the committee. A picture rail was also being installed for hanging pieces of art. We decided on the location to hang each piece at the committee meeting on March 9th, and were able to put them on display on March 11, the sixth anniversary of the earthquake and tsunami.

The readers of this trifling email newsletter visited City Hall lending us their artwork, including the large piece mentioned at the beginning, so we hope you'll come to view them. Most of the pieces will be shown for six months, and we look forward to receiving entries from many more of our citizens.

Because many citizens requested the use of the community hall on the first floor as a location for events, it is 990 square meters in size. Since it is deserted on days without events, the ornamental plants are wheeled into the room to make a small forest with tables and chairs for a nice mini park where you can rest even if you don't have business at city hall. Because we wanted to provide refreshments for those who come to city hall, there is an automatic coffee and tea machine. Although drinks are free, it is difficult to keep the space stocked with cream and sugar, so please feel free to bring your own.

Rebuilding Period — Chapter 5

(17) New community pool (Completed March 22, 2017)

Nickname: Red Brick Pool

Community pool
▽General pool (25 m, 8 courses, 1.2 m deep)
▽Kids pool (3.5 m x 10.5 m, 0.5 to 0.6 m deep)
*Glass roof that can be opened and closed

Community pool completion ceremony
(March 22, 2017)

(18) Seibu Children's Community Center (Completed April 5, 2017)

With a play room, childrearing salon, and after school kids club, this facility functions as a place for locals of all ages to mingle while raising their children

Seibu Children's Community Center Festival
Local kids and the elderly enjoy spending time together
(May 27, 2017)

Chapter 6 Fighting Radiation

(1) Preparing for worsening conditions at the nuclear power plant

Our initial thinking and action plan to deal with the accident at the nuclear power plant was introduced in the Acute Period in chapter 2, however it was necessary to formulate an action plan at the emergency headquarters if an evacuation order was issued by the Japanese government. The conveyance of the patients as well as the destination and the transportation has became a subject of challenge, especially conveyance for bedridden elderly, hospitalized patients and the patients requiring care level of three or above.

I called Chairman Torao Tokuda of Tokushukai to request that they accept these elderly people during the initial stages of requesting aid, receiving his approval for accepting up to 700 people at Tohoku Kanto area hospitals with available beds.

Of course we should also consider favorable conditions beyond Tokushukai Hospital in light of subsequent developments, however, the main priority of the emergency headquarters was to secure hospital beds in a worst case scenario. Because Chairman Tokuda was not well enough to speak to directly we used his secretary as an intermediary during negotiations, so I will always be grateful for helping us prepare for the worst case scenario.

The real challenge, however, was the transportation.

We negotiated with the permanent responsible person in Soma on a request to the Self-Defense Forces working in cooperation with medical care staff handling elderly patients and hospitals and elderly care facilities. One possible problem was the 46 bedridden people in their own homes who required care.

The emergency headquarters purchased 46 stretchers in case of emergency, storing them near the beds of patients in their homes or various fire stations. In addition to making preparations for the local fire departments to transport patients to the vehicles of the Self-Defense Forces, we were able to concentrate on emergency countermeasures and stay in Soma without evacuating for the time being.

Fighting Radiation

(2) Tap water countermeasures

To prevent internal radiation exposure, we do not eat any foods or drink anything containing radioactive substances.

On the other hand, it suffered us to decide to which extent we should pursue safety standard. Japan and the world have avoided primary goods from Fukushima, creating a significant rift between the responsibility of the shippers and the peace of mind of consumers. At that time even residents of Soma fed their family, children in particular, food produced in other prefectures, and it was common sense to avoid Fukushima produce at all costs.

The most worrisome thing at the beginning of the disaster was water. The water source for 70% of households in Soma comes from the Mano Dam situated in Iitate Village, which is purified, processed, and filtered at the Soma Regional Water Utility situated in the northern Ono area of Soma (Not only does this utility supply 70% of all household water in Soma, but also the Kashima area of neighboring Minamisoma and nearly all areas of Shinchi Town, resulting in a single partnership for all three cities). Because the remaining 30% of households receive purified water from underground water of the Utagawa water system (the high yearly speed of 50 to 100 meters means that surface pollution in high dosage areas is not immediately worrisome), residents were not worried. However, because of rainwater from Iitate Village, which was completely evacuated, ran directly into the dam, we paid particular attention to this situation.

Directly after the disaster we carried out testing of water samples from the source outlet on successive days and thankfully no cesium was detected even when testing at a rate of 10 becquerels per liter.

Bottled water for use as relief supplies

We lived with having the constant fear of cesium to be detected in our water supply. As it would be necessary to immediately cut off the water supply if any was detected, we urgently began to stockpile bottled water for distribution as drinking water.

At that point, local leaders from around Japan responded to our calls for aid on the Internet, sending many bottles of water to Soma, with thankfully resulted in sufficient stocks of water.

Testing for water contamination was not limited to the water source only, but has revealed no radioactive substances to date, even when rigorous testing was conducted on water being distributed in the pipes as well.

(3) Radiation dosage measurement and information disclosure

On March 13 when People from Minamisoma Odaka area asked evacuation shelters in Soma for assistance due to worsening conditions at the nuclear power plant, Soma General Hospital used the one dosimeter they had in their possession to begin taking measurements of radiation doses.

On March 13, dosages were measured at 3.25 microsieverts per hour (When adding the indoor dampening effect in a yearly conversion, the yearly dosage rate should not exceed 20 millisieverts.), and on March 14, the dosage was measured at 1.25 microsieverts per hour. Measurements never exceeded two microsieverts per hour thereafter, yet, one dosimeter was placed from March 14th onward to measure radiation levels all around the city, carrying out an independent study in Soma.

At the crisis response meeting on March 17, I ordered that all radiation measurements taken within Soma be posted on the reopened city website. The Japanese government announced data through the Ministry of the Environment and the Ministry of Education, Culture, Sports, Science and Technology, however, it was necessary to show citizens that we as a city were conducting our own independent investigation to confirm safety.

On March 30 FM radio station "Soma Saigai FM" opened at city hall began announcing air dose rates at each location within the city. Makoto Endo, who worked as a radio personality provided commentary on basic knowledge behind the differences between radiation and radioactive rays, however, residents did not seem to understand.

But myself and the directors of Soma General Hospital engaged in medical

Fighting Radiation 6

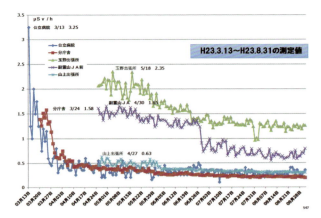

treatment while keeping radiation in mind were able to make rational decisions based on measured radiation doses. However, because city hall staff and general public had virtually no knowledge of radiation, they accepted groundless rumors flying about on the Internet as truth, which I believe led to a stronger feelings of worry in regard to policies from the Japanese government and those of the city.

Radiation measurement was carried out at dozens of locations on successive days across the city, however the results did not show heightened radiation due to worsening conditions at the nuclear power plant, allowing us to avoid evacuating Soma.

The graph shows changes in radiation in front of the main Soma city hall building. Thankfully the downward sloping graph did not rise. At heart, I was very nervous. We didn't have the luxury of wondering who had done something wrong. The only thing we thought of was what we would do in case measured dosages worsened.

(4) Vagueness of the Japanese government's expressions and their effects

To begin with, the expressions of the Japanese government were as difficult to understand as a cryptic Zen dialog.

"At the current stage, radiation is not at a level that poses immediate danger to health."

Upon hearing this expression, I believe many citizens were worried. At that time many foreign residents left Japan and the U.S. military moved 80 kilometers away from the nuclear power plant.

Although considerable unease spread among citizens, I believe the extra edition of my email magazine "Castle under siege (Rojo)" on March 24 helped people to keep calm and follow the city guidelines.

Many citizens who evacuated outside the city returned. At the crisis response meeting, we agreed to thank those who returned when we needed people for reconstruction efforts.

Actually, the hot water heater on the fifth floor of the Soma Central Hospital which I run had fallen over during the earthquake, and without a heat or hot water supply, medical treatment proved difficult. The person who was supposed to repair the boiler had evacuated, leaving it as it was, but after the extra edition of the newsletter, many people returned and it was repaired.

We were truly thankful for those who returned and helped add their skills to our reconstruction efforts.

Fighting Radiation

Chapter 6

(5) Limits of city handling

In order to formulate rational radiation measurements for the citizens, the main rule of "Correctly Fear and Wisely Avoid Radiation" was formulated to help with the difficult task of educating citizens and formulating radiation countermeasures in the initial stages of the disaster and during emergencies.

I believe that many citizens had the mindset that they should listen to instructions for the time being because there was no evacuation order.

For my part, I trusted that the Fukushima Office of Radiation Countermeasures would provide an explanation for area residents while indicating a direction to take action. Because the air dose rate was relatively high for the Tamano area bordering Iitate Village, I asked the prefectural government to provide an explanation for residents during the initial stage, however, they were unable to provide a satisfactory solution as Futaba county was affected by the disaster.

(6) Meeting professor Masahiro Kami

The following occurred right after the earthquake. On March 22 when Soma dispatched a truck to Tokyo to procure medicine because shipping companies were not coming into the city, a certain hospital within Minamisoma had already decided to evacuate. However, because it was impossible to transport patients on oxygen in the Self-Defense Forces vehicles, so the hospital director consulted with us to see if there was any way to arrange for helicopter transport.

When I told this to Deputy Chief Cabinet Secretary Sengoku, he suggested me to contact Tokyo University Institute Of Medical Science professor Masahiro Kami who has a wide range of contacts, and gave me the professor's mobile phone number.

While speaking to professor Kami on the phone, I could tell that he was a fearless/ brave person. Thanks to his instructions, I was able to request helicopter transportation for patients on constant a oxygen supply from Major General Norihiko Yamada, a medical technician in the Ministry of Defense.

Professor Kami later arranged for support in evacuating patients in Minamisoma and arranged for doctors at hospitals that were having trouble with dialysis due to the university pulling doctors out. He is an

265

Masahiro Kami

extremely skilled person, and more of a practitioner than a scientist.

At the beginning of April, along with doctors Masaharu Tsubokura and Yuko Matsumura, I was able to meet professor Kami at city hall. Although I had spoken to him on the phone many times previously and felt like we knew each other already, I was amazed to see that he was very young at only 43 years old.

As a specialist in hematology and with a wide range of knowledge in radiation, each and every piece of his advice was appropriate. In order to establish more objective policies on handling radiation in the city, on April 21, 2011, professor Masahiro Kami was delegated as radiation countermeasures advisor for the city of Soma. For the past six years, professor Kami and the previously mentioned professor Kenji Shibuya as well as specialists in various fields such as physicist and professor emeritus Ryugo Hayano and others from The Tokyo University School of Science have provided advice in helping Soma formulate radiation countermeasures policies.

(7) Information sessions in local areas on radiation and its health effects (from May 15, 2011)

On May 15, information sessions were held at 12 different meeting places in the city, beginning with the Kuroki meeting place, where we began educating citizens so they could gain accurate knowledge on radiation.

Instructors included professor Kami, Dr. Tsubokura and Dr. Matsumura who continued touring meeting places in the city until June 27.

Despite being incredibly busy with earthquake countermeasures, city hall staff did a terrific job arranging and promoting the information sessions. Of

Fighting Radiation

Chapter 6

course it is difficult to gain a proper understanding of radiation from just one or two information sessions, however, I believe it is beginning to permeate our local society through the help of teachers at our children's schools.

Area information session

Area	Location	Area	Location
Kuroki	Kuroki meeting place	Hatsuno	Hatsuno meeting place
Tamano	Tamano Junior High School	Otsubo	Otsubo meeting place
Nittaki	Nittaki Elementary School	Yamakami	Yamakami Elementary School
Iitoyo	Iitoyo Elementary School	Nakamura Seibu Nakamura Chubu	Hamanasu-kan
Nakamura Tobu	Tobu Community Center	Yawata	Yawata Elementary School
Isobe	Isobe Elementary School	Ono	Ono Elementary School

Explanation in sign language
Doctor Tsubokura
(June 6, 2011)

267

(8) Tamano Elementary and Junior High School schoolyard topsoil replacement (May 24 to 27, 2011)

Because there was a relatively high air dose rate measured in Iitate Village which borders the Tamano area, we began implementing countermeasures there as a focus area of the city.

First, we replaced the topsoil in the schoolyard at the Tamano Elementary and Junior High School as a way to reduce the air dose rate there.

As a result, the dosage at the Tamano Elementary School was reduced from 2.78 to 0.43 microsieverts per hour, and at the Tamano Junior High School it was reduced from 3.03 to 0.64 microsieverts per hour.

Tamano Elementary and Junior High School
Replacing the topsoil in the schoolyard
(May 24, 2011)

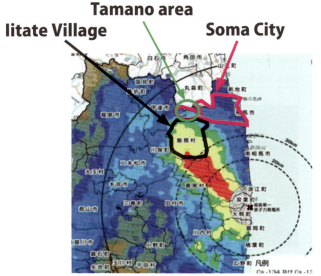

Areas with a high level of radiation according to SPEEDI

Fighting Radiation

(9) Tamano area residents' health examinations (May 28 and 29, 2011)

In addition to the area information sessions, we also provided health examinations to help alleviate Tamano area resident worries. A group of physicians including volunteers from the Soma County Medical Association along with professor Kami helped in this regard.

Because there were not enough doctors, I donned my white coat on May 29 to help. Compared with last year's results, there were no changes to the data including biochemical examinations, showing no significant effects due to radiation. However, we were unable to carry out examinations of the thyroid gland, resulting in relying on testing from the prefectural government.

For the most part, residents remained calm. However, because we understand that radiation is a delicate matter when it comes to children, we began preparations to move families with children to the temporary housing soon to be completed in the Ono area of the city if they desired to do so.

In such cases, we decided to transport children living in temporary housing to the Tamano Elementary and Junior High School by school bus. This was a necessary measure to maintain the Tamano Elementary and Junior High School and local community.

The author wearing his white lab coat

Tamano area health examinations

(10) Start of detailed investigation at all city schools and top soil replacement (from June 16, 2011)

We took children's exposure into serious consideration. At the emergency headquarters we established a policy to thoroughly investigate the hot spots in schools, which was a problem at that time.

We designated 50 locations as sites to investigate at each school, and measured radiation levels at 50 centimeters and one meter from the surface of the ground once a month. For these measurements we employed ISO9001 methods, which we captured in photos.

These photos are meant to provide an objective view of the results and as evidence that the investigation was carried out.

We also began topsoil replacement for all elementary and junior high schoolyards according to budgetary measures from the Ministry of the Environment. At the same time, concrete walls and road surfaces were decontaminated using high-pressure washers.

Measuring hot spots in schools

Decontamination using high-pressure washers

Fighting Radiation

(11) Distributing high-pressure washers and decontamination information session in the Tamano area (August 10, 2011)

Upon the request from four area administrators, high-pressure washers were distributed to 150 households in the Tamano area so that contaminants could be washed off the walls and roofs of homes in the area.

Because this was the first time we had experienced any kind of decontamination work due to the accident at the nuclear power plant, we held an information session on August 10 regarding points to keep in mind during decontamination procedures (wearing a mask, washing hands and face after finishing, replacing clothing, etc.).

Tamano area decontamination information session
(August 10, 2011)

Decontaminating homes using high-pressure washers
(August 11, 2011)

(12) Food contamination testing

Dealing with internal radiation exposure requires much patience. In particular, because the half life of cesium 137 is 30 years, it can remain solidified in the clay layer of soil even if cesium is not detected on the soil surface, meaning that we must remain vigilant for five to ten years.

However, keeping contaminated food out of the mouths of children was a particularly important issue at the beginning of the disaster. It was urgent that we equip the city hall and community centers with scintillation counters for food safety testing, but they were quite difficult to obtain.

We finally placed one in the first floor of city hall as soon as we received it on December 1, 2011, enabling citizens to carry out testing on their own. Later, we placed the devices in each community center as we obtained them, making it possible to check food safety among the daily lives of citizens. Sales of food by vendors such as supermarkets is based on the premise that all food is tested. On this point, the Ministry of Agriculture, Forestry and Fisheries and Ministry of Economy, Trade and Industry are providing vital support. The problem is when home-grown food that does not go through supermarkets is eaten by citizens after testing on the scintillation counters at community centers. In this case, one must rely on the common sense and mindfulness of citizens as they manage their crops.

In that case, the only method of testing for internal radiation exposure is using whole-body counting.

Fighting Radiation

(13) Radioiodine countermeasures

Because internal radiation exposure can cause serious damage to a person's body, this was an area that required particular attention from the administration.

Safety tests of radioiodine proved difficult, as this substance has an extremely short half life of only seven days. At the time, we considered various measures such as wearing a mask when outside and not drinking milk produced from cows grazing on possibly affected grass. Because masks were mainly intended to prevent inhalation of dust from asbestos and sludge caused by the debris from the earthquake, the biggest problem was radioiodine from food, milk in particular.

Although cases of thyroid cancer from Chernobyl are often raised, the risks of countries in the interior Eurasian continent such as Ukraine, Belarus, and Russia, are fundamentally different. As a maritime nation, the Japanese people take in kelp and kelp-derived soup stock on a daily basis, creating an environment where it is more difficult to accumulate radioiodine in the thyroid, as well as a quick prefectural and national government restriction on shipping milk, making the conditions completely different from Chernobyl. However, we believe it is our duty to carry out strict testing regardless, as well as thorough follow-up testing.

Incidentally, because the Fukushima government examination on the health of its citizens did not provide information to Soma, we faced the problem of not being able to follow-up on secondary testing of our residents. The reason for this was conflicting with protection of personal information. We faced serious difficulties in formulating appropriate measures to counter the risk of thyroid cancer, as managing the health of residents is the responsibility of municipalities.

Professor Shinichi Suzuki

For this reason, simply considering implementing an independent yearly testing system in Soma proved to be a major challenge. However, to help resolve this issue we consulted with thyroid surgeon Shinichi Suzuki of Fukushima Medical University, sharing secondary testing information with him, enabling us to avoid the double standard risk in independent testing in Soma.

A follow-up survey as conducted for the results of secondary testing on each and every person, and any points of concern were handled by a team of experts and hospital staff arranged by the city, along with further follow-up after secondary testing.

Professor Shinichi Suzuki consulted with us a number of times later on, proving to be a very reliable person who thoroughly understood the basic thinking of Soma. Afterward, we worked together with a common philosophy that required close examinations and calm handling.

Thyroid information session

Fighting Radiation

Chapter 6

(14) Systematic survey of radiation in all areas of the city and later progress (Starting June 18, 2011)

We laid out a grid at one kilometer intervals across the map of the city, establishing measurement points at 175 locations, first conducting a mesh survey of air dose rates at a height of one meter from the ground on June 18.

This was an important endeavor in order to track the course of air dose rates across the city, and the data for the past six years is quite interesting. Comparisons of each year showed that the air dose rate attenuates naturally as time passes. Although the test results over the passage of time can also be explained by the weathering effect, the investigation is still under way.

As a result, in June 2011 a dosage of 0.09 to 0.96 microsieverts per hour was measured in the city and on the coast, with a dose of 0.29 to 2.50 microsieverts in the mountains.

According to the Soma rules of "Correctly Fear and Wisely Avoid Radiation," we informed schools and conducted information sessions to warn people to keep out of relatively high radiation zones such as the mountains, etc.

The mesh survey was subdivided into 500 meter sections in 2012 for more detailed testing. The results of the survey indicate that the Tamano, Yamakami, and Yawata areas must be decontaminated due to comparatively high radiation doses, with the weathering effect (washed away by natural phenomena and dose reduced by settling underground) clearly visible in areas that do not need to be contaminated.

Two-person survey teams (mesh survey)

275

This enables us to conduct decontamination procedures with a focus on survey results, as well as formulate countermeasures that take the situation into account, mainly working on mini hot spots, etc. This also clearly shows that as of 2017 we have reached a point where we do not have to worry about the air dose rate in Soma at least during everyday living.

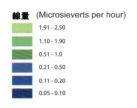

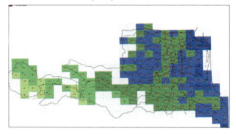

1 kilometer mesh survey results (2011)
Ground surface (soil)

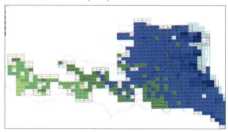

500 meter mesh survey results (2012)
Ground surface (soil)

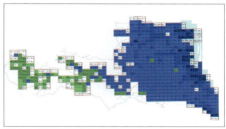

500 meter mesh survey results (2013)
Ground surface (soil)

Fighting Radiation — Chapter 6

500 meter mesh survey results (2014)
Ground surface (soil)

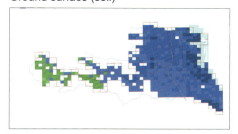

500 meter mesh survey results (2015)
Ground surface (soil)

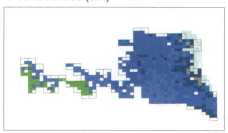

500 meter mesh survey results (2016)
Ground surface (soil)

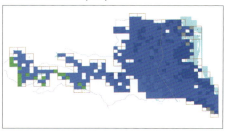

Measurements taken while checking survey points

277

(15) Start of education on radiation at schools (Beginning May 2011)

In addition to area information sessions, each year every grade in elementary and junior high receives two hours of education tailored to their developmental stages in order for the children to obtain correct knowledge on radiation.

This is intended to ensure that children act according to the principle of "Correctly Fear and Wisely Avoid Radiation." This knowledge serves as the foundation for beating radiation in Soma and continuing with reconstruction projects, and serves as a source of great expectation and confidence, and I would like to thank the school superintendent and principals of each school for their cooperation.

Radiation education at schools

Fighting Radiation

(16) External exposure survey and countermeasures for all schoolchildren in the city

I. 2011 (Year of the nuclear power plant accident)

Although the air dose rate survey is an extremely important part of radiation countermeasures in Soma, we asked questions such as, are children passing into danger zones and being exposed? What should we do if they are exposed? etc.

With this in mind, we formulated measures after measuring actual exposure among children. We measured external radiation exposure by having children wear film badge dosimeters for a period of three months.

This survey, conducted by obtaining the approval of families with schoolchildren in target areas in the city, was essential for formulating individual countermeasures for each and every schoolchild.

One challenge in this undertaking was setting an appropriate target level. During December 2011, there were no instructions for permissible exposure to children, particularly not from the government. The only indicators were "less than one millisievert per year of additional exposure at school" and "less than one millisievert of additional exposure per year for long term values."

When discussing what is the allowable annual rate of exposure for children in consideration of their health, regulating radiation exposure at school only is completely meaningless.

As an on-site mayor, we needed to establish standards and countermeasures that take into account the yearly exposure rate in all aspects of children's lives.

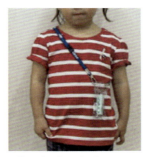

Film badge dosimeters

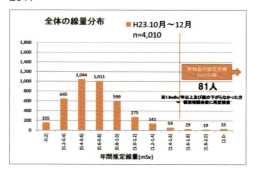

▽Survey months: October to December 2011
▽People surveyed: 4,010

The discussion resulted in determining that a total dosage of four millisieverts per year was appropriate if the additional exposure rate at school was one millisievert for the year.

From a preventative safety standpoint I determined that a rate of two millisieverts per year, which is half of the standard rate was appropriate, finally settling on an annual rate of 1.6 millisieverts taking into account an error rate of 20% during testing according to children's activities.

Out of 4,010 children tested in 2011, 81 showed a dosage of over 1.6 millisieverts. The maximum dosage of all children tested was 4.2 millisieverts.

The city then immediately began to formulate countermeasures. We began by first conducting thorough investigations into their living environments.

Although it was a delicate subject, we investigated the toilets, showers, hallways, and bedrooms of each house. We also conducted detailed surveys of their outside environments including garden trees and shrubs and hills behind their homes. What we learned from the results of these surveys was that one's exposure rate is higher when a sleeping on a futon close to a window, even in the same room, and that the dose is higher when there are trees in the hills behind one's home. We advised families to sleep on a futon closer to the hallway and to keep away from the trees in the hills behind their homes. Because cesium was stuck to the walls and roofs of homes as we suspected, contractors were hired to decontaminate these surfaces.

Fighting Radiation

Providing instruction at each home
Professor Shibuya and Dr. Matsumura

Measuring radiation indoors and
outdoors at each home

We also carried out health consultations for each individual family including cautions they needed to take in everyday life. It was necessary for them to recognize how serious exposure countermeasures based on detailed measurements of their home environment are. Nonetheless, we explained that even though the levels were not sufficient to be a health hazard, and that we would do our best to implement long-term safety measures, they needed to be smart in avoiding radiation whenever possible in their daily lives. Although we provided instructions on maintaining health in daily activities, the volunteer doctors of professor Kami's group from the Tokyo University Institute Of Medical Science was the main force behind this initiative.

We recommended that families with schoolchildren from the Tamano area, which was determined to have a comparatively higher level of radiation, move to temporary housing in the Onodai industrial park in the north, making the results of the testing particularly important.

II. 2012 survey results and countermeasures

A 2012 survey shows that of 4,135 people, 16 people exceeded 1.6 millisieverts. Also, the maximum value was 3.6 millisieverts per year.
In response, we further bolstered decontamination efforts in Soma. In 2012 the entire prefecture engaged in more active decontamination efforts.

Decontamination using high-pressure washers

2012

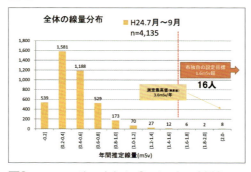

▽Survey months: July to September 2012
▽People surveyed: 4,135

Fighting Radiation

III. 2013 to 2015

Because there were no children who exceeded the initial target annual dose of 1.6 millisieverts in 2013, the city of Soma switched to the national policy of "less than one millisievert of exposure per year for long term values."

Because eight children exceeded the annual dose of one millisievert in 2013, we established measures for improving the air dose rates in the area. Although two schoolchildren exceeded the annual dose of one millisievert per year in 2014, we learned that instead of wearing the film badge dosimeter that it had been placed on the wall of the home entrance, and decided to wait for the results of next year's tests before taking further action.

The next year, in 2015, there was not a single child whose exposure rate exceeded one millisievert for the year.

2013

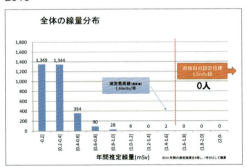

▽Survey months: May to July 2013
▽People surveyed: 3,173

2014

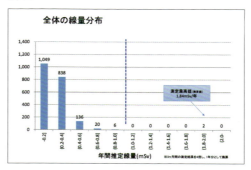

▽Survey months: September to November 2014
▽People surveyed: 2,051

2015

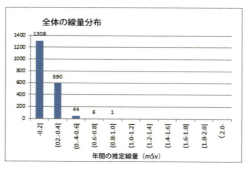

▽Survey months: September to November 2015
▽People surveyed: 1,949

IV. Actions in 2016 and beyond

As mentioned above, in 2015, the fifth year of testing, there were no cases that showed an exposure rate of one millisievert per year. However, when considering the future of the children, we will continue testing for a total of 10 years in order to completely do away with any insecurity regarding radiation, regardless of our initial goal of preventing external exposure.

Fighting Radiation

(17) Whole-body counting

The internal exposure testing conducted on all children using whole-body counting was an important issue carried out independently by Soma.

We first requested that the Reconstruction Agency provide the funds for purchasing equipment, however, because of the transfer of medical resources to the prefecture by the the Reconstruction Agency had transferred medical resources to the prefecture, they instructed us to contact the Fukushima government. They then told us that there was a request for the equipment from the United States and that they would send it to us as early as possible, but that we had to wait. However, there was no clear date when this would happen, and the performance of the equipment was also unclear.

Because this nuclear accident was virtually unprecedented, there were a variety of problems regarding the accuracy of whole-body counting. Some pointed out that portable equipment loaded onto large vehicles such as buses had a large amount of errors, so on its own, the city of Soma purchased the latest measurement equipment from Canberra, which is known for its precision. Surrounding radiation was thoroughly blocked to minimize measurement errors, and we began the plan to test all schoolchildren.

To deal with the problem of a stable location, the reception room of the Soma Central Hospital was modified, adding lead to the walls and reinforcing the floor. Several specialist staff members began whole-body counting measurement of internal exposure on June 11, 2012.

Whole-body counter

Whole-body counter test results

Number of subjects by cesium 137 dose in body

* Detection limit is 250 Bq/body.
  4 Bq/body approximation for a 60 kg subject.

▽Survey months: June 2012 to March 2013
▽People surveyed: 2,546 children (elementary and junior high students)

▽Survey months: April 2013 to March 2014
▽People surveyed: 2,583 children (elementary and junior high students)

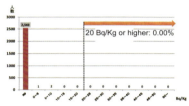
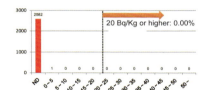

▽Survey months: February 2014 to April 2015
▽People surveyed: 2,519 children (elementary and junior high students)

▽Survey months: April 2015 to March 2016
▽People surveyed: 2,582 children (elementary and junior high students)

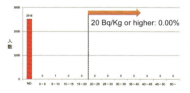
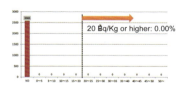

Fighting Radiation Chapter 6

Just as the results show, the danger to health due to radiation exposure is extremely low in Soma. When including the retesting up to 2015, there were no children showing signs of internal exposure in yearly tests, and two children in 2016. An investigation showed that this resulted from a family eating wild matsutake mushrooms in Minamisoma. Internal exposure (effective dose) equates to a minor dose that is smaller than a single chest x-ray, however, we provided instructions to the family just in case.

(18) The necessity of radiation education

Each year I have included the Soma countermeasures and results of combating the nuclear power plant accident, however, this is not as simple as single-mindedly avoiding the problem of radiation.

In Japan there are 53 reactors including some reactors planned for decommissioning at nuclear power plants, and none of them can be considered absolutely safe. For example, even if a reactor is decommissioned, or the nuclear fuel is removed from the power plant, contaminated structures such as the reactor will remain. At the risk of being misunderstood, considering the possibility of a certain nearby country firing a missile at Japan or suffering a terrorist attack, we must always be prepared for accidents.

Because the city of Soma is within 45 kilometers of the Fukushima Daiichi, we did not receive any benefits such as subsidies from the government such as were given to municipalities in close proximity to the nuclear power plant. For that reason, even if a nuclear power plant was operating in the Hamadori area of Fukushima, we were unable to postulate what might happen in case of an accident as residents thought it did not concern them.

Many patients were lost when evacuating local hospitals. If we had been fully prepared for an accident, and had basic radiation knowledge on the relation between degree of exposure and health risks, we could have avoided much tragedy.

The first instructions we received at that time were to evacuate immediately.

A schoolteacher I know was not allowed to go pick up some necessary items, and put on a bus to evacuate. It is likely that the central and prefectural governments both thought of distancing the people from the nuclear power plant as quickly as possible a matter of compliance.

We did not have the leeway to convert the annual air dose rate per hour,

287

Japan Association of City Mayors observing the Fukushima Daiichi Nuclear Power Plant

and the four to five percent concentration of uranium 235 was unlike the 90% concentration of the bombs dropped on Hiroshima, and we did not know that there was virtually no chance of an explosion, we could not provide systematic evacuation instructions.

The case of disaster vulnerable people, such as elderly bedridden citizens, was particularly tragic. Elderly who could not be rescued had no alternative but to starve to death. One surgeon I know conducted autopsies on his own for seven people died from starvation.

I believe that the decision of Kanno, the head of Iitate Village, was appropriate on this point. The city of Soma accepted 164 households of evacuees from Iitate Village who moved into temporary housing completed three months later when the full evacuation of the village was ordered.

The risk of leaving the elderly care facilities in the village was higher than the risk of low radiation exposure, necessitating that they remain there. The staff at facilities attached integral dosimeters to each person, controlling both work and the radiation doses.

The government's imperfect education on radiation was the reason behind socially damaging rumors in the area. An acquaintance's daughter's engagement was broken off because she is a woman from Fukushima. This type of thinking has remained basically unchanged even six years after the nuclear power plant disaster.

In November 2016 and April 2017, we invited the members of the Japan Association of City Mayors to view the decommissioning work at the

Fukushima Daiichi a total of four times.

A total of 75 mayors from Hokkaido to Kyushu came to observe, with each one donning an integral dosimeter to measure the air dose rate and experience actual radiation exposure.

Before the observation I provided a simple lecture on radiation and radioactive rays, however, many of the mayors did not understand the difference between the two, or the difference between sieverts and becquerels. This is true not only with the mayors, but you can imagine that knowledge about radiation has not spread common average citizens. Although I occasionally touch upon and appeal for the necessity of radiation education, just as the citizens of Fukushima used to think before the disaster, the citizens of Japan in general think it has nothing to do with them, despite our country having experienced a nuclear power plant disaster.

Right after the accident, radiation information sessions were conducted at 12 locations across Soma and at the fisherman's cooperative. However, very few people participated, and many adults did not take in the education on radiation. On the other hand, yearly courses in radiation are taught at elementary, junior high, and high schools where it is believed that the children have a better understanding on the subject now.

This knowledge is the best weapon children have for combating radiation. I believe that a better understanding on the part of the children will result in a more relaxed atmosphere across the region. I would like to express my sincere thanks to professor Masahiro Kami and other doctors for their cooperation.

(19) International symposium (May 7 and 8, 2016)

For two days on May 7 and 8, 2016, an international symposium on radiation and the disaster was held in joint participation by the Soma City Municipal Assembly and WHO at the Soma Community Center.

Soma and Minamisoma possess massive records of the air dose rate and measurements of radioactive substances in food and water for the past six years, along with a wealth of data on the previously described internal and external exposure measurements performed on children and residents.

We also conducted joint investigations into thyroid cancer of Fukushima citizens along with Fukushima Medical University, and that data was sent continuously to Soma on the day of the accident and thereafter by the university. Professor Seiichi Takenoshita (current president of the university) and professor Shinichi Suzuki of the same university were present at the symposium, with professor Suzuki presenting the testing data

Executive chairperson Dr. Sae Ochi   The author providing an explanation of initiatives since the disaster

Fighting Radiation Chapter 6

and conducting a panel discussion.

The symposium showcased the data, providing an objective viewpoint of radiation exposure due to the nuclear power plant accident, as well as hinting at actual measured values of nuclear disasters that mankind will unavoidably face in the future.

Many people participated in the event, and we plan on actively sharing the arguments held during the panel discussion and other data released during the symposium.

The data collected by Soma is available on the city website, but exposing the facts of our experience to researchers around the world will provide suggestions for the rest of mankind that faces the threat of radiation whether they like it or not. In this regard, we have created English translations of the records.

Nine-person panel discussion

Luncheon seminar

Afterword

In this work, I have sorted out how Soma City responded to this disaster based on records dating back to that event and my own recollections. As I think back, I am deeply moved to realize that we have been able to accomplish what we have to date precisely because we in fact received support from so many people.

While I did not mention it in the text, the two people who have been like brothers to me and buttressed my spirits as my most trusted advisors over the past six years are Nobuaki Sato, formerly a vice-minister at the Ministry of Land, Infrastructure, Transport, and Tourism, and today a member of the House of Councilors, and Jiro Makino, former Commissioner of the National Tax Agency.

I think everyone who works at City Hall has also been outstanding. The evening the day after the disaster, the then-chief of the General Affairs Department Toshimune Kikuchi said to me, "Mr. Mayor, at a time when this city's people are feeling the way they do, we are not going to be asking for overtime pay. Please just tell us whatever you want us to do."

I later received word from the Minister of Internal Affairs and Communications that they put measures in place to cover all overtime allowances related to the Great East Japan Earthquake and so through those allowances we were able to remunerate all the staff for their hard work, but the character they had shown buoyed my feelings. Even today, I am moved to tears when I think back on it.

I will leave it to later generations to judge whether the process we have followed in pursuit of recovery was the appropriate one or not, but for myself as the mayor who directed the disaster response effort this city's workers were the most powerful teammates I could have. For their abilities and strength of mind, I think they are the best workers in all of Japan. When it was time to put our lives on the line and confront the disaster, I was happy I could fight it with them.

Thoughts of the ten firefighters who on the day of the earthquake gave their lives when they were going around directing people to evacuate and were unable to escape the tsunami in time have never been from my mind over these six years. But I have come to believe that the best way to honor their memory is to be tenacious in carrying out our recovery effort and build a new Soma City. Soma's recovery as it stands today is built upon their sacrifice.

This book is dedicated to these fallen heroes.

■List of Reference Works

▽Interim Report, No. 1, issued August 1, 2011

▽Interim Report, No. 1 (additional printing edition), issued October 1, 2011

▽Interim Report, No. 2, issued April 1, 2012

▽Interim Report, No. 2 (detailed edition), issued July 1, 2012

▽Interim Report, No. 3, issued April 1, 2013

▽Interim Report, No. 4, issued June 1, 2014

▽Interim Report, No. 5, issued June 1, 2015

▽"A Five-Year Chronicle: Interim Reports Digest Edition,"
(March 1, 2016)

▽Interim Report, No. 6, issued April 1, 2016

▽Interim Report, No. 7, issued April 1, 2017

▽Tsubokura M, Murakami M, Nomura S, Morita T, Nishikawa Y, Leppold C, Kato S, Kami M. Individual external doses below the lowest reference level of 1 mSv per year five years after the 2011 Fukushima nuclear accident among all children in Soma City, Fukushima: A retrospective observational study. PLoS One. 2017 Feb 24;12(2):e0172305. doi: 10.1371/journal.pone.0172305. eCollection 2017. PubMed PMID: 28235009; PubMed Central PMCID: PMC5325236.

(Reports that the external exposure for all children from Soma City tested stood at 1mSv or lower five years after the disaster.)

▽Ishii T, Tsubokura M, Ochi S, Kato S, Sugimoto A, Nomura S, Nishikawa Y, Kami M, Shibuya K, Saito Y, Iwamoto Y, Tachiya H. Living in Contaminated Radioactive Areas Is Not an Acute Risk Factor for Noncommunicable Disease Development: A Retrospective Observational Study. Disaster Med Public Health Prep. 2016 Feb;10(1):34-7. doi: 10.1017/dmp.2015.102. Epub 2015 Sep 9. PubMed PMID: 26349438.

(Compiles the results of ongoing medical checkups in the Tamano area of Soma City. Reports that exposure amounts were remaining low, and chronic conditions were being kept from worsening.)

INDEX

●Number

46 stretchers   260

●A

Abukuma Higashi Road   247, 249–251
Akihiro Ota   163
All-Japan Association of Photographic
　　Societies Director   136
Alps Electric Co., Ltd.'s Soma Factory   84
Association for Aid and Relief   91, 92, 101,
　　108, 115
Association of Notary Publics   81

●B

Ban Ki-moon   145
Broadway (New York)   145

●C

Cart salespeople   120
Carts   117
Castle under siege (Rojo)   264
Children's museum   196
City hall community gallery   253
City of Soma Educational Rebuilding
　　Children's Fund   154
City of Soma Educational Rebuilding
　　Children's Fund Ordinance   124
City of Soma Reconstruction Advisory Board
　　Meeting   178
City of Soma Reconstruction Meeting
　　109, 111
City of Soma Reconstruction Plan   111
Clinical psychologists   86, 90, 101, 153,
　　192
Coffee and tea machine   256
Community gallery   255
Community Protection Association   234

●D

Daisei Kusamura   80, 85, 236
Decontamination information session   271
Dividing partitions   78
DMAT   32, 33
Donations to cover nearly all costs for college
　　153
Dow Chemical Company   132
Dream Soccer Soma   186, 191, 199

●E

Earthquake Disaster Orphan Scholarship
　　Fund ordinance   88
Earthquake Orphans Charity   150, 194
Eastern Rebuilding Association   210, 213,
　　215–217
Education on radiation   278, 288, 289
Emergency supplies storehouse   147
Emmanuel Prat   192, 195
Epson   135
Etsuko Enami   135
Examinations of the Thyroid gland   269
External exposure prevention   284
External exposure survey   279

●F

Fallen Firemen Monument Construction
　　Committee   150
FIFA Football Center   185, 190
Film badge dosimeters   279
Firefighter holding area and disaster
　　preparedness training center   149
Fishery warehouse   159
Fission product   39
Flowers Will Bloom (song)   253, 254
Folklore Museum   165–167
Food truck   235
Fukushima Daiichi Nuclear Power Station   38

297

INDEX

G

Great Keicho tsunami (1611)   160
Great Tenmei famine   73
Group Leader and Building Leader system
    109, 127, 128

H

Hamanasu-kan   21, 22, 32, 88, 146, 157
Haragama goods handling facility   244
Haragama Joint Distribution Center   228
Haragama Morning Market Club   116
Hazards maps   18
High-pressure washers   270, 271, 282
HIKOBAE (play)   145, 146
Hiroaki Ōmoto   104
Hiromichi Tsuji   237
His majesty, the king of Bhutan   138
Hisakazu Oishi   115
Hoeikai Hospital   204, 206
Hotoku Summit   43

I

Imperial visit   93
Inagi City   149, 170, 173
Influenza   64
Integrating dosimeter   288, 289
Internal exposure   287
International symposium   289
Isato Kunisada   172
ISO9001   35, 56, 114, 270
Isobe Seafood Processing Facilities   232

J

Japan Legal Support Center   80, 81
Japan Medical Association   63, 95
Jiro Makino   115
JMA (Japan Medical Association)   63
Joint Distribution Center   221, 228
Junji Otaki   63
Junko Mihara   67

K

Kan Suzuki   155, 194-196
Kanju Osawa   115, 177, 178
Katsuhiko Suzuki   64
Katsutoshi Kashimura   64
Kenji Shibuya   99, 204, 266
Kinichi Shida   84
Komono Town   173
Komoro City   34, 170
Kowa Yakuhin K.K.   65

L

Land and housing inspectors   81
Living support grants   60, 151, 153
Louis Vuitton Inc.   192
LVMH Kodomo Art Maison   87, 192, 196,
    197

M

Maibara City   149, 171, 173
Makoto Endo   262
Manifesto Awards Grand Prize   208
Mari Saito   196
Mariko Morita   242
Marumori Town   43, 49
Masaharu Tsubokura   266
Masahiko Usu   63
Masahiro Kami   115, 242, 265, 266, 289
Masataka Ishihara   173
Masataka Kataoka   85
Masayasu Kitagawa   115, 129, 208
Masayoshi Konaka   193
Mayors' Association to Consider Social
    Capital Improvements   43
Mayors' Conference on Medical Issues   43
Memorial Hall for the Repose of Souls   202
Mental Health Care Team   76, 102
Mesh survey   275-277
Michitane Soma   65
Mini bus service   205
Morgue   85

●N

Nagareyama City   62
Nakamura Highway   248
Nanako Kondo   101
Natural grass   185-189, 199
Neighborhood watch   229
New community pool   257
New emergency supplies storehouse   149
Nikon   135
Nippon Kodo Co., Ltd.   86, 193
Nobuaki Sato   293
Norihiko Yamada   265
Noriyuki Asahi   134
NPO Lifenet Soma   129, 130

●O

Odawara City   127, 149, 173
Ono City   149, 170, 173
Ordinance on living support grants   44, 89
Osamu Maekawa   235
Osteoporosis   205

●P

PDCA cycle   56, 114, 208
Plutonium-thermal project   39
Pool Gakuin Junior & Senior High School   193
Portraits of families standing together   134
Professor Shinichi Suzuki   273, 274
Psychiatric care   76
PTSD countermeasures   192
Public proposal   132, 133

●R

Radioiodine   273
Reconstruction Exchange and Support Center   187
Reconstruction Rice   181
Red Brick Pool   257
Regional revitalization strategy   222
Ryohei Suzuki   145
Ryu Matsumoto   32
Ryugasaki City   149, 173

Ryugo Hayano   266
Ryutaro Takahashi   86, 192

●S

Sae Ochi   290
Saijo City   149, 173
Scintillation counters   272
Seibu Children's Community Center   258
Seiichi Takenoshita   290
SEISA Group   86, 189, 192
Sharp curves   248, 250, 251
Shigeru Ban   192, 196
Shigeru Konno   163
Shiho-Shoshi Lawyers' Association   81
Shinichi Niwa   76
Shiseido   135, 136
Shuri   145
Sludge tilling, iron and steel slag rice   180
Solitary deaths, preventing   84, 113, 116, 118, 119, 241
Soma Central Hospital   32, 33, 63, 86, 242, 264, 285
Soma City Municipal Assembly   289
Soma City official records   49, 58
Soma crisis response meeting Excel spreadsheet   56
Soma District Medical Association   63
Soma Follower Team   86, 87, 90, 101, 153, 155, 193
Soma General Hospital   32, 39, 76, 82, 262
Soma Idobata Nagaya   125, 128, 130, 152
Soma Kids Dome   212
Soma Neighborhood Watch Council   229
Soma Nomaoi festival   121
Soma Photo Association   135
Soma regional revitalization strategy meeting   223
Soma Regional Water Utility   261
Soma Soccer Association   185
Soma Terakoya School   151, 155
Soma Tourism Reconstruction Information Center   198, 202

299

Strawberry Union   178
Street vendor truck   205
Strong Bones Park   203, 207
Susono City   149, 170, 173
Suzuhiro   127

●T

Tadashi Ara   80
Taiki Town   149
Takashi Haneda   183
Takashi Hanyuda   63
Takashi Komori   64
Takeaki Ishii   204
Takeshi Niinami   55, 115
Takeyoshi Tanuma   135, 136
Takumi Nemoto   183
Tamio Mori   170
Tamotsu Saito   163
Taro Aso   67
Tax Accountants' Association   81
Temporary housing   106, 119
Temporary incinerator   133, 174, 175, 214
Tetsuo Okubo   86
Their Majesties the Emperor and Empress of
    Japan   93
Thousands of Visitor Hall   198, 200, 201
Tobu Children's Community Center   226
Toho Pharmaceutical Co., Ltd.   65
Tokyo Medical University   61-63, 95
Tokyo University of Agriculture   115, 176,
    178, 179, 181
Tokyo's Adachi ward   34
Tomohiro Morita   241, 242
Torao Tokuda   260
Toshi Shioya   145
Toyokoro Town   149
Tsu shrine   93
Tsuneo Nishida   145

●U

Universal design   129, 243

●V

Village community   106
Volunteer Center   66

●W

Wada Strawberry Farm   182, 183
Weathering effect   275
WHO   289
Whole-body counter   285, 286
Women firefighters   69

●Y

Yamada Shokai   135
Yasuo Miyazawa   86, 192
Yasuo Takita   76
Yasushi Konno   45
Yonezawa City   53
Yoshimasa Hayashi   184
Yoshino Gypsum Co., Ltd.   79, 132
Yoshinobu Kuma   39
Yoshiteru Muto   155
Yoshito Sengoku   32, 47
Yuichi Ara   65
Yukie Osa   91, 101, 115
Yuko Matsumura   266

■About the Author
Hidekiyo Tachiya

Profile:
Born June 1951, Haragama, Soma City.
Director, Veteran's Circle Elder Care Facility

Major public offices:
Mayor, Soma City
Vice-Chairman, Japan Association of City Mayors
Chairman, Fukushima Association of City Mayors
Chairman, National Mayors' Association on Medical Science
Chairman, Mayors' Association to Consider Social Capital Improvements
Chairman, Mayors' Association to Consider Low-Carbon Societies
Chief Organizer, Community Protection Association
Vice President, National Council for the Promotion of Road Construction
Visiting Professor, Tokyo University of Agriculture

定価（本体2,800円＋税）

著　者　　立谷　秀清 ©2018 Tachiya Hidekiyo
発　行　　平成30年6月1日　　　（第一刷）

発行者　　近　代　消　防　社
　　　　　　　　三　井　栄　志

発行所
近　代　消　防　社
〒105-0001　東京都港区虎ノ門2丁目9番16号
（日本消防会館内）
TEL　東京（03）3593-1401(代)
FAX　東京（03）3593-1420
URL　http://www.ff-inc.co.jp
E-mail　kinshou@ff-inc.co.jp
〈振替　00180-6-461　00180-5-1185〉

ISBN978-4-421-00916-3 C0030 〈乱丁・落丁の場合はお取替え致します。〉